"First times are always a little frightening."

He sounded as if he knew what he was talking about. There had been many first and last times in his life, she was sure.

"I'm not frightened." That was true; she wasn't frightened. But the nervousness she couldn't do anything about. There hadn't been anybody, no special man, in her life. *Seth wouldn't be part of her life, not after tonight.* She had to remember that; she wanted it that way, yet it left an empty feeling deep inside.

He was looking at her again. She could feel his eyes on her. Laurel looked up into the midnight-blue depths.

"What are you thinking?" Seth's voice was as dark and velvety as the night sky.

"About beginnings and endings," she answered truthfully. "And about how much I'd like you to kiss me again."

ABOUT THE AUTHOR

Marisa Carroll is the pseudonym for a
writing team of sisters, Carol Wagner and
Marian Scharf. The siblings, who share
interests as well as backgrounds—Carol is a
nurse, while Marian is an X-ray
technician—describe themselves as being
"awfully ordinary" yet "hopelessly
romantic." They also write together under
the pseudonym Melissa Carroll. They live in
the small Ohio town where they were
raised, with their respective husbands and
children.

Books by Marisa Carroll

HARLEQUIN AMERICAN ROMANCE
127–NATURAL ATTRACTION
160–JENNA'S CHOICE
190–TOMORROW'S VINTAGE

HARLEQUIN SUPERROMANCE
268–REMEMBERED MAGIC

Come Home to Me

Marisa Carroll

Harlequin Books

TORONTO • NEW YORK • LONDON
AMSTERDAM • PARIS • SYDNEY • HAMBURG
STOCKHOLM • ATHENS • TOKYO • MILAN

For Joseph...
still with love
C.

Published July 1988

First printing May 1988

ISBN 0-373-16256-1

Chapter One

"Laurel Sauder! Have you been listening to a single word I've been saying to you?"

Laurel didn't answer her imperious questioner immediately. Smoothly she continued to count out small white pills, five at a time, pushing them into the indentation of the counting tray with a wide-bladed spatula, until she reached the number indicated on Mabel Jackson's prescription. She closed the clear plastic guard over the correct amount of medication, tucking a wing of brown hair behind her ear as she straightened to her full height, all five feet three and a half inches of it.

"I heard, Mabel, every word," she assured the small, wizened figure as she returned the excess pills to a large amber bottle, then set it back on the shelf behind her. "It beats me why anyone would spend good money to put eight-foot-high letters over the side of the elevator silos even for the President of the United States. I do have to admit they looked pretty impressive up there when I came to work this morning," she couldn't resist adding.

The unwary comment brought a rapid and scathing response. "There's plenty of better things to spend money on in this town. All I can say is it's a good thing Roosevelt or Eisenhower isn't President anymore. Where'd they put that many letters, I'd like to know? Probably hurry up and build a couple of new silos, spend another fortune showin' off.'' Mabel snorted and shook her head so hard that thin wisps of hair danced and bobbed around her ears.

"I don't think the town paid for the letters, Mabel," Laurel replied, offering the comment in the interest of fair play. "In fact, I know they didn't. Louis Christman was in here from the lumberyard a while ago. He told me the County Reelection Committee paid for them to be made." She'd been back home in Bartlow, Ohio, population 2,812 Christian souls, for less than a week. It never ceased to amaze her when she did return how little the place changed from one year to the next.

Take Mabel Jackson, for instance. She'd been complaining about one thing or another for as long as Laurel could remember. Nothing ever suited the woman. Laurel's father said she'd driven her patient, long-suffering husband, Henry, to his grave with her grousing. Just hounded him to death, Ralph Sauder insisted, until one day he gave up the ghost and keeled over dead in the field.

When Laurel was tired and her feet hurt, such as this afternoon, she could believe every word of her father's tongue-in-cheek assessments of his neighbor. But she was also fair-minded, a trait she'd inherited from her calm and intelligent mother. Lois Sauder always reminded her more volatile spouse that Henry Jackson, while a good man and a good farmer, had also been very fond of bending his elbow at the local taverns—and that had certainly contributed to his untimely demise.

"It's for the television people, I suspect," Mabel went on caustically, breaking into Laurel's thoughts abruptly. "They'll descend on us like a plague of locusts, you mark my words. Whose idea was it for the President of the United States to come here in the first place?"

"I suppose Congressman Willman had something to do with it." Laurel had lived in Phoenix, Arizona, for the past four years, but the congressman was an institution in himself. He'd been a fixture on Capitol Hill for almost thirty years. If his party wasn't in the minority he'd probably be Speaker of the House. As it was, he was the head of one powerful budget committee and sat on several others. He had a lot of clout.

"Just another campaign stunt," Mabel intoned darkly. "Why ever since Warren Harding's funeral train came through here back when I was a girl, they've been roostin' on our doorstep."

"At least the Republican ones," Laurel interjected unwisely, and was rewarded with another one of Mabel's hard looks.

"Why, even now, when there ain't no more passenger trains runnin', they resurrect some old batch of Pullman cars that FDR used and start it all over again."

Bartlow was situated at the crossroads of the east-west and north-south tracks of a major rail line, one of the few still making money in this day and age. Lots of freight trains rumbled around the wye curves in the middle of town, but the passenger station was used only for storage since the Amtrak lines had gone farther north.

"Remember when Harry Truman stopped here in '48?"

Laurel shook her head as she typed the information from Mabel's prescription into the computer on the counter beside her. Mabel's records appeared on the screen and Laurel began to scan her other medications to make sure this new one wouldn't cause any unwanted side effects. As usual, Dr. Mitchell had done his homework. Everything looked okay.

"No, I suppose that was before you were born." Mabel admitted the mistake grudgingly.

About ten years before I was born, Laurel said inwardly while she nodded.

"Well, I'm sure you've seen pictures of old Harry talking away. There's a big one over at the newspaper office. Why, you could march right up to the back of the train and shake his hand. Not like when it was Nixon's turn. Helicopters! Men on top of buildings with machine guns. It looked like Russia or one of them places in Africa or somewhere they're always having revolutions. Not plain old Bartlow, Ohio." Mabel sounded affronted that anyone, including the Secret Service, should feel as if the President needed protection from the good people of her hometown.

"It rained the day Nixon come." Caroline Insenmann, her father's longtime assistant, offered the information in a loud voice. She was in her mid-fifties, redheaded and with a fiery personality to match. "I voted for him, anyway."

"That makes about as much sense as anything else you do, Caroline," Mabel announced dryly. Caroline set her lips tightly, but didn't respond in kind.

Laurel tried not to laugh at the old lady's tartness. It was doing her good to be back here for a while. She needed to keep her thoughts on the world outside her own mind. She had to, or she'd find herself slipping back into the gray depression that had dogged her for so many months.

And it was getting easier. As long as she didn't remind herself that next month would have been the fifth anniversary of her marriage to Tom Keller. Or that their divorce had become final a year ago last week. Or that it had been three months since she'd seen Penny. That realization hurt far worse than anything else.

Penny.

Tom's daughter.

Only her stepdaughter, she'd found out during the legal proceedings to dissolve her marriage. She had no claim on the little girl she'd raised from a toddler. Nothing bound them legally, only ties of the heart. And those had no standing whatsoever in a court of law. So when the divorce became final and Tom was offered a very lucrative job on the East Coast, he'd gone and taken Penny with him, leaving Laurel alone, her heart broken for a second time.

"Congressman Willman must think that guy over Putnam County way has a chance of beatin' him this year. That's why he's callin' in the big guns." Mabel had returned to the subject that most interested her.

"Poor man," Caroline said with sympathy for the challenger. "There aren't a half-dozen liberals in a thirty-mile radius."

All three women laughed. Even Laurel, who lived two thousand miles away, could appreciate the joke. Willman's opponent didn't have a chance of unseating the congressman, no matter how many babies he kissed or Young Farm Wives' potluck dinners he ate his way through. Bartlow and the surrounding rural district had been sending the Honorable Barton Willman to Washington for twenty-eight years, nearly Laurel's entire lifetime. The outcome of this election would be no different for the wily veteran politician. Except that this time the President of the United States was coming to Bartlow.

And not just passing through, smiling his famous smile and waving from the back of an antique Pullman car, either. He was going to stop and make a speech.

"A major farm policy speech," Laurel's dad had told her as he bombarded her with last minute instructions for running the store. "Damn, I hate to miss it, but this reunion has been in the works for a year." His wife was dragging him toward the boarding ramp of the plane while he was still talking. "But a speech isn't going to do much good for farmers on the verge of losing their land."

Was the situation that bad around Bartlow? Laurel found herself wondering yet again. All the farms she'd driven past seemed prosperous enough. Her dad was carrying a few more people on his books, she'd noticed the other day, but the last recession had hit Ohio hard. A lot of people, not only farmers, were having a tough time getting back on their feet.

She'd been so wrapped up in her own problems and her work as Assistant Chief Pharmacist at Phoenix Medical Center for the past couple of years that she hadn't paid a lot of attention to what went on in the larger world outside her own.

What about people like Mabel Jackson, alone and childless? What would happen to the land she and Henry had worked all their married lives? Laurel smiled a polite goodbye as the old lady made her way to the door. Mabel had no one to leave her farm to, no one who cared enough for her to see that she got the most income she could out of the land her grandfather had wrestled from the Great Black Swamp a hundred years earlier. How very sad to be lonely and alone.

And how very sad to be so young and so self-pitying, Laurel scolded herself sharply. With a shake of her shoulder-length, straight brown hair, she put the melancholy thoughts from her mind and turned back to the list of medications she'd been preparing before Mabel came in.

In individual self-sealing containers, she placed the prescribed dosages of daily medications for the residents of Oakfork, the retirement home her cousin, Elinor Mieneke, managed. The twenty-five inhabitants of the big old house on Oak Street were among her father's best customers.

She'd ask Elinor to bring her up to date on the situation around town. She was still very fond of Bartlow and its people. She'd often thought of coming back here to live, especially since Tom had taken Penny back East with him. But she could never take over Sauder's Pharmacy. She just didn't have her father's touch, his easy charm and genuine love of his fellow man. You needed that in this one-on-one kind of life's work.

Laurel was a very private person, always had been, even as a child. A loner, Tom used to call her. For a long time after the divorce she'd worried about that part of herself, wondered if perhaps her reticence had helped contribute to her failure as a wife.

The marriage counselor they'd seen had told her to open up, not to hold back, to express her hostility. The trouble was she didn't have a lot of hostility to deal with, only sadness and pain. Where Laurel came from, love meant a marriage, and marriage was mostly forever. But she'd failed; so she remained silent, agreed to give Tom his freedom, never realizing it meant giving up Penny, as well, until it was too late.

The past few months she'd been substituting work for the uncertainty of love and building new relationships. The isolation of a big city hospital pharmacy suited her privacy-loving soul. She missed that isolation now, the atmosphere of noninvolvement that allowed her to immerse herself in her work for hours on end with no excess energy to spend on uncomfortable self-analysis.

The silver bell above the door announced a customer and was a welcome distraction from her aimlessly circling thoughts. Sauder's was on the ground floor of a long, narrow, two-story brick building that fronted on Main Street, just like all the others in town. It's only architectural distinction was a small tower room, like an old-fashioned sentry box, on the second floor that looked out over the railroad tracks.

The front three-quarters of the store was as modern and high tech as any you could find in the Midwest. Stainless steel shelves; white Formica; pastel letters on the wall identifying the different items for sale beneath them—hardware, jewelry, giftware, notions and snack foods.

But once you passed the carved walnut dividers at the back of the room, it was like entering another time. In her father's private domain, the decor was much the same as it had been at the turn of the century when the first pharmacy to locate in Bartlow had opened its doors.

There was even a soda fountain.

A real one, twenty feet long, solid native walnut with a black-and-white marble top and a brass footrail below. The stools were backless and swiveled in complete circles. The half-dozen small, round tables and chairs were twisted wrought iron, the floor, green-and-white hexagonal ceramic tiles. Three generations of Bartlow's kids had come here after school to drink real fountain Cokes, cherry phosphates and ice cream sodas. They still did, even though the high school had consolidated and been moved five miles north of town.

Her father had watched them all come and go with a benevolent eye from his elevated perch behind etched-glass dividers. Ralph Sauder was in his element up there. He loved kids and never seemed to mind the shrill giggles and noisy exuberance that on some days annoyed Laurel. But for the most part she had to admit the youngsters were polite and well-behaved—the more popular theories of minimal parental discipline and unstructured child rearing having pretty much passed Bartlow by.

The silver bell tinkled again as the door drifted shut behind a new arrival. Laurel glanced down at her watch. Not quite two o'clock. At least the school kids wouldn't descend on her for another hour or so. She squinted her big golden-brown eyes to bring the newcomer into focus. It was no use. The figure was feminine, but that was all she could make out. Laurel gave up and slipped her glasses onto her small, pert nose.

"Got time for a phosphate?" Elinor Mieneke asked.

Her low, smoky voice washed over Laurel like a silken breeze warm with summer sun. For years and years Laurel had envied her cousin that voice. She'd also envied her the four extra inches in height and the additional twenty pounds that on Elinor seemed to be deposited in all the right places. On Laurel the weight would have settled disastrously on her hips and thighs. Even in a severely cut white uniform and sensible shoes her cousin looked stunning.

Elinor was five years Laurel's senior. Only eight days separated her birthday and that of Laurel's elder brother, Kevin. Her hair was closer to being truly blond, and her eyes were hazel, not deep chocolate brown. She had the same snub Sauder nose, determined chin and generous mouth that gave Laurel her wholesome prettiness. But on Elinor these same features just looked better. The similarities between the cousins were more than merely physical. Laurel and Elinor shared many of the same likes and dislikes, the same views on life and living. And one thing more.

They were both divorced.

But Elinor, lucky Elinor, had a son.

"I'm buying. Name your poison," Elinor announced with a grand flourish as she slid onto one of the stools. "I want vanilla."

"Since it's your treat I'm going to splurge and have a double cherry Coke."

"You always were the piggy one," Elinor said without a trace of ill humor in her words as she propped her elbows on the marble counter. She rested her chin on her folded hands and watched Laurel work.

"I know," Laurel affirmed with a melancholy sigh. "I've got the hips to prove it." She looked down ruefully at the offending portion of her anatomy, skillfully camouflaged beneath a paisley dirndl skirt and long white lab coat.

"Oh, stop it. You're only a size eight," Elinor said with a sniff. "Quit tearing yourself down. I don't like it." Suddenly she wasn't joking anymore.

"Okay." Laurel made a wry face as she set the vanilla phosphate down in front of her cousin. "I've been indulging in some pretty heavy self-pity lately. I'll try to shape up."

"That's a terrible pun if you intended it that way." Elinor tasted her soft drink and nodded approvingly.

Laurel took a moment to think over what she'd just said. "I didn't. Elinor, do you have a few minutes to talk?"

"Sure, honey, Jack's on duty now."

Jack was Elinor's assistant. A former Vietnam combat medic, he'd recently completed a nursing degree at the university. The residents of Oakfork adored him.

"What's wrong?"

Hazel eyes met brown ones and held, reaffirming a bond of friendship that ran deep and strong.

"How long did it take you to get over divorcing Brian? I mean, really get over him?"

"Long enough," Elinor admitted bluntly. "And we both wanted out of the marriage."

"Some days I don't think I'll ever get over my divorce." Laurel knew there were tears lurking behind her words and punched the handle on the cherry syrup dispenser extra hard to combat that weakness.

"What I don't think you're getting over is losing touch with Penny. You always did have an overactive maternal impulse."

The last words were spoken in a gentle, teasing tone, more encouraging than scolding. Laurel knew her cousin wouldn't pry any further into her feelings than she herself wanted to go.

But Elinor's assessment of Laurel's character came devastatingly close to the mark. In this day and age of independence and two-career families, Laurel would have liked nothing better than to stay at home and have babies. At least for a while. Elinor was a very shrewd judge of character, and as an observer of human nature, she was without equal. At least as far as Laurel's human nature was concerned.

"I'm a reactionary," Laurel quipped, but she knew her lighthearted answer hadn't fooled Elinor for a second. "Probably the product of a disgustingly happy childhood. Do you agree with that diagnosis, Dr. Mieneke?" Laurel tried out her fake Viennese accent.

"Possibly." Elinor made a face at Laurel's mimicry. She watched her cousin closely in the mirror behind the fountain.

It was Laurel who looked away first. She ran Coke into her own glass and stirred the concoction with a long-handled spoon for a few seconds before she spoke again. "Did having Sam make a difference to you?"

"All the difference in the world." Elinor's eyes were bright with honest, unfeigned emotion. She paused for a few seconds, choosing her words with customary care. Laurel waited quietly for her reply. "Having a baby means you're never really cut off from loving someone. But it's also very difficult raising a child alone."

Laurel dropped the spoon into the tiny sink next to the Coke machine. It bounced against the stainless steel with a discordant clang. Had Elinor already guessed at the idea taking root in her mind? An idea so outrageous, so impossible, one buried so deep in her subconscious, that she hadn't even acknowledged it openly herself as yet? Or was

Elinor answering as honestly and directly as she could the question Laurel had put to her?

"You can't allow yourself to smother a child in love you can't share with another adult."

Laurel didn't say anything, only nodded silently, understanding.

"But Sam made it all worthwhile. Having him kept Brian and me from just plain hating each other. Still, it was so bad at the end it was a relief to call it quits."

Elinor's bright, brittle tone didn't fool Laurel for a second. It matched exactly the pose she always adopted when pressed for details of her own failed marriage.

"What happened to the two of you?" Laurel had never asked that question of her cousin before. Elinor had been married when she was seventeen, a pregnant teenager before the condition became a statistic. She'd married the boy who "got her into trouble." That's the way you did things in Bartlow—then and now.

Elinor was silent a moment before she answered. "We should never have gotten married in the first place. We grew up, that's all, and then we grew apart. Brian's very happy now with Andrea, and Sam adores their little boy." Elinor swirled her straw through the dark amber liquid in her glass. "She's pregnant again and this time Sam wants a sister."

"That's nice," Laurel answered automatically. *A little girl of her very own to love and cherish*. She felt like crying again because it would probably never come to be.

"Yes, it is," Elinor agreed with surprising ease. "Sam will have brothers and sisters to watch grow up. And I don't have to have them." She laughed suddenly and her laughter was every bit as lovely as her speaking voice.

"Children do make it all worthwhile, don't they?" Laurel said, her brown eyes darkening almost to black with bittersweet memories of watching Penny grow and develop from chubby toddler to active preschooler. *It wasn't fair. Penny had been Laurel's child as much as Tom's. It wasn't fair that Laurel had no more say in Penny's life. If she had a child of her own no one could ever take her away. No one. Ever.*

"Sure they do," Elinor replied, making slurping sounds at the bottom of her glass with the straw. "I've got to run. I'm dropping the medications off at Oakfork for Jack to log in. Then I have to race out to the school and pick up Sam from football practice, feed him and get him back out there in time for Driver's Ed."

"Driver's Ed?"

Laurel looked a little shell-shocked. Elinor watched her cousin closely from narrowed hazel eyes. "Time marches on, woman," she said with a shrug. She pushed a dollar bill across the top of the counter. "My treat, remember?"

Laurel pushed it back, anyway. "Driver's Ed," she repeated once more in a wondering kind of voice. That meant Sam was going to be sixteen.

"He'll be sixteen on his next birthday," Elinor said, echoing Laurel's thoughts. "Don't tell me you've forgotten? You're his godmother, for pity sakes."

"It just doesn't seem possible he should be old enough to drive a car," Laurel protested. Time was moving along so quickly. She'd be thirty on her next birthday. The future loomed long and empty before her mind's eye. So many years to spend alone. But not many years left for having babies of her own.

"I know. They grow up so fast."

Laurel experienced another stabbing pain around her heart. How would she ever know what it felt like to have a son who was almost old enough to drive a car? Or a daughter getting ready for her first date? She didn't have a husband to give her a child. She didn't even know anyone she cared about enough to consider an affair with, let alone marriage.

She never wanted to be married again. Watching love die once was enough for anyone in a lifetime. Twice was just too much heartbreak to contemplate. She didn't even want to think about a long-term relationship.

But it still took two people to have a baby as far as Laurel was concerned. Because you couldn't have a baby if you didn't have a husband. *Could you?* For the first time Laurel brought her buried wish out and acknowledged it, gave it life. *She wanted a baby of her own.* It was that simple. And that impossible.

"Did you see that official-looking car parked in front of City Hall?" Elinor was asking, unaware of the direction of her cousin's thoughts.

Or could she have a baby all her own? Was she strong enough to accept the challenge of single parenthood?

"Laurel Sauder! Have you been listening to a word I've said?"

"You're the second person to accuse me of not paying attention in the past half-hour." Laurel managed to turn her thoughts back to the conversation at hand as she moved across to the counter where Caroline was setting out the trays of medications for Elinor to take back to the nursing home.

A baby of her own. She couldn't turn off the glow the thought produced, try as hard as she might. For the first time in weeks, the aching pain around her heart had subsided and almost disappeared.

"It's so nondescript it has to be government issue," Elinor said in reference to the car.

"I haven't seen it. I haven't been out of the store since lunchtime."

"That's a shame," Elinor said. "It's a beautiful day. I love October." She accepted the tray of medications from Caroline, missing the flush of rosy color that stained Laurel's cheeks. "Thanks." She smiled as she turned back to her cousin and the interesting subject of the upcoming presidential visit. Laurel was very busy wiping off the counter and avoided meeting her eyes. "Very official. Secret Service, I'd guess."

"Secret Service! Already?" Laurel asked in dismay. "The President isn't coming for over a week."

"Eight days," Elinor corrected. She'd always been good with details.

"That's over a week," Laurel said, defending her generalization. She smiled and her whole face lit up. She always enjoyed trading quips with Elinor.

"Not much more." Elinor got the last word in as usual.

"Doesn't Clint Norris's boy work for the government?" Caroline asked as she handed Elinor a second tray clearly marked in Laurel's neat printing.

"Thursday's eight o'clocks." Elinor confirmed the tag. "Thanks, Caroline."

"I can't recall his name," Caroline said, shaking her head. "I must be getting senile."

"Seth," Elinor said to enlighten the older woman. "He graduated from high school with Kevin and me." She raised her voice a little. "You remember him, don't you, Laurel?"

"Tall, dark curly hair like his mother, and blue eyes. A bully," Laurel added promptly. "He's working for the government? Well, I always assumed he'd come to a bad end and he has. I'll bet he's a tax collector."

"Seth wasn't a bully. You were always just too much of a mouse to appreciate his sense of humor." Elinor's laughter at her cousin's indignant expression was without a speck of sympathy. "He was just a little wild, that's all."

"He got arrested for stealing a car," Laurel said righteously, pushing her glasses back up into her hair. She was only a little nearsighted and she usually wore them only to drive, but the store was so darn long and narrow she could never see who was coming in the front door without them. It nearly drove her crazy sometimes.

"Joyriding in old Henry Jackson's pickup," Elinor corrected her cousin again. She swiveled around on her heel to face the front of the building as she prepared to leave. "You're just mad because he talked Kevin into going along with him that night."

"Marshal Bemer arrested them." Laurel felt her lips tighten into a straight line, even though the incident had happened so long ago; then she smiled, tallying up just how many years had passed. It was ancient history. "I remember that night like it was yesterday, though. Dad nearly had a coronary when he had to go down to the jail in the middle of the night and bring Kevin home. Mom cried for hours."

"I suppose it was pretty traumatic for a thirteen-year-old." Elinor's voice held an echo of older-cousin condescension. "We all thought it was cool. The entire senior class gave them an ovation the first day they were allowed back in school."

"Well, I suppose Seth Norris is pushing a pencil somewhere in Washington these days and it serves him right. He scared me to death when I was a kid."

"I had a terrible crush on him." Elinor's hazel eyes took on a dreamy, faraway look. "But Dad thought he was a little too wild, too. He didn't want me to date him, so I started going out with Brian. Look where that got me."

"It got you Sam," Laurel said, her voice tight with emotion. She looked at her cousin sternly, but made the mistake of leaning too far forward. Her glasses came dangerously close to falling off her head. She brushed them back too quickly and banged her hand against her nose. "Ouch."

They both laughed. It broke the serious mood.

"You're right," Elinor agreed. "No more reminiscing. We're two successful, independent women who have made some mistakes in life. Who hasn't?" She shrugged philosophically.

Laurel smiled, too, and it was genuine and quite enchanting. The silver bell above the door jangled loudly. She was standing at right angles to the door and couldn't see who had entered so precipitously. "We're just lousy at picking our men, that's all."

"Excuse me."

Laurel spun around at the sound of a soft-voweled Texas accent. A large, very official-looking black man in a well-tailored three-piece suit was standing in front of the counter.

"May I help you?" Laurel was more than a little surprised to see him there. Not because he was black, although that was unusual enough in itself around Bartlow, but because he was wearing a suit. In the middle of the day, in the middle of the week. That was unheard of in Bartlow. He showed her his badge and ID card.

"I'm Special Agent McManus, and this is my partner, Special Agent in charge—"

Laurel got a quick impression of broad shoulders beneath tailored black pinstripes, intelligent cobalt-blue eyes and a shock of curly black hair before Elinor broke in on her polite greeting with scant ceremony.

"Well, as I live and breathe! Seth Norris, is that really you?"

Chapter Two

Special Agent Seth Norris took one look at the small, tawny-haired woman behind the soda fountain of his old high school hangout and the earth moved under his feet.

Literally.

The 2:55, heading north, three Chessie System diesel engines towing a hundred coal cars, roared by the building. As a result, conversation slowed to a standstill.

"This is my cousin, Laurel Sauder. You remember her, don't you, Seth?" Elinor hollered above the racket.

He heard about half of what she said, guessed at the rest. *Laurel?* Could this possibly be Kevin's shy, mousy tomboy of a sister?

The woman behind the counter held out her hand in greeting. It was slender and fine boned, with long shapely fingers. He closed his hand around hers. Her grip was firm, but her fingers were soft and warm to the touch.

"Hello, Laurel," he said when the noise of the engines had died away to a rhythmic clatter. "You've changed." He wondered briefly if she'd ever married. Or if she was married but continued to use her maiden name. She wasn't wearing a ring, but that didn't mean much anymore—except in places like Bartlow.

"So have you."

She smiled then, and it was Kevin's smile. Seth smiled, too, because the connection was a happy one. Kevin Sauder had been his best friend all through school; yet almost fifteen years had passed since he'd seen him.

Elinor was introducing herself to McManus, so he took the opportunity to talk a little more with Laurel. "I see your dad didn't let them remodel this part of the building. It sure takes me back." He was certainly outdoing himself with banalities, but he felt strangely off-balance in this small, intact portion of his past.

Hell, he was more than a little off-balance; he was a nervous wreck. He hadn't set foot in Bartlow for the past ten years. If everybody here had changed as much as Laurel Sauder, he wouldn't recognize a soul. Yet he'd known Elinor the moment he'd walked in the door. But their relationship had always been special: two rebels in an isolated world of rule followers. You didn't forget a friend like that.

Laurel smiled again and his heart accelerated a couple of beats. That smile changed her whole face, taking it from pleasantly pretty to something close to beautiful. Her eyes smiled, too, he noticed. They were still her most striking feature, too large for her face and the deep, rich brown of a Hershey bar. The same and yet different. They were a woman's eyes now, not a girl's, and there was a faint shadow of lingering sadness deep within their gold-laced depths.

How old had she been the last summer he'd lived at home? Thirteen? Fourteen? Her hair had been shorter then, he recalled suddenly, frizzy at the ends from a new permanent, but the same warm, tawny color. She'd been skinny as a rail fence, and small. It looked as if she hadn't grown an inch since then. The top of her head still only reached his chin. Her figure was still slight, her breasts small, but today all the curves were in the right places and her legs—at least what he could see of them—were long and shapely. Laurel Sauder had definitely grown up.

Seth smiled and the effect on Laurel's memories was also strong. Vividly she remembered the tall, laughing boy who could always talk her brother into anything. Even up to, and including, auto theft. Or Bartlow's equivalent of it. Nearly twenty years ago everybody left their keys in their cars, day or night. At least once a year one group of teenagers or another ended up daring someone to get in one and take a drive. It was always a vehicle parked behind one of the two bars in town. That's how Seth and Kevin had picked Henry Jackson's truck. The trick had been to get it back before the owner noticed. Or someone recognized it being driven around town.

Seth and Kevin's problem had been a flat tire and Henry's annual attempt to go on the wagon occurring within a few minutes of each other. They'd been caught. Henry hadn't pressed charges, of course. No one ever did in Bartlow. But the consequences had been traumatic just the same.

And something else she recalled, now that her memory had been jogged. Seth's punishment had been far more severe than Kevin's. His father had made him quit the football team. He'd missed the last three games of the season, and that had hurt the team. The Bartlow Pirates had missed the playoffs by a single game. Looking back, she could see how the incident must have contributed to Seth's estrangement from his family.

"Seth, are you going to be staying in town part of the time since you're the agent in charge?" Elinor looked impressed as she glanced at her watch and picked up her trays of medications, reluctantly getting ready to leave. "Seth Norris working for the Secret Service. Who'd a thunk it?" She shook her head in mock wonderment, her eyes sparkling with pleasure at seeing her old friend.

"Times change, Elinor." Seth laughed, bending forward to give her a quick, hard hug, which he accomplished with such controlled and fluid ease of movement that not a single pill in her trays was disturbed.

"Don't I know it. Do you have any free time with this job?"

He nodded.

"We'll have to get together for coffee or a beer." She grinned wickedly. "I'll catch you up on all the goings-on around town. But now I have to run. Give me a call. I'm in the book."

Laurel swallowed an uncomfortable metallic taste of irritation. Elinor was actually flirting with the man. It wasn't like her cousin. And it wasn't like Laurel to be censorious of other people's actions. They were old friends, for heaven's sake. They hadn't seen each other in a decade. Why shouldn't Elinor flirt? Seth Norris was probably one of the best-looking men Laurel had ever seen.

Just a shade over six feet, Seth was several inches shorter and probably forty pounds lighter than his fellow agent, but his shoulders were just as broad and his legs as long. His waist and hips were narrow, his hair still as black and curly as when he'd been a boy. But his face had changed. It was all rough angles and rugged planes. He'd finally grown into the prominent blade of a nose he'd inherited from his mother's family.

And those eyes. She'd bet half a month's salary that if she dug Kevin's high school album out of the attic, Seth Norris would have been voted the senior boy with the most beautiful eyes. They were blue as a north country lake, shot through with silver and black lights. His lashes were dark and straight and so long they threw shadows on his high cheekbones.

He wore no wedding ring, no jewelry at all except for a plain gold tie bar. She wondered if he was married. If he had children . . . Did he feel as strangely out of place in Bartlow as she sometimes did? His expression was polite and alert, but his eyes were wary, his emotions locked away behind reflecting blue surfaces. He wasn't a man to cross for any reason, Laurel decided suddenly. No one would lie to this Seth Norris and not live to regret it. She wasn't sure why she felt so strongly about that judgment, but she did.

"Ms. Sauder." It was Seth's voice pulling her back to the present.

"Call me 'Laurel,' please," she replied, automatically setting her glasses back on her nose. Elinor was gone. She couldn't even remember if she'd said goodbye. Laurel felt a flush of color mount to her cheeks. "Is there anything I can do for you, Agent Norris?"

"Call me 'Seth,' please," he answered in turn. "Yes, I'd like to speak to your father, if I may."

"I'm afraid Dad's out of town. You'll have to make do with me." Good Lord, whatever had made her say that in such an antagonistic tone of voice? "I mean, I'll be happy to be of help." Laurel set her lips in a firm straight line, drawing the slipping folds of her dignity around her once more, as she tried very hard to look businesslike and professional.

"Thanks. I'd like to look over the building before I head back to Toledo." Seth set his own jaw and accomplished what Laurel had been attempting with no apparent effort whatsoever. "I'm afraid that due to the building's proximity to the railroad tracks we'll have to make periodic security checks all week. And the day of the visit we'll have to cordon it off."

"How can I take care of our customers?" Laurel asked in dismay. "Dr. Mitchell isn't going to close up his office.

It's three blocks over on Maple. What if there's an emergency at Oakfork?'' Laurel shook her head emphatically, and silky strands of tawny brown hair caught and held the light. ''That's impossible.''

''That's the way it will be.'' Seth's voice was cool, his words clipped, but his blue eyes twinkled briefly. ''Laurel, don't get yourself all worked up yet. This is my job, remember? We'll make it as easy as possible on all of you. But the President's safety is paramount.''

There was no arguing with that statement and Laurel didn't try. ''What do you want to see first?'' She capitulated as graciously as she could manage. ''Everyone else on Main Street may not be such an easy touch,'' she couldn't help adding with quite a bit more asperity in her tone. Surely Seth hadn't been away from the area so long that he didn't realize there was going to be plenty of opposition to having businesses shut down arbitrarily on a day when the largest crowds the town had ever seen would be pouring onto Main Street. She wondered just how he did intend to handle it.

Laurel watched Seth confer with Agent McManus, and decided she'd find out soon enough. All the promise of leadership Seth Norris had shown as a boy had borne fruit. His voice was low and steady and filled with command. They conferred quietly for a few moments, then McManus nodded and held out his hand to her.

''Nice to meet you, ma'am,'' he said in his slow Texas drawl. ''Be seein' you around.'' He headed for the door.

''He's going over to City Hall to find the mayor. Is Dewey Whitman still His Honor?'' Seth waited patiently for Laurel to tidy up behind the counter and then wash her hands.

It was three o'clock, Laurel noted. In ten minutes or so the high school senior who ran the soda fountain after school would be showing up for work. She could leave the store in Caroline's hands in the interim. "Of course. He's running for reelection next month. Unopposed."

"He's been mayor for twenty-five years." Seth shook his head in a marveling gesture.

"Twenty-six. And it's a pretty thankless job, if you ask me. Doesn't pay enough to keep body and soul together," Laurel said tartly, and thought she sounded a little like Mabel Jackson. Bartlow was already rubbing off on her, and she'd been back in town only a few days. "Caroline, I'm showing Seth around in the back and upstairs," she called as she wiped her hands on a towel and pushed her glasses into place on top of her head. She wouldn't need them to show Seth around the building. "I assume you want to see the upstairs, also?" she added with admirable calm, although her heart skipped a beat or two as he moved close to follow her into the storage room.

"Yes."

Again that switch in tone and stance. There was going to be no banter when it came to his work.

"This way." Laurel gestured to the doorway that led into the long storeroom where most of the inventory was kept. Seth wasn't a big man compared to his partner, or even to her father and brother, who were six foot two and four respectively, but he towered over her. Usually with strangers she didn't like being reminded of her lack of height, but today she didn't mind.

"Do you have a security system?" Seth asked, looking around the big, almost empty room. There was no heat and it was cool and slightly musty smelling.

Seth took a step that brought him closer yet. He smelled good, like soap and pipe tobacco and some spicy aftershave.

"Yes." Laurel swallowed hastily. She wasn't used to encountering men who were so potently male. It was unnerving, to say the least. "It's some kind of infrared sensing device. See it there above the door and window?" She pointed to the small, unobtrusive box fixed to the walls. "It's hooked into Marshal Armstrong's office over at City Hall. An alarm goes off here, too, if the connection is broken. Dad hates it...but the insurance company insists, even though all the narcotics and other controlled substances are kept locked in the safe. Only Dad and I know the combination."

"I see." He nodded and walked forward to better survey the security system. For the first time, Laurel noticed the slight bulge under his left arm. A cold shiver swept down her spine. The coat of his suit fit so well that if she hadn't been looking directly at the broad sweep of his shoulders, she'd never have noticed the gun.

Handguns weren't that common in Bartlow. A lot of people owned rifles or shotguns. Hunting small game was still a popular sport, and there were always grain- and poultry-eating varmints to be eliminated. But handguns were a different matter altogether. Laurel shivered again. As far as she was concerned, handguns were used only for harming others.

"I'm ready to see the upstairs." Seth turned on his heel with the deceptively casual speed that marked all his movements. He noticed that Laurel jumped slightly as he caught her staring at him. She'd seen his gun, obviously, and she didn't like it. Thank God, in Bartlow even the marshal probably didn't keep his weapon loaded. There weren't many places like this left on the earth, more the pity.

"Of course." Her voice was tight and small. She cleared her throat and her next words came out more normally. "Right this way."

She led the way up the steep, narrow steps that opened directly into a big, dusty sunlit room. Her hips swayed slightly beneath the soft, colorful print skirt she was wearing and Seth caught himself lagging a step behind to better appreciate the totally feminine grace of her movements.

He usually didn't pay that much attention to the details of a woman's walk. He generally watched people far more objectively than that, always on the lookout for a suspicious action, any out-of-character mannerisms. It was an occupational habit that wasn't easily shrugged off. It had probably cost him some friendships over the past couple of years. Most people didn't care to be scrutinized that way. When he was off duty he often had to consciously turn off the working part of his brain to relate to people as one human being to another. *Someday he was going to have to get out of this end of the business or he'd lose his soul.*

"I'm sorry, what did you say?" Seth felt like kicking himself. What in the world had caused such an introverted and melancholy turn of mind? He'd missed what Laurel was saying entirely, but it took only a second to come up with the answer to his own mental query.

It was being back in Bartlow, being within two miles of his parents' home. He hadn't seen them in five years and the last time they'd been together had been at his place in Washington, the year before he'd split up with Gina. There were too many memories in the town, too many unresolved conflicts within himself, and they were playing havoc with his concentration. He should have refused this assignment, but he'd been the only senior agent on the White House detail familiar with the area. He'd had no choice but to accept.

"I said," Laurel began, watching him quizzically as she paused at the top of the stairs with her hand on the railing, where it looked small and fragile against the dark, sturdy wood, "this would be the perfect place to listen to the

President's speech. The tower room windows look right out over the Main Street crossing.''

"The perfect spot for an ambush," Seth said dryly. He walked across the room as soon as she moved away from the top of the steps. He'd made her blush and he was sorry. His voice was softer as he continued to explain. "The President's private car will stop just about even with City Hall. We'll have sharpshooters on every roof. And most likely in this room. I'll have to coordinate all the details with the security teams. I'm sorry, but as I said earlier, the building will be off-limits—to all civilians."

"I'll have to stand in line with all the others to get to see the President?" Her voice was filled with mock affront.

"When Nixon came through, Kevin held you on his shoulders. You're not much bigger than you were then." Seth surprised himself with the memory and his willingness to banter with this woman. "Should I make it my duty to find another volunteer for this whistle-stop visit?"

Laurel laughed, and it was a sweet, pretty sound in the big, echoing room. "You remember that? I don't have my big brother around to help me out this time." She smiled, pleased out of all proportion to the casualness of the words.

"I do have a little pull with the powers that be. I could find a spot for you right down front where you can stand on your own two feet." He rested one hand on the window frame, hooking his left hand in his belt as he bent toward her slightly. "Will that help make up for some of the inconvenience we'll be causing you?"

"Yes. Thank you."

She didn't move away as he half thought she might. She stood looking out the window, one slim, pearl-tipped nail making abstract patterns on the dusty glass.

"Do you think Bartlow has changed much?"

"I'm afraid I've only been back in town about half an hour." Seth straightened abruptly. "But, no, it looks just the same. I guess that's not all bad, considering the state of the farm economy and the way so many towns this small are going downhill fast."

"Umm." Laurel cocked her head and once again stray beams of sunlight were caught and held in the brown, silky waves. "It never changes. I'm glad. I like to think it will always look like this in the fall, red and gold leaves on the trees, smoke in the air and the sound of tractors at work in the fields. And for Christmas there'll probably be snow."

"You don't live here?" Seth found he was far more interested in her answer than he should be. He relaxed again, leaning closer once more. Something in him was responding to the hint of homesickness in her voice, which he was positive she didn't hear herself.

"I live in Phoenix," Laurel divulged, turning toward him. She shoved her hands into the pockets of her coat. "I'm Assistant Chief Pharmacist at Phoenix Medical Center. I'm just here to help out while Dad's attending a reunion of his old army outfit."

"Is there someone in Phoenix waiting for you to come back?" Seth clenched his jaw and the fingers of his hand, still hooked in his belt loop. *Damn!* He was coming on to her as if she were one of the many one-night stands that were always readily available to a man in his position.

Laurel looked as if he'd slapped her. "I'm divorced," she returned bluntly. "No children, no ties."

"Sorry." Seth rubbed his hand across his chin. "I didn't mean that the way it sounded. It's just . . ."

He touched the nameplate pinned above her heart. His fingers brushed the swell of her breast so lightly the contact was almost imperceptible, but Laurel felt the heat of his touch through her clothes. She was amazed at the faint stir of pleasure she experienced. She stepped backward, momentarily confused, and nearly stumbled. Seth's hands shot out to steady her. It was all over in a heartbeat.

"Maybe you should put your glasses back on, Squirt." His voice was level, composed. He obviously felt nothing at all.

"No one calls me 'Squirt' and lives these days," Laurel said, deciding to go on the attack. "Are you married?"

So the timid little Laurel Sauder was gone for good. And in her place was a very appealing and provocative woman. "Divorced, no children, no ties." He repeated her terse words. They moved across the room in silence. "Laurel, would you have dinner with me?" Seth halted at the top of the stairs. "I'd like to ask you about Kevin," he added hastily, so she wouldn't think he was coming on to her again, although he was. "I'd like an update on my old buddy Kevin Sauder, World Famous Wildlife Photographer." He spread his hands, smiling disarmingly again. "How is he? Where is he?"

"He's in South America." Laurel answered his last question first, stalling a moment before responding to his request. "I'd like to have dinner," she surprised herself by saying. "I'll tell you all about Kevin's latest adventure. He's in Brazil doing a study on the effect of disappearing habitats of tropical birds. He's sent me some marvelous shots. Discards, if you can believe that." She shook her head in amazement. "The stuff he's keeping for his new book must be dynamite."

Seth laughed at that and Laurel nearly missed a step. His laugh wasn't the same as it had been when he was a boy. It was low and deep and hesitant, as if he didn't find a lot of things funny enough to laugh at. In his business she supposed there weren't but she liked having made him laugh, anyway.

"I have all three of his books. My favorite is the one on antarctic mammals. Does he actually write the text?"

This time it was Laurel's turn to laugh. "No. He only takes the pictures, but he does a lot of research, anyway." She opened the door into the storeroom and continued on into the pharmacy. "You know as well as I do that Kevin's writing abilities are...limited. He still can't make two complete sentences in a row when it comes to writing down his thoughts."

"And I know for a fact that he'd have flunked biology if I hadn't helped him cram for every test we had. How did he ever make it through college?"

"You have been gone a long time," Laurel said thoughtfully, wiping a spot of dust off her white coat. "He dropped out after his freshman year and joined the navy. He got into photography then."

"Well, I'll be darned. Old Kevin really made something of himself, after all. 'Who'd a thunk it?'" he said, echoing Elinor's corny expression.

"Kevin always had the ability," Laurel retorted in her brother's defense, "just not the desire to succeed. At least that's what my mother's always said. We're very proud of him." She reached up to straighten a display of aspirin boxes. "And now I've told you all about him, so I won't hold you to that dinner invitation." Laurel found herself lifting her chin to look Seth straight in the eye, and was shocked and slightly appalled at her own boldness.

What would he say, this stranger who had once been her brother's closest friend? Would he back out gracefully, or ask her again to have dinner with him? She found she was holding her breath, and let it out in a long sigh.

"I want to hear everything about him. I have a lot of catching up to do. You've made me very curious to know how the Sauder kids are getting along in the world." Seth hoped he wasn't making a mistake. He couldn't deny it. It was there between them, fizzing and sparking in the quiet store. He'd felt it before, the instant physical attraction that usually preceded a short but pleasant interlude with a woman. But he didn't particularly like the feeling now, here, with this grown-up version of Kevin's little sister. Especially not back here in Bartlow, where the kind of casual liaison he was used to wasn't common practice at all. Seth pulled himself up short and made his second request much more formal. "I'd still like you to have dinner with me, if you're free."

"Thank you, Agent Norris," she replied with equal formality, but there was a definite sparkle of mischief in her warm brown eyes. "I'd be honored."

"Great." He was overreacting, as he had to so many things today. It wasn't sexual attraction he felt for this woman, he reminded himself. He wasn't merely responding to Laurel as a lovely, intriguing woman, but as the younger sister of his best friend. "Know any place good to eat around here?"

They both laughed at that. The bars served breakfasts and lunches. In the evening the menus ran pretty much to sandwiches and pizza. If they wanted to have any variety in their choice of restaurants, they'd have to drive twenty-five miles in any direction.

Laurel was about to suggest going into Toledo, when the earsplitting wail of a police siren cut off her words.

"What the hell?"

Seth didn't actually reach for his gun, but Laurel had the impression he could do so at the flicker of an eyelid. A police car screeched to a halt directly in front of the fire hydrant on the corner. Flashing blue and red lights had people coming to the doorways of every store on the street. Pedestrians stopped to stare.

"Rudy Sunderson," Caroline said with a sniff from be-hind the glass partition of the pharmacy. "Will that old fool never learn?"

Laurel stifled a grin and tried to look serious as the small, roly-poly deputy lumbered into the store. "The town coun-cil passed an ordinance against using the lights and siren in-side the city limits unless it was a real emergency," she whispered. "Rudy's just so darned proud of that car he gets carried away. According to my dad, the Sunday morning he stopped Mayor Whitman's wife in front of the Presbyterian church just as service was getting out to give her a scold for having a taillight burned out was the last straw."

"I'll bet it was," Seth said dryly. He straightened his tie, put on a poker face and held out his hand

Rudy halted. "Hello, Laurel," he said politely, touching his forefinger to his cap before shaking hands with Seth. "Nice day, isn't it?"

"It sure is, Rudy."

"Deputy Rudy Sunderson reporting for duty..." The middle-aged man stopped and blinked twice. "Well, I'll be damned. Aren't you Clint Norris's oldest boy?"

"Seth."

"Seth. I'm looking for the Secret Service guys."

In Seth's opinion Rudy resembled nothing so much as a teddy bear in a policeman's outfit in his black shirt and pants that strained at the seams, but his badge was polished and his tie was spotless.

"Seth is the Secret Service, Rudy," Laurel said gently.

"Glad to have you to back us up, Rudy." Seth sounded as if he really meant what he said. Laurel found she'd been holding her breath, and let it out. For some reason she couldn't immediately analyze, she hadn't wanted Seth to be patronizing to her father's old friend. Rudy meant well; he was just overeager, that was all.

"Well, I'll be damned! Seth Norris a Secret Service agent. Wait till I tell my wife."

Seth didn't have to find an answer to the last remark because a second police car joined the first. Now Bartlow's entire force was visible through the plate-glass windows of the store. The second cruiser parked conventionally in front of the hardware across the street.

"Marshal, over here," Rudy called as soon as his boss was inside the door. "Guess what? Clint Norris's boy here is the one we got the phone call about. *The agent in charge of the advance team for the President's visit.*" Rudy's reverential tone underlined each and every word of the title.

"Marshal Armstrong." Seth held out his hand once again. Wade Armstrong was a few years older than he was, probably thirty-six or thirty-seven, Seth decided. And he knew his business. He'd read the files on the area law enforcement agencies on the plane. The lean, auburn-haired man before him was a veteran from the Chicago police force. He'd been in Bartlow about three years. Seth wondered briefly what had brought Armstrong to his hometown. Shrewd hazel eyes met blue ones as the two men took stock of each other.

"Agent Norris, you'll have our full cooperation."

"I appreciate that. It's your town. You'll know sooner than anyone if there's something going down."

Wade nodded his understanding and Laurel realized yet again that Seth was in deadly earnest about his job. The presidential visit, a source of excitement and pleasant anticipation to the citizens of her hometown, was an exacting, dangerous job for the man with her.

"I'd like to talk over some of the preliminaries with you if you have the time." Seth had no qualms at all about laying his plans before Wade Armstrong. In some towns the police departments were more of a hindrance than a help to the Service, but that wouldn't be the case here.

Bartlow might not have the manpower or the facilities to coordinate a massive security effort, but Seth was certain Armstrong knew his job and his town. He would also have some suggestions for securing the outlying farmlands along the presidential route. It was going to take one hell of an effort to bring this two hundred mile whistle stop off without a hitch. Seth needed all the help he could get.

"I'll be in my office," Wade said. "Rudy, don't you think it's time to turn off the lights? We're attracting a crowd."

"Sure, Marshal." Rudy's red face got redder still. "Nice seeing you again, Agent Norris."

"'Seth.'"

"Seth, it is." Rudy beamed. "'Bye, Miss Laurel." He was gone in a whirl of black and silver, each step he took reverberating through the building.

"My office is just inside the main entrance of the city building, on the left." A flurry of activity heralded the entrance of a group of high school students. Laurel barely glanced in their direction. "I'd offer you a ride," Wade Armstrong continued, "but it's quicker to walk." He touched his finger to his cap in the same half salute Rudy tried so hard to emulate, and left.

"Is everybody going to call you 'Agent Norris'?" Laurel asked with a wicked little smile curving her lips.

She wasn't wearing lipstick, Seth was sure, but her lips were a rich, smooth coral color just the same.

"I'm not," a sullen young voice said from behind them.

Laurel spun around in alarm, but Seth only stood a little taller before turning to confront the speaker.

"Mike." The name came out harsh and low. He hadn't expected to see him so soon.

"Big brother."

The boy in the royal-blue-and-gold jacket stared back at him without blinking. God, the kid was going to look just like their old man. His hair was the same dark red, almost bronze, and his nose—well, that was the same as his, if you got technical. But Clint Norris's features were stamped deep on his brother's face.

"Why didn't you call Mom and Dad and let them know you'd be coming?"

"I wasn't sure when we'd be getting here. I only got the assignment forty-eight hours ago. I was with the advance team in Nevada last week...." Seth found himself stuttering over the explanation and shut his mouth with a snap. "You've grown, Mike."

"Most kids do in five years."

Laurel wished she were somewhere else, anywhere else. She didn't like being caught in the middle of a family quarrel. Seth had been more or less estranged from his family for a long time. She didn't like being sandwiched between these two tall Norris men when the animosity was so strong between them it could be felt in the air around her.

"How are the folks?"

It didn't take an expert in human relationships to discern how hard it was for Seth to speak those words.

"I have to be going," Laurel said into the sudden silence. "It looks like Rudy's light show has attracted some extra customers for the soda fountain. Ruthie's swamped." She made a move to step past Seth, but he blocked her way with a long arm. The hair on the back of his wrist was dark and curling. His watch had a black leather band and was plain and serviceable, no nonsense, like its owner. Laurel stayed put.

"About that dinner." There was a shading of apology in his words and in the deep blue of his eyes.

"Some other time." It was absurd how disappointed she felt about breaking such a casual date. She wanted to spend more time with him, hear his deep voice, learn more about him. "Goodbye, Seth."

"Goodbye, Laurel."

She was gone in a swirl of colors and the scent of lilacs.

"Are you coming out to the house, or are you going to make Mom come up here looking for you?" Mike asked, still belligerent.

Seth wasn't exactly sure what was wrong with his brother. It had been a long time since they'd seen each other, but he was unprepared for the hostility he felt radiating from the tall youngster. "I don't have a car," he said bluntly, as much to stall for time as anything else. "They're bringing extra vehicles in from the regional office in Cleveland. They won't arrive in Toledo until tomorrow."

"Your old room's all ready. The President isn't coming for over a week. Can't you stay the night, surprise her?"

"Why not?" He didn't really have a good excuse not to stay over. There was nothing going on at the motel where they'd established their base that McManus couldn't handle himself tonight. "Have you got a razor I can borrow?"

Mike grinned, and some of the wariness with which he'd been regarding his brother faded from his gray eyes. "At least you think I'm old enough to shave. Mom sure doesn't," he admitted with a sheepish grin. "Welcome home."

Seth ignored the outstretched hand and took Mike into his arms for a quick, hard hug. "Thanks." Something was wrong with the kid, but what was it? He'd stayed away too long, letting the rift between his family and him grow wider and deeper.

He'd always had an excuse for not coming back. First it was his marriage heading for the rocks. Then the divorce, and finally his being assigned to the White House detail. All legitimate, all convenient for not mending fences. And if Mike hadn't forced his hand, he'd have gone on avoiding a meeting with his father at least another day by taking Laurel Sauder out to dinner.

No, if he was honest with himself, that wasn't strictly true. For some reason he couldn't quite come to terms with, Laurel Sauder had put every other thought out of his head for most of the time he'd been alone with her. Or at least it seemed that way, as he replayed their conversation in his thoughts. A woman hadn't had that kind of effect on him for a long, long time. He wasn't sure he wanted it happening now.

Chapter Three

Laurel contemplated the mound of orange and red maple and oak leaves at her feet. She leaned on the handle of the rake and pushed at the old blue bandanna confining her hair. *Should she?* She narrowed her eyes to better assess the midafternoon activity up and down the street. The action didn't help much. She wasn't wearing her glasses and most of the people and objects beyond the sidewalk were a fuzzy blur of color and movement.

Her visual perception of the scene might be flawed, but there was still too much going on to indulge in the very childish desire to fall spread-eagled backward into the pile. Laurel Sauder, registered pharmacist, could think of a hundred very good reasons not to do so. Laurel Sauder, former tomboy, couldn't think of one.

She straightened and rolled her head to ease the strain in her neck. She wasn't used to this kind of work, but it felt good to be outside without the fierce Arizona sun beating down on her. Excited squeals and laughter caught her attention. Two houses down, the Cooper children were doing exactly what she'd been contemplating, rolling and tumbling in the mound of dry, fragrant leaves they'd been raking.

Laurel sent two more sweeps of leaves flying onto her own pile. She liked autumn best of all the seasons. The days were usually warm and mostly sunny, the nights cool, and harvest was getting underway. In the distance she could hear the steady drone of a big combine making trial passes through a field of soybeans to test for yield and ripeness. In a week or so, if the weather held, they'd be going full speed, day and night, until the crops were in. Her parents' big old frame house was located at the very end of Elm Street. Golden fields of soybeans and tall, yellow corn stretched away on two sides of the house.

When she was back home in Bartlow, Laurel always realized how much she missed the changing rhythm of the seasons in a farm community. Living in the desert southwest was so very different. She'd been born to this land and this way of life; it would always be a part of her, no matter where she lived.

She wondered if Seth Norris felt the same about coming back to Ohio? Did he sometimes yearn for the slower pace of rural life, as she often did? She hadn't seen him, except at a distance, since their first meeting two days previously, but he was often in her thoughts. She would have liked to go to dinner with him. They were kindred spirits by virtue of being expatriates temporarily returned to their place of origin. It created a bond, no matter how subjective, how fleeting.

Temptation beckoned again as a gust of wind swirled and danced across the grass, changing the tenor of her thoughts, threatening to undo all her work and her good intentions. Down the street the Cooper girls were starting a leaf fight. The youngest hopped around like a scarecrow, with leaves clinging to her hair and sweater like molting feathers. Laurel laughed aloud at the image and whirled in a circle, abandoning all thoughts of her dignity as she fell backward into the pile she'd so carefully created.

The sights and sounds of happy children sent her thoughts skipping onto forbidden ground. Was she wrong to be harboring dreams of having her own baby? What had started as a nebulous, wanting ache during her conversation with Elinor had become an obsession occupying a great deal of her thoughts. Was she crazy to contemplate such a course of action? How could she find a partner? A lover? Laurel's heart contracted at the reality of trying to seduce a man who would be, essentially, a stranger. She couldn't. She'd never been aggressive in her relationships with men. It wasn't in her nature.

The problem was too complicated, too complex for storybook-simple solutions like Prince Charming showing up with a glass slipper exactly in her size. She wasn't thinking clearly, and after all, it was only just a lovely dream. Laurel lay quietly for a few more minutes, focusing her attention outward, away from the loneliness at the center of her soul. She let the noisy rustling of leaves all around her settle into silence as she studied the pattern of bright October sunlight filtering through half-bare branches. A leaf dropped off a big maple. Laurel watched it glide closer. At the last moment, caught in an eddy of air, it veered to the left and landed on her nose.

It must be some kind of omen, Laurel decided with a giggle. She was taking life too seriously. Someday she'd find love again and it would be strong and lasting. She would have a baby of her own. She was young; there was plenty of time to take a second chance on love. She puckered her lips and blew the leaf away. The loneliness and wanting retreated but didn't fade completely; somehow she was sure they never would.

A car pulled up before the house and stopped. Laurel held her breath. Who could it be? Everyone in town knew her parents were away. Perhaps it was Elinor? Her cousin was the only person she could feel comfortable revealing her whereabouts to at the moment. She lay very still, hoping for a clue to the unknown person's identity without having to roll over onto her stomach to see who it was.

It was hard enough for some of her father's customers to believe she was grown up and competent to run his business. It was certain to be all over town in an hour if someone like the mayor's wife found her lying here in a ratty flannel shirt and jeans with leaves in her hair. She'd be the prime topic of conversation at tomorrow morning's coffee break at the Family Kitchen bakery's small dining area. Just as she would bet Seth Norris's arrival, choice of occupation and unexpected visit to his parents had entertained the matrons yesterday and today. An extremely fast, efficient and not-always-accurate network of information on the public and not-so-public activities of Bartlow's citizens originated in those morning coffee klatches. It was one of the things about small town living that wasn't so attractive.

"Jeez! I know I've been in the jungle too long," a low, deep, wonderfully familiar voice stated. "But if I'm going to conjure up a woman lying on my parents' front lawn, it shouldn't be my brat of a sister. What are you doing in Bartlow, Squirt?"

"Kevin?" Laurel wondered if she was dreaming. She rose to her knees in a flurry of leaves. "Kevin! What are you doing here?" She must be dreaming. Her brother was thousands of miles away in a South American jungle. It wasn't possible. She blinked to clear her vision, but the male figure before her didn't fade away. "Kevin!" She launched herself into his arms with such force that the tall blond man took a step backward to keep his balance.

"I'm AWOL, so to speak," he answered, laughing and somewhat breathless from her assault. "I flew out of the jungle with a priest making his monthly visit to an Indian tribe a few miles down the river, hopped a cargo plane to Rio, then on to Miami." He made it sound like nothing more than a Sunday afternoon drive in the country.

"But why? Is something wrong? Are you ill?" Laurel clung to his arm as though she intended never to let him go. It had to be something serious to take Kevin away from his work.

"I'm fine," he assured her. "But I broke a lens. The Mirachi. I can't finish my work without it." He looked tired and dejected. Grim self-reproach had replaced the boyish laughter in his green eyes. "I can isolate a grasshopper on a leaf at three hundred yards with that lens. It's like a kid to me. I've done some of my best work with it."

"Can it be fixed?" Laurel began walking toward the house, relieved that Kevin was all right—physically, at least.

"Mirachi's working on it now."

Kevin sounded confident, and Laurel nodded automatically. She'd never met the elderly Japanese lens maker who'd custom crafted much of Kevin's photographic equipment over the past few years, but she'd heard a great deal about him. Eccentric, wizened, ancient; he was a genius in Kevin's opinion.

"It could be ready tomorrow. Or it might be next week. Mirachi still has the magic, but he moves slower every time I see him." He rubbed his hand across his eyes. "It's Saturday, isn't it? I've sort of lost track of time." He smiled, but his offhand remarks couldn't hide his worry or fatigue.

"You look exhausted."

"I could sleep for a week," Kevin admitted. "But I heard this TV news spot at the airport in Miami. About a whistle-stop..."

"The President is coming to town." Laurel confirmed the report.

"Just like Truman?"

Laurel threw up her hands. "That's what everybody says."

"Every cloud has a silver lining, they say. Since I had to come out of the jungle, I might as well take the opportunity to photograph some of our native exotic wildlife."

Laurel looked up at him with a question in her brown eyes.

"National politicians."

"And the press," Laurel added with a laugh. "They're all over here already. The phone company's got a whole bank of phone lines set up in the council chambers at City Hall."

"Do you think Dan Rather will come?" Kevin looked wide-eyed with feigned excitement.

Laurel giggled in appreciation at the performance. "No way, big brother. I imagine we'll be able to pick out a face or two in the crowd, though," she added with a consoling pat on the arm when he looked down at her in exaggerated disappointment.

"Oh, well," Kevin said with a sigh. "Hey, I'll still be a great surprise for Mom and Dad." He held open the solid walnut front door with its center oval of beveled glass that was their mother's pride and joy.

"They'd be delighted—if they were here." Laurel turned to Kevin with regret. "They're in St. Louis attending Dad's army reunion. That's why you found me with leaves in my hair on the front lawn. I'm minding the store." She pulled the bandanna off her head and shook her hair free.

"When will they be back?" Kevin's green eyes darkened with true disappointment this time.

"Next week. I'm free till the thirtieth, so I told them not to hurry."

"I'll be back up the Amazon by then."

"We'll call the hotel and leave a message. Dad just checked in last night, so I don't expect to hear from them for a few days."

"So much for my big surprise homecoming, huh, Squirt?" Kevin looked around the cluttered, comfortably furnished living room he hadn't seen in nearly two years. "Hey, Mom got new carpet."

Laurel ignored the observation. "You're the second person to resurrect that odious nickname in the past forty-eight hours." She glared at her brother's back as she followed him into the room.

"You're kidding." Kevin spun on his heel. "I didn't think anyone else in Bartlow would even remember it except maybe Elinor."

"It isn't anyone from Bartlow," Laurel answered. "Kevin, you'll never guess who's back in town."

"Probably not, unless you tell me, Squ—Sis," he finished in his teasing way.

"Seth Norris." Laurel was rewarded by the expression of amazement on her brother's face. Kevin really did look a lot like their father. He was tall, blond and broad shouldered. She took after her mother's family: small, darker and heavier. "And guess what else?"

"He's a Secret Service agent," Kevin answered, effectively taking the wind out of Laurel's sails.

"How did you know that?"

"I talked to his mother the last time I was home."

"Oh." It didn't surprise Laurel. Kevin was outgoing and easy to talk to. He liked people and they liked him.

"Listen, you put in that call to the folks' hotel and I'll go out to the car and get my gear. Then we can get something to eat before I crash. How about a pizza at the Station?"

"What else?" Laurel asked in resignation. "Let me wash my hands and face and comb my hair."

"I'll race you for the bathroom." Kevin caught her up in his arms and whirled her in the air just as he always used to do.

Laurel giggled with delight. "Put me down," she ordered, but her voice lacked conviction. "Oh, Kev, it is good to see you." She gave him a hug, clinging so tightly to his neck he grunted. She loosened her hold and caught his clear gaze. "Sometimes I wish you'd give up chasing all over the world to photograph animals whose names most people can't even pronounce. If you'd settle down someplace civilized with some nice girl, we could spend Christmas and Easter and the Fourth of July together like other families." Laurel heard her voice start to tremble, and stopped speaking abruptly.

Kevin held her at arm's length and searched her face. She was afraid he could see the sadness beneath the surface happiness she tried to project for everyone else. "If I don't take pictures of those strange animals, no one will know the danger they're in. It won't take very many more years of exploitation and neglect to lose them all."

Laurel nodded. "You're right, of course."

"But I know what you mean," Kevin added. "Living out of backpacks and sleeping on the ground isn't quite the high it used to be." He changed the subject abruptly, catching Laurel off guard so that she couldn't evade answering. "Are you doing okay, Squirt?" His voice was filled with gruff love and concern. Laurel didn't admonish him for the use of the detested nickname.

"I'm fine. Just feeling a little sorry for myself, that's all." She could tell Kevin how much she missed Penny and he would understand. But could she tell him how often lately she'd been dreaming of a child of her own?

"Tom Keller is a jackass," Kevin declared, his face set and hard.

Laurel abandoned any thought of confiding in her brother for the time being. Suddenly she saw him as others must. A commanding man, a master of his craft, successful and admired, even a little famous. In her eyes he would always be her idolized big brother, but for the moment her dreams were too private even for Kevin's ears. "No, Kevin. He was selfish and a little immature, but not bad." She found she believed what she was saying and it helped a little. She tried for a big smile and almost pulled it off.

"Any man who lets my sister slip through his fingers is a jackass." Kevin ended the discussion. "Let's eat, I'm starving."

Laurel loved him for his loyalty and his willingness to drop a subject that would always be painful. "You can tell me all about your new book while we eat."

"Saturday night in Bartlow. The excitement may be too much for me."

"We'll make an early night of it. You can sleep through Sunday school, too, since no one knows you're in town."

"Good."

"And Monday night we'll go to the town meeting."

"Town meeting? This is Ohio, not Maine. I've never heard of anything like that in Bartlow." Kevin sounded intrigued.

"It's for the merchants whose properties will be affected by the security restrictions for the presidential visit. Seth Norris will be there." Laurel found she was looking forward to seeing him.

"Sounds interesting. Let's go eat."

"Not till you change your clothes." Laurel surveyed his wrinkled shirt and grubby jeans with a stern eye.

"I shaved off my beard," Kevin said, running his hand over the blond stubble on his chin.

"Good. You look like a shaggy dog with a beard," Laurel replied candidly. "It won't take you five minutes to change."

"I get the hint." Kevin brushed at his pants with a strong brown hand. He gave her a rueful, lopsided grin. "Laundry facilities are few and far between where I've been for the past six months, you know." He looked at her hopefully.

Laurel ignored the opening to offer to do his laundry. "I've got another surprise for you. Mom has a new washer and dryer. They work like a dream. Get your clothes in here and I'll show you how to punch the buttons." She gave him a saucy look over her shoulder as she started up the stairs.

"I'll get you for this—"

"Don't even think of calling me by that name." Laurel held up a warning finger. She tried to look stern but spoiled the effect by giggling. "I might just forget to make that phone call to Mom and Dad's hotel if you cause me too much grief."

"You wouldn't dare." Kevin took a menacing step toward her, his lean, tanned face screwed into a furious mock scowl. "You may be all grown up, Laurel, but I can still take you over my knee."

Laurel retreated up a couple of risers, pretending terror, laughing all the way. "You still have the scar from the last time you tried to spank me, remember?"

"Don't remind me." Kevin's scowl was replaced by a pained grimace. He lifted his left leg to rub his shin. "Lord, I'll never know why the folks got you that cowgirl outfit that Christmas. Those boots had points on them sharp enough and hard enough to dent steel."

"Truce?" Laurel inquired with a triumphant smile. She leaned over the banister to extend her hand.

Kevin reached up and caught her fingers between his own big rough hands. "Truce. Now get going."

"I know, I know. You're starving."

SETH RESTED BOTH HANDS on the kitchen table and sniffed appreciatively. "Smells good, Mom."

"Fried chicken always smells good. I'm glad you could find the time to eat with us tonight." Helen Norris set a covered basket of flaky biscuits alongside the heaping platter of chicken in the middle of the round oak pedestal table that had occupied the same spot in the farmhouse since his father was a boy.

Clint Norris had been born in this house. So had his father before him. Seth's great-grandfather had built it at the turn of the century when Bartlow was still mostly swampland. Clint had always expected his eldest son to live here, too, someday, but Seth had had different dreams.

A bowl of sliced tomatoes made their appearance on the table. "That's the last of the Big Boys," his mother announced. "I'm not sorry to see them go. I put up twenty-five quarts of juice and sixteen pints of sauce, not to mention the beans and corn I froze."

"And the strawberry jam and applesauce. You work too hard."

His mother was almost sixty. She was starting to show her age in the deepening lines around her eyes and the hint of a double chin. But her blue eyes still sparkled brightly and her hair was just as dark and curly as it had ever been. She looked at him sharply, hands on rounded hips, making Seth aware how harsh his words must have sounded. He erased their sting with a smile. Helen smiled back.

"I'm boasting, not complaining. You know how much canning our own fruits and vegetables saves on the grocery bill. It beats going to work at Bartlow Industries or driving a school bus for extra money to make ends meet like most of my friends. Mike eats like a horse and there's his college tuition to think about next year." She sighed and blew a wisp of wavy black hair off her forehead.

"Has he decided on a school?" By dint of a lot of extra hard work and cutting corners, his parents had managed to put him and his sisters through college on the income from the three hundred sixty acres they farmed. Now his sisters both lived on the West Coast and had families of their own. He visited them occasionally when he was assigned to accompany the President to his California hideaway.

"No. He's dragging his feet and I don't know why. His grades are good. The best of the four of you, really. He could even get a partial basketball scholarship to a small school if he wants to play."

"What's the problem then?"

"I don't know," Helen repeated, slamming the silver drawer with more force than necessary. "He reminds me a lot of you, Seth. So hard to talk to about things that mean a lot to you. He just clams up around me and your dad."

"He's bullheaded, you mean," Seth said with a rueful grin as he fiddled with the silverware his mother handed him.

"You get that from the Norris side of the family." She didn't contradict his character assessment. She opened the back door and hollered across the barnyard. "Clint! Michael! Come in here. Supper's ready." Helen shut the door and shook her head in disgust. "They can't hear me with that tractor running. Go get them, Seth. It's only an hour until the town meeting starts. You don't want to be late."

"I'm not so sure. I understand there's going to be some pretty vocal opposition to closing off Main Street." He recalled for a moment the quick flash of anger and dismay his announcement had kindled in Laurel Sauder's big brown eyes. He hadn't seen her since that first afternoon, but she was often in his thoughts. He wondered if she would be at the meeting tonight. He also wondered how she felt being back here. For her it wasn't quite such a shock, he imagined. She visited often, from what he'd gathered from their conversation in the loft. Still, her life in Phoenix must be vastly different. But was it any richer or more fulfilling?

"You can handle it," Helen predicted. "It'll only be Earl Conklin and one or two other malcontents moaning about losing business. But you'll never convince me anyone's going to be wanting to buy flowers or potted plants while the President's in town."

"I hope I can persuade our local florist that easily."

"Tell him I said so." Helen set a pitcher of milk on the table with a flourish.

"That'll do the trick," Seth said deadpan. He held back a grin and concentrated on lining up forks and knives beside the plates.

Helen wasn't fooled. "Quit making fun of me and do as you're told." She turned back to the stove with a chuckle. "It's good to have you home."

"It's good to be home, Mom." Seth wasn't even surprised to realize he meant it.

He stepped out into the October twilight. The crewneck sweater he was wearing over his white shirt felt good in the cool air. The day had been warm and sunny, but there would likely be fog by midnight when he officially went off duty. He'd probably stay here again tonight and send McManus back to the motel headquarters they'd established in Toledo as soon as the meeting was over. His partner would let him know if there was anything pending that needed his attention. McManus had been born and raised in Dallas. He was more than happy to spend most of his time shuttling between Dayton, where the President would board his special train, and Toledo, where the campaign trip was to end. Even those two cities, with over a half million people each, were a little too small town for his taste. Bartlow, with its rural isolation made him downright nervous.

Seth had felt that way, too, once upon a time, confined and cut off from life, from the "real world." Now that he was part of it, a small cog in a very important wheel, there was nothing there, he'd learned, worth holding on to. He paused to watch his father and brother working on the motor of the new John Deere diesel tractor. What did a piece of machinery like that cost these days? Seventy-five thousand dollars? No wonder his dad's dark red hair was liberally sprinkled with gray. Farmers were going bankrupt all over the country. Land values were down, grain prices at the lowest level in years, yet his dad hung on. Still committed to a way of life that had endured for centuries, still coaxing a living from the stubborn, black clay, still his own man and proud of it.

As he grew older, Seth was beginning to wonder if his father had been right all along. Maybe he should have stayed on the farm. Maybe he should have committed himself to the land. Then perhaps he wouldn't be midway through his thirties with no ties to bind him, no wife or children of his own to make getting up each day worth the effort. Maybe then he'd be at peace with himself.

"Supper's ready and Mom's hopping 'round on one foot waiting for you two." Seth halted just inside the door of the barn. It smelled of eighty years of dust and hay, cows and chickens, machinery and manure.

"Be right in." Clint straightened slowly and rubbed his hands on an oily rag. "Best not to keep your mother waiting when she's got a meal on the table." He motioned to Mike to switch off the big green tractor.

"She's a beauty, Dad." Seth bent forward to peer into the engine casing.

"Don't get too close," his father cautioned gruffly. "You'll get grease all over your clothes."

"You should have called me out to help."

"You're on duty. What if the White House called while you were out here tinkering with a balky mule of a Deere."

"Good point." Seth laughed at his father's pun. Clint allowed the edges of his mouth to curl into a smile before he said seriously, "You always were good with machinery. I could have used your help."

The motor died and Michael hopped down out of the cab. "What would Seth know about a tractor engine anymore? He hasn't even turned a strip of ground in nearly twenty years."

Seth bit back a sharp retort and held his peace, because what his young brother said was true. He hadn't shown any interest in the farm for what amounted to Michael's entire life. Why should the boy believe he was interested now? Clint looked down at the scuffed steel toes of his work shoes and said nothing. The tension between the trio was thick enough to cut with a knife. Once again it was brought home to Seth that for all intents and purposes he was an outsider and had no business trying to mediate problems between his father and brother.

"Extra hands are always welcome," Clint said finally.

"We can take care of this place. You've got your own job to do," Michael continued sullenly. "Isn't your job what really matters? If Dad's told me once, he's told me a thousand times, that protecting the life of the President of the United States is a hell of a lot more important than getting a crop in the fields."

"Mike! That's enough. Your brother's work is important."

Seth wasn't sure what to say that wouldn't make matters even more tense. He'd always thought he was hot tempered himself, but the dark red hair his brother and father had inherited from their Norris forebears carried with it added fractiousness.

"I'm sorry." Mike grabbed his royal blue jacket with the familiar gold emblem across the back. Future Farmers of America. It brought back a lot of memories for Seth, not all of them pleasant. Mike looked embarrassed by his outburst. "I'll go get cleaned up while you eat. See you at the meeting, Seth."

His voice was less quarrelsome. It was as close to an apology as he could come at the moment. Seth accepted it as such. "I didn't expect you to attend."

"Our government teacher is giving us extra credit," Mike confessed with a grin. "He said this is history and we should be a part of it whether we want to or not."

"That's probably the only reason I'd have gone at your age myself," Seth admitted with a laugh. "I'll be glad for your support. Mom says Earl Conklin's going to raise a stink over having to close his flower shop. I wouldn't be a bit surprised if Ralph Sauder's daughter doesn't try to get her two cents' worth in, also." He smiled inwardly at the memory of sparkling brown eyes. "She's not very pleased about having the drugstore sealed off."

"You can handle those two. Earl's seventy, if he's a day, and Ms. Sauder hardly weighs a hundred pounds, I'll bet." Mike grinned and faked a punch at Seth's shoulder, his bad temper forgotten with adolescent quickness.

"I hope so."

"And if they don't cooperate you can always have them thrown in jail." Mike got in his parting shot and took off. "I'll see you later. I have to pick up a couple of guys." His long strides covered the distance between the house and the barn in a matter of seconds.

Seth was alone with his father. He could count the minutes they'd been alone together over the past fifteen or so years on the fingers of both hands. Seth searched his feelings for the familiar angry ache and found it missing. Sometime, somehow, the old animosity had disappeared. The silence between them now would only become uncomfortable if he allowed it to. A younger Seth would probably have done so. But he was twice Michael's age. He hoped he had twice his sense. "I'd like to know what I've done to get under his skin."

Clint looked sharply at his eldest son. He, too, was silent a moment, as if choosing his words with extra care. "It's his age, I suppose." Clint's tone was carefully everyday. If he was aware of the giant step he was taking in reestablishing contact with Seth, he wasn't about to let the knowledge show. "He's wanting to make all these decisions about his future for himself. He don't particularly want to go to college. We've been arguing about that for a couple of years now." Clint balled up the oily cloth he was still holding and threw it hard against the wall. It landed with a soft plop. "I've spent half my life working to give you kids an education. I don't intend for it to stop now."

"What does he want to do, Dad?" Seth didn't like having to ask what his brother's wishes for the future might be. If he'd been around while Mike was growing up he'd know what dreams he cherished.

"He wants to farm." Clint's voice was hard, laced with old pain. "It's too late for this place, Seth. Maybe if you'd stayed we could have taken on enough land to make a go of it...." He shook his head as he switched off the overhead bulb that hung from the rafters spanning the two haymows. Darkness descended like a heavy, aromatic blanket, smudging details, hiding his father's rough-cut features as effectively as a mask. "But not anymore. This place is all your mom and I have. It won't support two families, not the way things are today. And I'm too old to do anything else."

He grabbed his jacket from a bale of straw and started for the house. Seth shoved his hands in the pockets of his gray wool slacks and walked alongside his father. He didn't say anything.

"A man's a fool to want his children to go into this crazy business these days. You were right back then, son. I was wrong."

He kicked at a stone in the driveway, then took a deep breath and let it out in a long whistle. Seth felt the tension and stress in the older man like a physical pain. It had cost him a lot of pride to say those words.

"Mike'll do as I say come next fall. He hasn't got any choice."

Seth felt his stomach tighten with anger at his father's intractable tone. He knew his reaction wasn't rational, but this didn't make the feeling any less intense. Clint was probably right. Farming wasn't exactly a growth industry these days. And how in hell could he tell his father, after all this time, that he'd changed his mind, too? That he wanted to come back home? After all, the chasm growing between Mike and their father was a reflection of his own defection all those years ago.

No wonder the boy resented him. For over fifteen years, almost Mike's entire life, he'd been a stranger. Now, when the youngster was ready to begin making decisions that would affect him for the rest of his life, Seth's leaving home was being held up to him as an example yet again. This time as the right choice. It was ironic and it hurt like hell.

How was he going to convince his father, so bitter and so tired of carrying on alone, that he should allow his younger son to farm the land he loved? Clint's attitude was mostly Seth's fault. He couldn't heal the breach by simply asking to come home. Or could he?

The need to return to his roots had been growing steadily within him for a long time. That old saw about not being able to take the country out of the boy even if you took the boy out of the country was more true than anyone realized. He just hadn't recognized the longing for what it was until he got back home. He doubted anyone he knew right now would understand his yearning to return to the land.

Except one person. A small, determined woman with haunting brown eyes. Laurel Sauder was another lost lamb searching for her way back to the fold. It would be nice to think they might find their way together.

Chapter Four

The meeting was going smoothly. The main room of City Hall was full of people: the mayor, council members, most of the merchants, the Methodist and Lutheran ministers, and what she would guess was at least half of the senior government class from the high school, including Michael Norris. Seth's parents were also present and Laurel wondered how things were coming between them.

"Agent Norris." She spoke loudly enough to carry over the whir of the exhaust fans working overtime to deal with the smoke and heat of sixty bodies pressed into too small a space. Seth was bringing the subject of business closings to a conclusion. It was time for her to voice her own misgivings.

Laurel had to admit she was impressed with his handling of the situation so far. Earl Conklin had raised a fuss, just as everyone knew he would, but it had amounted to a tempest in a teapot. Seth was polite, willing to listen to Earl's opinion, and impossible to influence, just as he'd been that first day in the storeroom.

He'd explained to the irate florist in a few concise, chilling sentences just how big a job it was to keep the President safe from harm. Earl had hemmed and hawed and blustered through a few more complaints. But when Seth asked him point-blank how much responsibility he would be willing to accept if anyone were hurt during an attempt on the President's life—brought about by his lack of cooperation with the Service—he agreed, although still grudgingly, to go along with the closings.

"Agent Norris." Laurel stood as she repeated his name. Obviously her voice hadn't carried over the scraping of chair legs and secondary conversation. Seth looked up from his notes.

"Ms. Sauder." He looked out over the crowd, narrowing his eyes to counteract the glare of the overhead lights. He'd spotted her early on, sitting at the back near the door, dressed in a blouse of some soft blue-green color that complemented the warm golden tones of her skin and made her eyes seem even bigger and darker than he remembered.

"I understand the necessity of safeguarding the President during his visit." She paused a moment to clear her throat, then rushed on. "But I need access to the pharmacy if an emergency should arise."

There were murmurs of interest from the crowd. A faint stain of color tinted Laurel's cheeks. She twisted her thumb through the belt loop of her jeans in a gesture of nervous tension. Even from this distance, Seth could see how nicely the soft denim hugged the curve of her hip and thigh. She shifted her weight, and her breasts pressed against the fabric of her blouse.

She wouldn't meet his eyes directly, instead fixing her gaze at a point somewhere near his left shoulder. She didn't like being the center of attention now any more than she had as a child. Seth pushed his more private deductions to the back of his mind and stepped deliberately back into his role as liaison, explaining that the Service tried to be as flexible as possible where the disruption of citizens' daily lives was concerned.

"We'll run a security check on you, and you'll be issued a special pass just like the other village officials who need access to the restricted area. That is—" he paused for dramatic effect "—if we don't find any skeletons in your closet. You aren't, by any chance, a double agent working for an unfriendly foreign power, are you?"

Appreciative chuckles from the crowd indicated his small joke was a success. He smiled to reinforce the humor. Laurel didn't smile back. Her color darkened several shades. She looked uncomfortable, and Seth regretted prolonging her ordeal as the center of attention. Yet he thought he detected a sparkle of amusement in her brown eyes. He decided to follow up on it and find out for sure. "There isn't any reason you might be turned down, is there, Ms. Sauder?"

"Just a parking ticket I forgot to pay before I left Phoenix." Laurel tilted her head slightly to the left, a reluctant smile curving the corners of her mouth. "Will that show up on your computer check?" The laughter was general this time.

"Yes, it will."

The crowd shifted their attention back to Seth once more. Several people shook their heads in amazement. Somebody mumbled something about not keeping anything secret from a computer. Seth pretended not to hear.

"But I doubt if that alone will qualify as grounds to deny you access to your place of business in an emergency. I should have all the necessary information in twenty-four hours. By Wednesday afternoon at the latest."

"Thank you." She sat down, her face still slightly flushed.

She was nothing at all like Gina, although both women were successful and independent. His ex-wife had been bright, sharp, polished to a brilliant sheen. She had her own interior design business now in Baltimore and she'd probably cleared three times his salary last year alone. He was happy for her. She'd been as eager to be out of their failing marriage as he was.

He wasn't certain what adjectives he could use to describe Laurel Sauder, though. She was softer somehow, less driven to succeed. He didn't know why she was divorced, but he'd bet it wasn't because having a husband took too much time away from her work. The bitterness of his memories of Gina startled him and he cut off that line of thought.

Laurel was far more like his mother and the women he remembered growing up with. That wasn't unusual; they shared the same background, after all. Women who were strong and resilient, able to juggle families and careers. Partners in increasingly complex agri-businesses, working alongside their husbands in the fields, weathering good years and bad and still managing to lead secure and relatively happy lives, turning out intelligent and well-adjusted children in the bargain.

Laurel Sauder would make a wonderful mother. The judgment came out of the blue and he didn't know quite what to make of it.

The mayor rose from his seat at the head of the table, disrupting the train of Seth's private thoughts. "If there are no other questions at this time, we'll adjourn the meeting." He paused; people fidgeted in their seats, searching for purses and tugging jackets off the backs of chairs. No one spoke.

"Okay." The mayor banged his gavel on the table. "A schedule of events will be in Thursday's edition of the *Bartlow Flag*. Marshal Armstrong has told me to warn you that any car found parked on Main Street after eight Friday morning will be hauled away." The mayor held up his hands in dismissal. "We've got quite a show lined up to keep everyone entertained until the President's train arrives. Better show up looking your best. We might all see ourselves on the *Six O'clock News*." Laughter and catcalls greeted his last announcement. "Good night, folks. Any questions you have you can refer to Agent Norris or his men."

Laurel was already on her way out the door when Seth managed to get away from the mayor and several council members who'd descended on him. She had linked arms with a tall, fair-haired man, whom Seth hadn't noticed before. A dart of envy knifed through him. Then he took a second look. There was something about him; the set of his shoulders, the red highlights in his blond hair, that struck a memory chord deep within him.

Kevin would look like that now.

Laurel's companion glanced back over his shoulder and his green eyes caught and held Seth's gaze. He grinned and Seth was certain of his identity. It was Kevin Sauder. Jerking his thumb in the direction of the street in a wordless invitation to follow, his old friend walked out the door. Others had recognized Laurel's brother and Laurel and Kevin were becoming the center of a noisy, exuberant group.

Seth envied them. He didn't have many friends outside the Service. Most of the friends he'd shared with Gina had drifted away after the divorce. And that was his fault too; he'd quit accepting invitations long before people had quit asking him.

It wasn't hard to rationalize his reclusiveness. The White House detail was grueling physically, especially when the President traveled. Seth had even spent six weeks in Africa that spring, making advance plans for a trip that was canceled when the regime was overthrown in a lightning fast coup. Rotating eight-hour shifts seven days a week left little time to socialize, even when he was back in Washington.

But, as with so many other things these past few days, the tug of the past was too strong to ignore. He made his way to the group surrounding Kevin and Laurel. She looked small and fragile at the center of a half circle of a dozen men. Most of the people were vaguely familiar to him, teammates, classmates, only older, heavier and with thinning hair. They were all dressed casually like Kevin.

His friend's bare, sun-streaked, blond head towered over them all. The two old school chums clasped hands. Men didn't hug other men in Bartlow. The closest you came to physical contact was a hearty slap on the back. Kevin hadn't forgotten the rules. Seth had to brace himself against the force of his greeting.

Kevin's green eyes sparkled with devilment. "Old buddy. It has been too long," he said unnecessarily.

"Way too long." Seth gave Kevin's hand a bone-crushing squeeze to retaliate for the overzealous blow between his shoulder blades. He was pleased to see the taller man wince, although none of the satisfaction showed on his face.

Kevin wasn't fooled by Seth's bland expression. "Will you look what living with all those bureaucrats and politicians has done to this man?" he addressed the group in exaggerated, mournful tones. "All dressed up and wearing a tie." He reached out and flicked the knot of Seth's subdued, blue-and-gray tie with the tip of his finger. "Damn it, man, don't you know it's a weekday? Neckties are for Sunday school and funerals." The others laughed.

"Company policy," Seth replied, keeping his face stern, but there was laughter in his eyes. He'd always been Kevin's straight man. That was something else that would never change.

"You know, I can't believe my eyes. Seth Norris, a T-man. Good thing old Marshal Bemer never wrote us up for joyriding in Henry Jackson's pickup."

"I'd never have gotten this job with a criminal record," Seth agreed, shaking his head at their youthful folly.

"You were juveniles." Laurel's voice was sharp, but both men turned to her with smiles. She only noticed Seth's. She smiled back. "I know, I know. It was ages ago."

"We scared you that night, didn't we?" His voice was low and warm. It touched her like a caress. She nodded.

"We have a hell of a lot to catch up on," Kevin announced, breaking the spell of Laurel's eyes finding his. Seth looked away from her with an effort that was almost physical.

"And I want to know what you're doing here in Bartlow instead of paddling a dugout up the Amazon."

"That's another long, sad story. Let's go over to the Station and get a beer, and I'll tell you all about it."

Several other voices chimed in to second the idea. One or two of the men at the edge of the group suited action to words and headed for the tavern. Laurel decided she'd be walking home alone.

"I can't go with you, Kevin." Regret laced Seth's words. "I'm on duty until midnight."

"Damn." Kevin frowned. "When do you have a couple hours free of this glorified baby-sitting patrol?"

"Tomorrow afternoon." Trust Kevin to cut right to the heart of things. *Glorified baby-sitting patrol.* In a very serious and deadly way, it was. "I'll look you up."

"I'll be staying at the house. It's been too damned long, Seth." Kevin shook Seth's hand.

The two men seemed to have forgotten Laurel existed. She tugged on her brother's sleeve to bring his attention back to her. "I'm going home, Kev. It's been a long day and I need to search my memory for any other misdemeanors that Seth's computer check is liable to dredge up. I want to have my defense ready.''

"Time enough to worry about that when we come for you with handcuffs, Laurel." He couldn't help teasing her. He was recalling more and more half-forgotten occasions when he and Kevin had ganged up on the exasperating twelve-year-old she'd been.

"Why don't you walk Laurel home? You can't have that much to do before midnight." Laurel was looking down at the toes of her shoes and missed the calculating gleam in Kevin's eyes. "You can get in a little third degree along the way."

Laurel's head snapped up. "Kevin, don't be ridiculous."

"You're a dangerous character, sister mine. Or hadn't you noticed?" He directed the last remark to Seth.

"Oh, I've noticed, all right." He didn't elaborate. He didn't have to. "Laurel?" He looked at her with a question in his blue, blue eyes.

"I have to check in at the store before they close." She took a deep breath, aware of several pairs of interested eyes. "And then I would like to have some company on the way home."

"Fifteen minutes, while I check with McManus, then I'm free until I make my final rounds and report in to the night shift."

"Fine."

Seth was gone with a wave of his hand that included all the group.

"I'll get you for that, big brother."

"What?" Kevin looked sublimely innocent.

"Setting that poor man up so that there was no way he could refuse to offer to walk me home." They turned their steps down Main Street, nodding greetings to other pedestrians as they walked.

"I'm only looking out for you, Squirt." Kevin called a hello to his old coach, who was coming out of Earl Conklin's shop with a small potted plant.

"You are not. You're setting us up. I'll never see Seth Norris again after Friday." The words struck oddly in her mind. *Never see him again.* Laurel refused to connect them to any other thought.

"I wasn't setting you up, not intentionally, anyway." Kevin had the grace to look slightly sheepish. "I just thought you might enjoy each other's company. Seth's a swell guy."

"The Seth Norris you knew almost twenty years ago was a swell guy. This man is a stranger to both of us."

They were in front of the tavern. Music swelled out of the door that was open to the mild October evening. Noise and laughter made talking in a normal voice difficult. Kevin stared down at her. He was almost a foot taller than she was and she had to tilt her head back a long way to meet his gaze.

"Maybe you're right." He didn't look as though he wanted to concede the point. "None of us are the same kids we were back then." He looked a little sad at the realization and Laurel was sorry she'd brought the matter up at all.

"I can take care of myself, Kevin. That's all I really wanted you to understand. I like Seth. I'll enjoy our walk. Now go shoot the bull with your friends and quit worrying about me."

"You are all grown up, aren't you?" Kevin shook his head in wonderland. "Maybe I shouldn't stay away so long next time."

"Maybe not." Laurel shot him a challenging look. "You may not be able to manipulate me at all next trip." With a giggle at the look of consternation on his face, she hurried across the street and into the store.

"THE MOON IS AS BIG as a volleyball."

"Did anyone ever tell you you have a very poetic turn of mind, Laurel Sauder?" There was more than a hint of sarcasm in Seth's low, raspy voice. The sound of his words washed over her skin like rough smoke. She shivered and hunched her shoulders inside her lightweight cotton jacket.

"Frequently." She giggled, more from nerves than amusement. Silvery light cascaded through the half-naked branches of the trees overhead, catching in the sable waves of his hair. He'd taken off his tie and the top button of his shirt exposed the taut skin of his throat. He'd rolled back the sleeves of his shirt and his arms were strong and lightly muscled. She felt very odd and unlike herself walking alone with this man.

Laurel cleared her throat and pulled her skittering thoughts back into line. "Let me try again. The moon is as big and shiny as a ripe honeydew melon." She looked at him from the corner of her eye, awaiting his opinion on her latest effort.

"More appetizing," Seth conceded. "But still not exactly poetic."

"You try." Laurel stopped walking and looked out over the flat countryside at the patchwork pattern of fields and farm lots bathed in pale October moonlight.

They were standing on the banks of the old railroad reservoir. It had been deeded to the town years ago when the steam locomotives were replaced by diesel engines. Now it was a park and recreation area. In winter, the fifteen-foot embankments were the closest thing to a sledding hill Bartlow kids ever saw. It was a popular spot for bike riding, bird-watching and leisurely evening walks.

Tonight they had it all to themselves.

Seth was silent for a long moment. "Okay, I'll take a stab at it. It looks like a silver medallion given to a beautiful mythical princess by a gallant warrior to remind her of him while he's away on a great quest."

"What kind of quest?"

Laurel wasn't aware of the note of whimsy in her voice, but Seth was. He was aware of a lot of things: the way she walked, the sound of her laughter, the flowery, spicy scent of her straight brown hair swinging free just above her shoulders.

"To bring the lovely lady the moon itself, of course." He smiled down at her, small and strong and determined at his side.

"Of course. Not bad," Laurel admitted with a smile that rivaled the brightness of the full moon.

"I can't remember the last time I've been out when you could see the stars this plainly." The nearest streetlamp was a hundred yards away. Above them the autumn stars were grace notes to the beauty of the harvest moon. He felt isolated from reality, here alone with Laurel, and he liked the feeling.

"Want to stay a little longer?" Laurel motioned to the base of a cottonwood tree that had a trunk as wide as a park bench. He dropped down and stretched one leg out before him, resting his right arm on his upraised knee. Above them the cottonwood's leaves were already yellow and half of them had fallen. The grass was thick with them.

"I'd forgotten how quiet it could be here." Crickets chirruped around them. A frog croaked at the water's edge a few feet away, but the night air was growing chilly and he soon gave up. An owl hooted in the distance. Behind them, town sounds were muted and indistinct. "The air smells good, too." He took a long, deep breath, scented with wood smoke and damp earth.

"I'm not looking forward to all the dust when they start fall plowing," Laurel answered matter-of-factly, for all the world as if she had a home here to keep clean. "And the chaff from the elevator, ugh." She picked up a twig and started swirling it through the fallen leaves. Their sharp, musty scent rose to his nostrils.

"Are you always so prosaic?" Seth cocked his head and grinned over at her, his teeth white and gleaming in the near darkness.

"Not prosaic," Laurel defended herself. "Just practical."

Her knees were drawn up close to her chest. Her chin rested on top of her folded hands, the twig dangling from her fingers, forgotten. She looked young and desirable and far more fragile than she really was. In another time, in another place, she might have been the mythical princess of his story. A slight frown drew her delicately arched brows together. It was too dark to see the color of her eyes, but Seth drew the rich, warm brown shade from his memory and smiled at the recollection.

"You're right, in any event." Her thoughts were obviously of a far more serious nature than fairy tales. "Bartlow isn't heaven, or even close to it. But it's home and it has big cities beat all to hell."

"I miss it, too." She twisted around, tossing her stick into the water behind them.

"Where do you go next, Seth?" Laurel couldn't keep herself from asking the question. Her skin tingled from being so close to him. Only inches separated their shoulders; his hip was so near that if she shifted her weight they would touch. She hugged her arms tighter around her knees.

"Back to D.C. I'll get my next assignment there. I think the President is scheduled for a series of speeches in the Pacific Northwest. It's hard to keep track during an election year."

"Sort of, if this is Tuesday, it must be Portland, kind of thing?"

"Sort of."

"But not quite that simple." The moonlight picked out the angle of his jaw as he leaned his head and shoulders against the tree. The lean, strong lines of his wrist and hand were etched in silver light as they rested on his knee. Hands trained to kill if necessary. "Dangerous and exciting."

She said it so quietly Seth wasn't sure he'd heard her at all, but he answered, anyway.

"Once you've spent three or four nights in a row standing in the drafty hallway of a hotel in some city five thousand miles away from home, you'd be hard-pressed to find any excitement or glamour about the job."

"All right, listening to the President snore on the other side of a hotel room door all night may not be exciting, I'll agree. But the danger is always there, isn't it?"

She sounded so young and so innocent and so earnest. Seth hid a smile, but when he looked into her eyes he found himself answering seriously. "The danger is always there. My job consists of being prepared to put myself between death and the man I protect every minute I'm on duty. It could come from anywhere, any way, at any time. I might never know if I have what it takes to deal with it. Or if I do face it, I might not live to know."

"I see." Her voice was a whisper in the moonlight.

God. Why had he said that? He didn't ordinarily talk too much. And never about the dark side of his work. He didn't know why he'd said anything at all.

"So how about a kiss? I'm shipping out tomorrow, sweetie, and who knows if I'll be coming back? It would be a lovely memory to take with me." He made his tone deliberately light and teasing, his expression a hopeful leer.

Laurel blinked and shook her head as though to clear her thoughts. Then she laughed, and the sound echoed out across the field of rustling soybeans at the bottom of the bank. "I'll bet you say that to all the girls."

It was Seth's turn to laugh. He had diverted her thoughts from his inadvertent disclosure of private doubts, but it always amazed him when she turned and stood her ground so quickly. As a youngster she'd been shy and tongue-tied around him. Now she was a woman and the tables had turned.

"Most of the time I don't even have to say that much." He meant to keep the conversation light and as meaningless as possible because he felt the same sweet stirrings of desire that he'd experienced that first day in the storeroom. And they were no more appropriate tonight, beneath the moon and stars, than they'd been a few days ago. Laurel Sauder was a woman for all the nights of a man's life, not the companion of a few pleasurable hours.

"Well, I should hope not," Laurel said with frosty indignation so exaggerated it was comical. She sniffed in disdain. "It's a hokey old line."

All at once she stopped smiling and it had very much the same effect on his senses that the moon's suddenly going behind a cloud would produce. Disappointment and impatience for the soft, bright light to return. Her next words caught him off guard again. "But everything else you said is true."

She held his gaze, refusing to look away. Seth broke the contact of their eyes first. He half turned on his side to face her and looked down at the ground. "Yes. But it's something I can live with."

Laurel was silent a long moment. His voice had changed. It was harder, cool, unemotional. He wasn't going to allow the discussion to continue any further along these lines. She didn't want to feel him withdraw any further from her. She took her courage firmly in both hands and spoke.

"I would like a kiss." She wondered if it was truly her voice coming out of her mouth. The words sounded strange, even a little forlorn. Suddenly she wished she were on the moon hanging high and aloof above them.

Seth reached out and pushed a strand of her hair behind her ear. His fingers barely brushed her skin, but he felt the heat of her body beckoning to him. "A gentleman always gives a lady what she wants."

She unwrapped her arms from around her knees and leaned toward him. Seth didn't move closer and it was Laurel who came to him. He braced his shoulders against the tree and she rested her weight on her hands. Only their lips touched for a long, waiting moment. She leaned a little closer; the pressure of her lips on his increased. Their touch was still light, tentative.

He cupped her face between his big, rough hands. His kiss was tender and gentle, passionate but restrained, and in no way threatening. Laurel sighed and opened her mouth to accept the pleasant, searching thrust of his tongue. She relaxed slightly, feeling the hard expanse of his chest press against the rounded fullness of her breasts. He moved one hand to cradle the back of her head, his fingers splaying through the fine silken strands of her hair. His other hand lowered to rest just beneath the swell of her breast.

Laurel let her hands curl around the broad slope of his shoulders. She felt his muscles tense beneath her touch. She responded to his exploration of the velvety moistness of her mouth with delicate, seeking flicks of her tongue. He smelled good; warm and woodsy. The faint odor of tobacco smoke she'd noticed before was gone. She wondered if it was McManus who smoked a pipe, not Seth. He tasted good, too, like coffee and mint and . . . Seth.

He would be a thoughtful, exciting lover, she realized with a small, still active portion of her mind. He was also the kind of man she'd always admired: strong, composed, with convictions and ideals she could share and respect. A small, cold knot of tension deep inside her began to unwind in thin, silvery strands like the moonlight shining on the water behind them. Being in his arms felt right and good.

Seth ended the long, soul-satisfying kiss and held her close while their breathing slowed and steadied.

"That was nice," Laurel murmured against the soft wool of his heather-blue sweater.

"By far the nicest kiss I've had in a long, long time."

Seth's voice was a low rumble in her ear. She could feel the rise and fall of his chest beneath her fingers.

"You are a very special lady, Laurel Sauder."

"And you are a very special man."

As quickly and easily as that, she made her decision. She could make love to Seth Norris with no qualms. She trusted him; she respected him. She could give herself to him and not be afraid.

She would give herself to Seth Norris for a single night.

And he would give her something very precious in return—a baby of her own.

Chapter Five

"I don't want you to say good night, Seth."

Laurel held her breath. All the way home she'd been silent, her thoughts scurrying around in ever smaller circles inside her head as she tried to find just the right words.

She'd never asked a man to make love to her. What would he think of her for asking? Seth had touched something precious and fragile inside her that she'd kept shut away for a long time, but he was still a stranger. She wasn't sure she had enough courage to go through with it, even for the sake of her dreams.

"Laurel, are you sure you know what you're saying?" They were standing at the bottom of the front steps to her parents' home. It didn't look much changed to Seth in the dark, but in the daylight he knew the clapboard siding would be a warm colonial blue instead of the white he recalled. And the gingerbread trim on the porch and eaves was a darker blue that repeated on the frames and shutters of the big double-hung windows. Fifteen years ago it had been green.

"Yes. I know exactly what I'm saying." Laurel ran the tip of her finger over the last faded bloom of a geranium in the planter by the railing. Its scent rose, pungent and musty around them.

Seth reached out and drew her into his arms. He kissed the top of her head and held her close for a moment before speaking. "I can't think of anything I'd rather do than make love to you tonight." He held her close for a few seconds longer. He couldn't seem to help himself. She felt so soft and warm in his arms, so right, as if she belonged there.

Laurel tilted her head back and searched his face with eyes that were bottomless and shadowed by the night. "I want you, too."

The words lodged themselves deep inside him, warming and exciting. Seth forced himself to answer the way he knew he had to. "Laurel, I don't think you understand. It would be only for tonight, a one-night stand." She stiffened in his arms. He could feel her muscles tighten beneath his fingers. She closed her eyes for a brief moment and he regretted the abruptness with which he'd spoken. But what he said was the truth. "I can't offer you any more than tonight."

Laurel wished desperately she could read his thoughts, but his expression was guarded and it was too dark in any case. She couldn't go through with it if she thought he might want to see her again. The realization hurt more than it should have. She was only a one-night stand. That's what she wanted.

"I'm not asking you for anything more. I know you can't make any promises. Neither can I. All I want is tonight, Seth."

It was as though the words were coming from somewhere outside her body; almost as if another woman were speaking through her. Laurel closed her mind to the thousand clamoring questions in her thoughts. She was attempting to make her dreams come true the only way she could. She was doing the right thing; that was all she needed to know.

"I see." Seth took a deep breath. He'd taken both her hands between his own. She was cold, so he pressed their joined hands to his chest to warm hers. "I would like to be with you, Laurel, very much. Perhaps we can share something special even if it is for so brief a time. But I don't want you to be hurt."

Suddenly Laurel felt her doubts slip away like so many clouds in the sunlight. He was lonely and alone, too. They could share something tonight that would enrich both their lives. "I'm willing to take the chance." She smiled at him.

Seth was powerless to retreat from that moment on. He overrode the warnings of his wary heart with a ruthless hand. He would make love to Laurel tonight and the memory of her tenderness and caring would be something to cherish for the rest of his life.

"I have to check in and give my report to the night shift. I'll pick you up after that. Kevin..." Laurel sensed rather than saw the frown that pulled his dark brows together.

"I'll explain to Kevin." But what would she say?

Seth lowered his head to kiss her. Their lips met and clung. Laurel could feel the tension ease, then rekindle between them as sweet desire. She didn't hold back and was amazed at the wave of longing that swept over her, weakening her knees and confusing her reason.

"If you have second thoughts I'll understand." Seth kissed her once more, gently, lingeringly.

"I won't." She said it aloud to convince herself as well as him. She'd made her choices; she was prepared to accept the consequences.

Laurel watched Seth turn and walk away into the night. He was headed in the direction of Main Street. It was too late to retreat now even if she wanted to. Physically the timing was right; she knew her body and its cycles very well. Emotionally she wasn't so serene. Laurel thrust her hands deep into the pockets of her jacket. How would she explain her actions to Kevin? She didn't want to lie to him, but she had to. Secrecy was essential to her plan.

Laurel mounted the steps to the porch and entered the house, her mind still a jumble of half-formed sentences. Ordinarily she would have told Kevin at least part of the truth. She was attracted to Seth Norris; she wanted to spend some time alone with him. Kevin would understand even if he didn't approve of her spending the night with a man. Some protective traits were just too deeply ingrained in most brothers ever to be totally erased, but he wouldn't stand in her way.

Yet, if she was lucky enough to become pregnant tonight, Kevin would know at once who the child's father was. That was too dangerous. There must never be the slightest connection between her and Seth. She couldn't stand the pain of losing a child again. This baby, if she conceived, must be hers alone. She had no choice but to deceive her brother and everyone else.

Kevin was standing in the kitchen doorway at the end of the long, wide front hall that bisected the house. "Laurel. Good. I was just writing you a note." He waved a piece of paper at her.

"I thought you were at the Station with the guys." Her hands were shaking so badly she knew her brother would notice, so she stuck them in the back pockets of her jeans. Her legs felt rubbery and she had to keep reminding herself to breathe.

"I was there. I came home to check in with Mirachi." He grinned sheepishly. "I'm like a hen with one chick, aren't I?" Laurel nodded, but her smile was understanding.

"And . . ." she prompted.

"It's a good thing I did. He's got it fixed. Good as new."

"Kevin, that's wonderful."

"I told him to book a seat for it on the next flight out of Miami to Detroit. Nothing flies to Toledo this late at night."

"You paid for a plane ticket for a camera lens?"

"Coach, Sis. On the red-eye. Hey, don't look like I'm burning a wad of hundred dollar bills right under your nose. I earn my living with that lens. And my insurance will cover it." He grabbed up a canvas duffle bag that had been sitting on the kitchen table. It still had his navy ID numbers stenciled on it and was as much a part of him as his camera case and light meters. "I have to get a move on. The plane gets into Detroit at one-fifteen. It's after eleven now."

"You aren't going to drive all the way to Detroit and back tonight." Laurel was adamant, but she couldn't help the quick stab of relief she felt. Now she wouldn't have to lie to Kevin. She wouldn't have to tell him anything.

He shook his head. "I'll stay up there someplace and drive back in the morning. Will you tell Seth I'll see him anytime he's free? I sure hate missing him . . ."

"But that lens means a lot to you." Laurel finished his sentence for him. "Drive carefully, big brother." She reached up on tiptoe and planted a kiss on his cheek. "I'll tell Seth what happened."

"I'll be back by noon tomorrow."

Laurel didn't move from the spot where she was standing until she heard the garage door close and the sound of the rental car's engine fade into the night. There was no turning back now.

SHE WAS SITTING on the porch swing an hour later when Seth drove up in the nondescript Ford sedan Elinor had pointed out the first day he was in town. She'd left a lamp burning in the living room window. It threw a half circle of light onto the porch, but where she was sitting the shadows were as thick as black velvet.

Laurel turned up the collar of her jacket. It was chilly now that the dew had fallen. It sparkled in heavy wet drops on each individual blade of grass under the streetlamp. It wouldn't be much longer until it was cold enough to turn the dew to frost, and that would take the last of the leaves and the chrysanthemums, too.

Seth closed the car door quietly and came up the walk. His hands were stuck in the back pockets of his slacks. The thought crossed her mind that he might be nervous, also. If he was, he certainly didn't show it in any other way. He paused at the bottom step.

"I'm over here." Laurel swallowed hard and tried again, hoping her voice wouldn't betray her unease. "I think it would be best if you parked your car in the garage, don't you?" Seth didn't reply and she rushed to explain.

"Kevin left for Detroit Metro almost an hour ago to pick up an important package. He's so sorry to miss you, but Mr. Mirachi, the lens maker, has repaired his telephoto lens. That's why Kevin's back in the States, did you know that? He can't finish his work without it." She was babbling, and forced herself to slow down. She took three deep, steadying breaths and brought her ramblings to a halt. "He won't be back until tomorrow."

"Kevin's being away makes this easier for you, doesn't it?"

"Yes." She stood and walked toward him.

"I don't think you're ready—" Laurel placed her fingers over his mouth to still the words.

"Don't mention it again, Seth, please. Come inside. I'll make some coffee."

But when they got inside she was all thumbs. The second time the coffee measure clattered against the side of the can Seth reached around her and took it away. "Let's skip the coffee."

"All right." She couldn't say, "Let's go upstairs." For some reason the words wouldn't come. She stood there looking up at him.

He made it easy for her then. He put his hands on her shoulders and bent his head to kiss her lightly yet thoroughly. He tugged the sleeves of her jacket over her hands and draped it over the back of a kitchen chair. He flicked off the light switch and started down the hall. At the foot of the steps Laurel moved past him, not meeting his eyes, and led the way to her room.

She hadn't made the bed when she'd gotten up that morning, but somehow that was only a small uncomfortable pinprick of embarrassment compared to the utter strangeness of having a man here with her. Everything in her room was just the same as it had been the September she'd left home for college.

She'd never slept in this room with Tom. The white iron bed with its brass scrollwork and yellow ruffled eyelet spread was too narrow for two adults, he'd always said. He'd slept alone in the guest bedroom down the hall. Laurel, slept in her own room and shared it with Penny, who had slept on a cot close to the closet, though the memory of soft little girl snores and early morning snuggles was bittersweet.

"I apologize for the clutter."

"I like it." Seth dragged the knot from his tie and dropped it on the desk beneath the window. Laurel turned to watch him as he continued speaking. "I spend too much time in motel rooms. I miss what real houses look like and feel like and smell like." This room smelled like Laurel; like a woman, with a dozen unfamiliar sweet and exotic odors competing against one another.

"I'll change the sheets." She brushed a strand of fine brown hair behind her ear.

Seth wanted very much to kiss that ear. She was blushing. He could tell even in the dim light shining through the half-open door from the hallway.

"Don't." They would be exchanging polite small talk for hours if he didn't take matters into his own hands. Seth reached out and circled her wrist with his hand. He drew her a step closer. She didn't resist, but neither did she initiate any movement. He began unbuttoning her blouse. Laurel's eyes got big; then she looked down at his hands. He felt a tremor go through her.

"Actually, I just put fresh sheets on the bed yesterday...." She closed her eyes on a rush of nervous desire that surprised her with its strength, its urge to be fulfilled.

"Be quiet." Seth chuckled and leaned over to kiss her again. She opened her mouth to accept his caress and answer it with quick delicate thrusts of her own. She moved half a step closer. He slid the blue-green blouse down over her arms. She shivered again, but this time he thought it was from the rush of cool air skating over her bare skin. Her bra followed the blouse to the floor.

"It's cold." Laurel couldn't think of anything else to say. He pulled her close and the soft fuzzy wool of his sweater teased her breasts. She slipped her arms around his waist and held on tight.

"Are you going to stay that way all night?" There was the faintest hint of a smile in his question.

"Yes." Laurel nodded against his chest to emphasize her point.

"First times are always a little frightening." He sounded as if he knew what he was talking about. There had been many first and last times in his life, she was sure.

"I'm not frightened. I like it here." That was true; the strong steady beat of his heart was soothing but exciting, too.

Seth unwound her arms from his waist. He stepped back and pulled his sweater over his head. His shirt followed hers to the floor. Laurel was suddenly glad she didn't have to manage all those buttons. She was glad he didn't expect her to unbutton it for him; she wasn't ready for that. She didn't think her stiff fingers could accomplish what seemed all at once a very intimate task.

She wasn't frightened. But the nervousness she couldn't do anything about. There hadn't been anybody, no special man, in her life since Tom had left. *Seth wouldn't be part of her life, not after tonight.* She had to remember that; she wanted it that way, yet it left an empty feeling deep inside. He was looking at her again. She could feel his eyes on her. Laurel looked up into the midnight-blue depths, trying to guess at his thoughts.

She looked innocent in the near darkness, and unprepared. "Do you want me to be responsible for birth control, Laurel?" He didn't know any other way to say it. She wasn't the kind of woman to indulge in casual sex. She didn't make a habit of going to bed with a man; he'd bet his life on it. The women he usually made love to were so practiced in their affairs that he never gave more than a passing thought to protecting them from an unwanted pregnancy. But not tonight, not with Laurel. Everything was different here and now; none of the old rules applied.

"I . . ." Her eyes were huge pools of shimmering brown. Flecks of gold swam to the surface and were reflected by the moonlight peeking through the lacy curtains at the window. "I . . . it isn't necessary, thank you." She got the last words out in a rush.

"I'm spoiling your fantasy."

He sounded regretful. "No." She'd told her first lie, but she wasn't going to tell another one if she didn't have to. "You're not a fantasy." *You're the answer to a prayer.* She cupped his face in her hands and met his enigmatic blue gaze head on. His beard was heavy and felt rough against her fingers. It also felt very good. "This is all very real to me."

"What are you thinking then?" Seth's voice was as dark and velvety as the night sky.

"About beginnings and endings," she answered truthfully. "And about how much I'd like you to kiss me again." He covered her hands with his and she stood on tiptoe to meet his lips.

Those were the last words she spoke for a long time. The rest of their clothes were discarded with little fuss. She stepped into his embrace and felt the long hard length of him along every inch of her body.

Seth kissed her over and over again and she felt herself unwinding from deep within, melting, the nervous tension growing less acute but returning in a new form, one more tactile and harder to describe. It left her feeling jumpy and needing to be touched.

They moved to the bed. His hands were strong, yet gentle. He kissed her breasts and she arched into the caress. He kissed the soft golden skin of her neck and she wrapped her arms around him to hold him close. Laurel let her hands roam over the hard lines of his body, through the thick dark waves of his hair.

It was good to feel a man's body under her fingers again. She liked the hard ridges of bone and muscles she felt pressing against the softer curves of her own body. She liked the heavy satisfying weight of him on top of her.

Seth was patient and skilled. Laurel tried to give herself up to the loving of the moment, but one part of her brain refused to relax. *What if it didn't happen?* She might never be given another chance.

What if it did? Would she be a good mother? Could she make it all work? Was she robbing Seth of something pre-

cious, something that was his alone to give? Was she stealing a child from this unsuspecting man?

He sensed her restraint but not the reason for it. He would
have liked to make this experience something Laurel would
never forget, but he wasn't sure he could. She was like a
fever in his blood now that he was so close to possessing her.
That's how he felt, as if he could brand his imprint on her
so deeply that she'd never forget him or this night. The
beckoning, mysterious hollows of her body called out to him
so loudly his ears rang with the sounds. He caressed her
gently, then more boldly, and though he could still feel some
part of her holding back, her body at least began to respond.

He entered her gently, slowly, paving the way with a kiss
that kept her silent and mimicked the more intimate join-
ing of their lower bodies. She stiffened, then began to relax
beneath him as he felt her body readjust, then open more
fully to him.

She kissed him back; she moved with him, but she didn't
follow him into completion. He led her on with slow deliberate strokes, prolonging the pleasure of their union, but
when his release broke over him like a tidal rush he knew she
had not experienced her own.

"I'm sorry," she said automatically as he relaxed against
her.

He wondered what kind of a fool she'd been married to.
Had she been in the habit of apologizing to him each and
every time he left her less than satisfied? For Seth that
seemed the ultimate act of male selfishness. Right now he
couldn't think of anything better in life than the feel of
Laurel's breasts pressed against his chest, her legs tangled
with his, except filling her again and again and taking her
with him all the way.

"I'm not sorry. Next time it will be better, much better for you." He smiled over at her and brushed a damp strand of hair from her cheek. It was silky and soft. The scent of lilacs mingled with the musky warmth of their lovemaking.

"Next time?" He felt her tense beneath him once again. The movement pushed their lower bodies closer. He hadn't withdrawn from her and felt familiar heaviness building in his lower stomach as she tightened around him.

"And the time after that." His mind was swirling with desire, and need, and the beginnings of dreams. Laurel wasn't a one-night stand, not for any sane man. She was a woman for the rest of your life. He wondered if there might be a possibility of a continuing relationship—even if it had to be a long distance one. He wanted out of the Service. He wanted to come home, come back to the land. He wanted a woman like Laurel to share his dreams. *He wanted Laurel.* "We have all night." He hooked a finger under her chin and bent to kiss her.

"All night." Laurel repeated the words against his lips and opened her mouth for his kiss.

LAUREL, I WANT to see you again. How many times in the past three days had her brain repeated that sentence? One of the bands at the back of the crowd had been playing the "Colonel Bogey March" all afternoon and the words had taken up the rhythm in her head. It was driving her insane.

Lois Sauder leaned closer and said something that Laurel couldn't make out. She smiled and shrugged, and her mother smiled back and put her hands over her ears. Ralph Sauder was standing on his wife's other side. He looked tired and drawn. Laurel was worried that it wasn't merely travel fatigue, although they had arrived home at a late hour the night before.

Laurel, I want to see you again. How could everything go so disastrously wrong so quickly? How could it hurt so much to say no to a man she barely knew?

The military helicopter that had been scouting the whistle-stop route roared overhead. The huge crowd cheered. Two men with guns could be seen at the open doors, but they waved and the crowd waved back.

Three hours ago two very serious young men in army fatigues, carrying high-powered rifles, had escorted her and her father from the store, locking it behind them. If she turned around now she would see them in the storeroom windows, watchful and sober above the bunting and crepe paper streamers and waving flags. Two more men were silhouetted high up on the elevator silos. Wade Armstrong and a highway patrolman were on top of the city building to her left.

The Bartlow High School Pirates struck up "Hail to the Chief" for probably the sixth time. The helicopter was back overhead. Her mother shaded her eyes and watched it until it was out of sight. Laurel hadn't been at all surprised to get a call that her parents were cutting short their trip. But she was surprised to hear her father dismiss his wartime buddies as a grouchy bunch of sick old men. That wasn't like him and she'd exchanged worried glances with her mother over the lunch table.

Twenty feet in front of her, as close to the cordoned-off security area as he could get, Kevin hung precariously from a railroad signal post, happily snapping individual faces in the huge crowd. He seemed completely oblivious to the risk he was taking. Using the Mirachi lens, he focused on young and old alike. He was capturing for all time a small child on his father's shoulders; an elderly farmer with weather-beaten face and hands, a small American flag stuck in his shirt pocket; a group of noisy youngsters perched on a display of farm machinery near the old depot. Michael Norris's red head was easy to pick out even at a distance, because today Laurel was wearing her glasses. He didn't look much like Seth, except for his blade of a nose and the determined jut of his chin.

Why couldn't she stop thinking about Seth? She'd been avoiding him for three days—a last-minute shopping trip with Elinor, driving to Toledo to pick up her parents, just plain hiding out in her room. She hated the way she was acting but couldn't seem to make herself change.

Last night had been the worst. The presidential train had made its trial run through town. For forty-five minutes it sat majestically on the Main Street crossing, the gleaming, dark green Pullman cars a reminder to lots of old-timers in town of bygone glory days. Kevin had been on hand, obligingly snapping shots of excited youngsters and nostalgic adults in front of the brass plaque proclaiming Ferdinand Magellan to be U.S. Car No. 1. Even if they didn't want a photograph, most people couldn't resist running their hands over the big round presidential seal hanging beside the plaque. Laurel knew exactly what was going on, because for that same forty-five minutes she had hidden in the empty room above the store and watched her brother—and Seth.

Kevin had come home much later raving about three-inch-thick plate glass windows, armored plating, escape hatches, the pictures of FDR, Truman and Eisenhower lining the walls. He said Seth would be staying with the train after the President flew out of Toledo on Air Force One, for at least as far as Dayton. That meant he'd be in town one more time. He wanted to see her, Kevin mentioned casually, to say goodbye. The train would be getting in around eleven, he thought.

Her mother had interrupted then, wanting to know all about Helen Norris's son being a Secret Service agent, and Laurel was saved from lying to her brother once again.

She had no intention of being anywhere near the Main Street crossing at eleven o'clock. She had no intention of speaking to Seth Norris again as long as she lived.

SETH LOOKED at his watch. Fifty-seven minutes behind schedule. He brushed a stray red dot of confetti from the lapel of his subdued gray pinstripe suit. His hand grazed over the cool surface of the small round pin that identified him as a member of the White House detail. The train slowed to a crawl.

They'd already turned the press corps loose from their confinement in the first four cars of the train. The print media guys were doing okay—their deadlines were still several hours away—but the video crews were chomping at the bit. Being an hour behind schedule meant it would be dark when they got to Toledo. They'd have to make their six o'clock leads here in Bartlow.

Seth watched them scurry for position from the front of the presidential car. He frowned in disgust as they barreled past a group of little old ladies and knocked signs out of the hands of a couple of kids. What a bunch of jerks they were. The networks kept teams of guys like that outside every function the President attended. They called them "the body watch" and they served no other purpose than to have cameras rolling in case there was an attempt on the man's life.

Seth leaned out from between the cars and took a quick look around. Rudy Sunderson was proudly patrolling the cordoned-off area behind City Hall, where three very long and very shiny black limousines were parked. If there was a problem farther along the track, the President would be whisked away by car. Seth waved and Rudy saluted smartly before returning to his measured pacing.

Seth glanced up and spotted Wade Armstrong on the roof of City Hall, a rifle held casually, comfortably, in the crook of his arm. He touched the brim of his cap in acknowledgment and Seth returned a thumbs-up gesture.

Turning back into the car, he moved past the dining room with its green-and-gold damask chairs and gold-plated fixtures and on toward the observation platform at the rear. He wondered if Laurel would be standing in the VIP section down front. He didn't have time to think of her now, but later, when the train came back through town, he intended to track her down and make her talk to him. He wanted her to know he'd meant every word he said to her that night. He didn't want what they'd shared to end like any other brief stopover affair. He wanted to see her again, as often as they could manage.

The President was getting ready to make his entrance onto the platform. In Bartlow he'd speak from the same spot as Harry Truman had in '48. The media loved it, and it made Seth's job easier, too. At least the man was staying within three feet of the door to the armor-plated Pullman car.

He could hear that old windbag Barton Willman droning on. The President was getting antsy. He never liked to wait on other politicians to speak. Seth held out the heavy bullet-proof vest the President would wear under his suitcoat. The older man hated the thing and never hesitated to say so. For the most part Seth didn't blame him. The vest weighed a ton.

"I understand this is your hometown, Norris," the President said as Seth fastened the straps that held it closed.

"Yes, sir."

"Nice little town, Willman says. Good crowd?"

"The highway patrol estimates twenty thousand."

The President looked pleased. He buttoned his coat over the vest and lifted his shoulders, trying to get comfortable. His face was screwed up in a grimace. "Damnable thing."

"Yes, sir." Seth adjusted his own tie. He slipped the mirrored sunglasses he'd been wearing earlier into an inside pocket. The sun was low on the horizon and hidden behind the buildings. He saw the other three agents in the car doing much the same thing. Heaven help an agent on duty caught looking less than well-groomed.

"We're about ready for you, sir." An aide stuck his head around the corner.

"Let's go, Norris."

Seth gestured the other agents to move ahead. He wouldn't be able to think of Laurel again. His job was to protect the man behind him with his life, if necessary, and that's exactly what he would do. He wouldn't think of the soft, exciting feel of her body under his, the tiny moans of pleasure he'd coaxed from her lips, the passion they'd shared in the long dark hours of the night.

And most of all he wouldn't allow himself to think about the stricken look in her eyes when he'd told her he wanted to see her again. That reaction, above all, he couldn't understand or accept.

"Dempsey, Markham. You guys take the steps at this stop. Springer and I will stay up here on the platform with the President."

A voice sifted through the background static of his earphone. Some piece of equipment in the communications car had been interfering with his reception all afternoon. It was another routine surveillance report. "Green lights all the way." A band was playing "Hail to the Chief." Willman must have finished his speech. A cheer went up from the crowd. Seth unbuttoned the jacket of his suit so he'd have easy access to his weapon. He adjusted the shoulder holster a fraction of an inch. It felt awkward and heavy. He'd gotten out of the habit of wearing a gun during his time in Bartlow. The cheers grew louder. It was the President's cue. "Move out," Seth ordered.

The sea of humanity that stretched before him was a little disconcerting at first, as it always was. How could you ever single out an individual troublemaker in that press of bodies? As always, Seth didn't have an answer to that question. He'd probably never know unless an assassination attempt occurred.

He began to focus on separate faces. He didn't hear a word the President said; he never did. He let his eyes scan the crowd, a split second for each face, each body, then move on to another, always searching.

Then he saw her. For half a breath brown eyes locked with blue. Then she looked away. And turned away.

And in the brief heartbeat of time he allowed himself to think about it at all, Seth realized he was never going to see Laurel Sauder again.

Chapter Six

"I'm going to have a baby." Laurel savored the words on her tongue. They felt right and good. She repeated them with more conviction. "I'm going to have a baby." She'd been longing to say it aloud to someone for three whole days, since the morning she'd gone to the Planned Parenthood Clinic and had her suspicions confirmed by a doctor.

"You're pregnant?" Karen Hollister's voice rose a pitch or two. Her dark eyes, set wide apart in an even darker face, began to sparkle with more than friendly curiosity. "I don't believe it."

All at once Laurel began to wish she hadn't confided in her co-worker. Would that surprised, rather calculating gleam be everyone's first response to her wonderful news? *Surely it wouldn't be Elinor's reaction.* She wanted desperately to talk to her cousin, to share her joy and her fears, but it wasn't possible, not now, not yet.

"When?"

Karen leaned forward, her elbows on the tabletop. She'd come to work at the medical center shortly after Laurel's divorce had become final. She was a friend; not particularly close, but, then, Laurel knew that was her own fault as much as anything. She'd kept most people at a distance these past months.

"I'm sorry?" Laurel apologized for her wandering thoughts.

"I said, when is the baby due?"

A cigarette dangled from the fingers of Karen's right hand. She and Laurel were sitting under an umbrella on the staff patio. It was Friday, the first week in December and payday. The other employees taking their breaks were in a festive mood. It was hot and sunny, noisy and crowded. A fountain bubbled away in the center of the patio, effectively screening their conversation from the others.

Laurel hesitated a little longer, then fudged her answer. "The end of July, I think." Actually, she was due before the middle of the month, but she didn't want Karen or anyone else to associate her vacation in Ohio with the date of her baby's conception. People liked to count backward on their fingers; it was human nature. Her friends would be no exception. She refused to think about how the world in general might view her pregnancy. *But would her parents welcome a baby born out of wedlock?* She was certain they would. Still, it would take them a while to get over the shock. She wasn't that naive or lost in her own dreams. Karen's next words brought Laurel back to reality with a jerk.

"Well, I'll be damned." She sat back in her chair, lighting a second cigarette from the embers of the first.

Laurel hadn't as yet experienced a great deal of morning sickness, but she wished Karen wouldn't smoke nonetheless.

"Who's the father, anyway?"

Laurel's fingers clenched involuntarily around her glass of orange juice.

"When's the wedding? I didn't even know you were seeing anyone seriously."

Laurel forced herself to relax slightly. She was going to have to get used to this kind of interrogation. Karen's reaction was probably typical, if somewhat more direct. The tall black woman was nothing, if not blunt. She wasn't going to change just because Laurel was feeling particularly fragile and vulnerable these days.

The sun was making her squint, giving her a headache, so she pulled her glasses out of the pocket of her long, white lab coat and set them on her nose. The lenses were photosensitive and started to darken after only a few seconds. She took a deep breath to cover her hesitation.

"There isn't going to be a wedding, Karen. I'm not going to marry the baby's father. It wouldn't have worked out between us." She rattled off her carefully rehearsed speech and wondered how she was going to explain her actions to Kevin when he came home in the spring. *Would Kevin ever settle down long enough to help her teach her baby some of the things he should really learn from his father?* That way of thinking was maudlin and self-defeating, she knew. "This is my baby. I'm going to raise him alone." She spoke aloud, as much to reassure herself as to convince Karen.

"Well, I'll be damned." Karen crushed her cigarette stub out in the Styrofoam cup that had held her coffee.

Laurel's stomach lurched and she swallowed twice to quell the rising nausea in her throat.

"I've always pegged you for the hearth-and-home type, even if you are an ace pharmacist. And even if you did let your ex take his kid away without putting up a fight."

"I did what was best for Penny," Laurel whispered.

Karen softened her next statement somewhat when she saw the stricken look in Laurel's eyes. "I wish you luck, honey. If anyone can pull this single parenthood stuff off, it's you." She shook her head and wiry dark curls bounced in agreement.

"Thanks for the vote of confidence."

"It's going to be a hell of a tough row to hoe." Karen was repeating in her own fashion exactly what Elinor had said that October day in Bartlow. It wasn't going to be easy. But the rewards, a child of her own to love and cherish, would make the sacrifice worthwhile.

"I know."

"I have to get back to the lab." Karen gave her one more direct, unwavering stare, but when she spoke her tone took on a kind of gentle roughness. "You're one hell of a brave sister, you know that?"

"No, not brave. I'm scared silly, but I've never been happier."

Karen didn't reply. She stood, moving abruptly and decisively, as she did everything else. "I'm going to give you a piece of advice, even if you don't want it. Your eyes are full of pink and blue stars, your daydreams are all tied up in frilly ribbon bows. You aren't looking past the end of your nose. Reality hasn't set in yet, but money is a hard fact of life. Even if you don't want to marry the kid's father, make the bum pay child support."

"I don't want his money." Laurel didn't think Karen had even heard her. She watched the other woman walk away. What good would it do to tell Karen that Seth knew nothing about her child?

Already she knew, deep in her heart, that her fears that Seth might find out about her baby and claim him were irrational, but it didn't make them any less worrisome. Still, just as intensely, she wished to thank him, to see his dark face lighten with joy and delight at her news.

Sometimes in the middle of the night she'd come awake and see his face: strong, composed, but gentle and caring, too. And she'd long for him, for the brief happy hours they'd spent together, for the short sweet night of passion they'd shared. But at other times she saw a different Seth.

The man at the whistle-stop: a warrior, tall and commanding, still strong and composed, but lethal and ruthless, too. A stranger. The way he must always remain. Then her happy memories were overshadowed by uncertainty. *If she'd only had the chance to know him better.*

There was no way she could bring that about and that was why, when their eyes had caught and held for a split second that October afternoon, she'd panicked and turned away. Run away, if the truth be told, and returned to Phoenix on the next available flight.

"I'm doing what's best." But was she? Still, she felt satisfied and fulfilled as never before. Seth had given her what she wanted most in the world and she would always be grateful to him for that gift.

An orderly burst through the sliding doors of the lounge, Walkman earphones on his head, his face contorted in an effort to catch every word he was hearing. Some urgency in his actions, the look of disbelief in his eyes, caught and held Laurel's attention, constricting her with a sense of dread. Something was very wrong in the world, in her world.

"Hey, man, listen up! Somebody just tried to shoot the President!"

EVERYTHING WAS SET. The President's motorcade was right on schedule. The cold, early December day had already faded into twilight when the entourage of hulking, black limousines, smaller government cars and a motorcycle escort set off for the short trip up Connecticut Avenue to one of Washington's landmark hotels.

Seth and McManus had driven the route so often they'd lost count, but that fact made them no less vigilant. However, the only variation in routine they expected tonight was that the President would be addressing a small, select group of two hundred fund-raisers in one of the hotel's smaller banquet rooms, rather than the customary three or four thousand who usually thronged the main ballroom to hear him speak.

The preliminary preparations had gone smoothly. About a dozen agents would be covering the event and they all had their assignments. The security screen was already in place. It looked as if the President's appearance would be routine in every way.

Seth and McManus, along with two other agents, arrived first. The usual contingent of newsmen and TV cameras was positioned outside the side entrance to the hotel that the President always used. There would be more TV cameras inside, Seth knew. A few hecklers were also present, anti-nuclear, pro-life and pro-abortion; the standard bunch, most of whom Seth knew by sight. As long as they made no threatening moves toward his charge, they were left alone. The Secret Service was responsible only for the President's safety and answerable to the Treasury Department, not the White House staff. As far as Seth and the other agents were concerned, these people were only exercising their right to free speech and lawful assembly.

The President smiled and waved at the crowd as he walked inside. He didn't stop to answer questions shouted by several newsmen, although Seth knew he probably would pause for a few minutes on the way out.

Inside the building Seth caught a glimpse of the occupants of the banquet room as he entered the hallway leading to wide double doors near the podium. The glitter of champagne flutes was refracted into rainbow prisms by the light of a dozen chandeliers.

Dancing sparks of rich gold and warm fire, like the flecks of color in Laurel's eyes. Thoughts of her had begun to invade his mind even during working hours, but he ruthlessly banished them. Dreams of her, long and exciting and intensely erotic, had tortured him throughout the lonely nights with even greater frequency.

Seth and McManus walked ahead of their charge, as always. A scan of the crowd from the doorway showed nothing amiss. It was a black tie affair; the President was wearing a tuxedo, although Seth and his agents wore conventional three-piece suits.

An aide advanced to the microphone when he noticed Seth in the doorway. He announced the President in stentorian tones that brought an immediate hush to the crowd. A chamber orchestra struck up "Hail to the Chief." The martial strains sounded incongruous coming from flutes and violins instead of trumpets and trombones. At least they hadn't attempted "Ruffles and Flourishes." For that small mercy, he was grateful.

It was the last extraneous thought Seth allowed himself before habit and instinct took control of his actions. His eyes ranged over the crowd yet again. All the guests had been screened by metal detectors. Nothing was out of place. He gave McManus a curt nod. They moved forward.

The President was only a step or two behind them. He would go directly to his seat on the dais; then Seth and another agent would station themselves on either side. The rest would take their places among the crowd. Uniformed Washington police were in the hall.

McManus held his walkie-talkie in his left hand. Seth's was inside his coat, clipped to his belt. The President halted in the doorway a moment, trying to adjust his eyes to the brilliantly lighted room.

A brief flicker of movement high up in the shadows along the wall, where no living person had a right to be, caught Seth's eye. Something was wrong. He opened his mouth to holler a warning to McManus.

It was already too late.

A long time later Seth would wonder who screwed up and let the disgruntled former hotel employee slip through the security screen undetected. Now he didn't have time to think about it at all. Gunfire from a single semiautomatic weapon began to erupt from the spot where Seth had noticed the telltale movement a mere heartbeat before, a sealed-off, supposedly unreachable balcony, high up on the far wall.

He threw himself backward against the man he'd sworn to protect, making himself a target, arms and legs outspread. Time warped out of sync. Seth saw people, their mouths open to scream or curse, begin to drop to the floor all over the banquet room. He squeezed off three shots, firing over the crowd, trying to pick off the sniper on the balcony. He heard McManus fire twice before a white hot streak of pain slammed him back against the wall. His left side seemed to be on fire. He ignored it; the President's condition was his only concern. He was sprawled on the floor just inches away from Seth's right foot, two agents shielding him, pinning him down. His tuxedo was torn, his tie bunched under his ear, but he didn't seem to be hurt and he was swearing a blue streak.

"Get him out of here," Seth yelled, but the words came out rough and slow. It took most of his breath to utter them at all.

McManus fired again and the shots from above ceased as suddenly as they had begun. The two other agents, now joined by uniformed Washington police, grabbed the President unceremoniously and dragged him out of the room, down the hall, toward the waiting bulletproof limousine.

Seth blinked, trying to clear his eyes of a strange, debilitating black haze that impaired his speech as well as his vision. In front of him one of the President's aides lay as still as death. A woman in a low-cut green gown wiped blood from her cheek and screamed repeatedly, making it even harder for him to concentrate. An agent, new to the White House detail, was slumped against the wall across the narrow hallway down which the President had disappeared. He was still breathing. Seth wasn't so sure about the aide.

"We got the bastard." McManus signaled to two more uniformed officers to get someone up to the balcony. An agent had taken over the microphone and ordered everyone to stay where he was until the room could be secured. For the time being, people seemed too stunned not to follow orders, but Seth began to wonder if he'd be crushed in a rush of panicked citizens at any moment. He was still leaning against the doorway and he couldn't seem to make himself move out of the opening.

He knew he should be following the President. He knew he should be conducting a sweep to ensure that no other gunman lay in wait. But his legs refused to obey his brain. He straightened with an effort that made the room appear to lurch. His earphones crackled into life and he tried to make sense of the jumbled words filtering into his mind.

The President was safely inside his limo and apparently unharmed. Seth reached for his radio to order the car back to the White House, the most secure building in Washington, until it became certain that the gunman had acted alone, but when he slid his hand inside his jacket, it came away covered with blood. His blood.

An alert cameraman set up to cover the President's speech panned away from the dark figure slumped over the balcony railing. Now the scene he framed in his lens was even more dramatic, a vignette to open newscasts and preface special bulletin reports for days to come. The tall, dark, Secret Service agent, upright among the fallen, gun still in hand, as he stared down at his blood-stained hand. He shook his head like a wounded animal, consternation and disbelief overriding the pain etched deep on his features, as he fought to stay upright. Slowly he lost the solitary battle, sinking to his knees and toppling forward to lie facedown on the floral carpet of the banquet room floor.

"HI, MOM. How are you? I...I just thought I'd call. I..." Laurel let her words dwindle off into nothingness. She couldn't bring herself to ask the next question aloud.

"What's the matter, honey? Have you seen those awful pictures on TV, too?"

Her mother's voice sounded strained. Laurel couldn't decide if it was because she was so upset herself or if something was wrong at home. She'd been increasingly worried about her father's health as autumn slipped into winter, but now her need to know about Seth Norris was even greater than her concern for her parent.

"I've been watching the news. Mom, have you heard? Was one of the Secret Service agents, the one on the videotape... Was it Seth Norris?" If she closed her eyes she could see him bleeding and bewildered and it tore at her heart. She shouldn't care so much, she told herself. *She couldn't care so much.*

"Yes, Laurel. I heard it from the mayor's wife not an hour ago, but of course we recognized him right away. It was awful. And, Laurel, his mother saw it, too. Imagine. They had it beamed out to the networks before the government could even call Clint and Helen and let them know how badly he'd been hurt."

Laurel wrapped her free hand around her middle in an instinctive protective gesture. "How badly was he hurt?"

"They don't know for sure. They sent a plane for Clint and Helen. They took off for Washington about two hours ago. He was already in surgery by then, of course. Your father thinks it looks bad."

Laurel couldn't say anything for a long time. She sat there listening to the static of long distance and the faint ghost sounds of other conversations that were almost words, but not quite. She felt like a ghost herself at the moment, a shell of the woman she'd been when she'd gotten up that morning, so full of plans and dreams. She hadn't thought it was possible to hurt so badly, to feel so strongly about someone who was a stranger in all respects but one.

"Laurel, have we been cut off?" Her mother's voice sounded anxious.

"Sorry, Mom. It's just kind of hard to take. I mean, not having seen him for so many years, then to have something awful like this happen so soon after meeting him again." She wasn't being very coherent, but for once her astute and intelligent mother didn't notice her vague and rambling explanation.

"We're all upset. But if the good Lord is willing, it will all turn out right in the end."

"I'll say a prayer for him, too, Mom." She'd already done that, a hundred times, short, disjointed pleas from her heart. "Can I say hello to Dad?"

This time the hesitation was on her mother's end of the connection. He must have had bad news from the series of tests he'd undergone at the Cleveland Clinic right after Thanksgiving. There couldn't be any other reason for her silence.

Laurel stared at the off-white adobe walls of her apartment with unseeing eyes. A young girl in an impressionist print over the mantel stared back at her. The rooms were laid out in traditional southwestern style with low archways and tile floors, with a central courtyard filled with plants and falling water. But inside the apartment was pure country, and home. Summer colors abounded and small floral prints covered the sofa and chairs; lacy curtains at the windows filtered out the direct desert sun and filled the too quiet room with golden warmth.

"Mom?" Laurel heard the faint edges of hysteria in her voice and took a deep breath to quell the suffocating sense of panic that hadn't left her since the orderly's announcement of the assassination attempt that afternoon. She wondered how much more she'd have to deal with tonight.

"Your father's already in bed, Laurel."

"What did they find out at the clinic?"

"They want to do more tests tomorrow."

There was a definite break in her mother's voice, as though she were trying very hard not to cry. "Mom, tell me the truth."

"They think there's something wrong with the valves of his heart. They recommended open heart surgery as soon as possible, but he's refusing to go. Dear God, Laurel, I'm so scared." She was crying openly now and Laurel could hardly keep from sobbing, too. Instead she bit her lip and made her voice as strong and steady as she could manage.

"Don't cry, Momma. I'll help you convince him to listen to the doctors. I'm coming home as soon as I can make the arrangements."

HE'D BEEN DREAMING about Laurel again, but the sweet memories of her passion kept fading away, replaced by images of blood and fear and pain. Sharp, cutting pain that stayed with him, grew stronger and wouldn't let him rest. Seth opened his eyes.

It was dark and he couldn't move. His head felt like a block of wood, his throat hurt, his side and back hurt. The only thing he could be sure of at the moment was that he wasn't dead. Being dead didn't hurt and he hurt like hell. The small room revolved before his eyes, the walls and ceiling tending to trade places in a slow, dizzying whirl. He closed his eyes and waited a moment. When he opened them again the room was still. He focused thankfully on a figure sitting in a tall chair in the corner.

"Are you awake, Seth?"

It was his mother's voice. How had she gotten here? Where was here? He couldn't remember much of anything. He lay quietly for a moment, listening to her rise from the chair, trying to assess the source of his pain, trying to fill in the blanks in his memory. He tried out his voice, but his mouth was as dry as tinder and the fire in his throat made the words come out as nothing more than a croak.

Her face appeared over the side of the bed. She looked tired and anxious, the dark curls of her hair mussed and standing on end.

"How about an ice chip? They put a tube down your throat when they operated. Does it hurt a lot?"

He let the ice chip melt on his tongue. It helped a little. "Hurts." His mother smiled faintly, so he knew she'd understood the garbled sound.

"They'll be giving you some pain medication in just a little while."

Bits and pieces of memory were crowding back. "President?" That one was harder to get out.

Helen frowned thoughtfully for a moment, then repeated the word. "He's fine. So's the other agent who was shot. Do you remember that?"

Seth shifted on the high, hard bed and the agony that knifed through his back and side was swift and hot. "Ouch."

"I don't know about the President's aide or the man who shot you." She looked very fierce all of a sudden. "I hope he dies."

Seth tried to shake his head.

"I'll ask the Lord's forgiveness later on," his mother replied with more of her usual spirit. "But not tonight."

She was whispering. Except for the continuous beep of a monitor somewhere above his head, the Intensive Care cubicle was quiet. It must be the middle of the night. He'd lost all track of time.

"Time?" The more awake he became, the more pain he was in, but his brain was at least beginning to function a little better.

"It's three o'clock in the morning. You were in surgery for almost six hours."

"That's why you need your rest."

A strange woman's face appeared over his mother's shoulder.

"He's really awake this time. Good."

She adjusted the IV tubing running into the back of his right hand. That's why he couldn't move his arm, Seth decided. It was strapped down. He began to relax a little as he figured out more of his surroundings.

He watched the nurse with detached interest as she injected the pain medication directly into the IV. Almost at once he could feel it starting to work. His body got lighter; sounds faded away. Another thought penetrated his consciousness with enough force to bring him back from the fuzzy edges of healing sleep. "You came alone? Dad... Mike...?"

"Michael stayed on the farm to look after things. Your father is with me. He's taking a nap. He'll be here when you wake up again." There were tears on his mother's cheeks, but he couldn't gather the strength to lift his hand and brush them away.

IT WAS DAYLIGHT when he woke again. His dreams had been hazier this time, less clear, but still he knew they'd been filled with images of Laurel Sauder. As his mother had promised, Clint Norris was sitting in the high-back chair in the corner. His eyes were closed and he looked tired. And old.

Somehow Seth had never thought about his father getting old, but he had. The realization made him anxious to voice his thoughts. He shifted position but found he was lying on his side, propped up against blankets. He wanted to turn over on his back, but he couldn't manage the feat. "Damn." The word came out strong and clear.

"Seth?" Clint stood but didn't move toward the bed. "Should I call the nurse, son? Do you need something?"

"Ice." There was a glass of ice chips on the table beside the bed. It was close but still maddeningly out of reach. Clint hesitated a moment, then took a plastic spoon and slipped two pieces between his son's lips. Seth rolled the cool ice around on his tongue. "Thanks." He thought the word sounded more normal. He tried to swallow and was relieved to find the fire in his throat had been quenched. "I feel like hell."

Clint leaned both arms on the rail of the bed. "The bullet ruptured your spleen. You were lucky the hospital was this close. You almost bled to death."

"I don't remember a thing." Seth frowned as he tried to recall what had happened to him. "Dad?"

Another nurse had appeared out of nowhere on crepe-soled shoes. It was a different face, older, wrinkled. It must be morning. He craned his neck to see out the long narrow window. Daylight, gray and wintery, streamed through the narrow casement. The nurse had already pumped more medication into the IV tubing. Seth knew how fast it worked now. He wanted very badly to say something and he had to work to get the words out in order. For a minute he was afraid his father couldn't understand. He searched the familiar lined face that was already growing blurred.

"Is that really what you want, son?" Clint reached down and squeezed his left hand, lying across his chest outside the blankets.

Seth managed to nod and repeat the sentence one more time. "I want to come home, Dad."

Chapter Seven

"I never expected to be Christmas shopping with you this year, Elinor. Mom and Dad had planned to spend the holidays with me in Phoenix." Laurel shook her head, experiencing one of the fleeting, bewildering moments of disorientation that seemed to come over her so often lately. Some of it probably had to do with the time change and the change in climate. Mostly it was from her own unsettled, and unsettling, emotions.

Small pellets of sleet chattered against the car windows on the driver's side. Eddies of snow, blue-white in the twilight, swirled around the small car, pushed forward relentlessly by the fury of the north wind. Laurel shivered as she felt around on the floor for the one or two small packages she'd acquired at the mall in Toledo.

"I know how you feel," Elinor said, "but admit it. Isn't it easier to get into the spirit of the season in weather like this?" Her tone was dry as she pointed to the snow-encrusted tree branches bending low in the cold, wet wind.

"Uck." Laurel's reply was succinct.

"All right, I get the message." Never one to give up easily, Elinor waved a gloved hand toward the Rafferty house next door to Laurel's parents' place. Mrs. Rafferty and her teenage son were draping a string of colored lights over a six-foot yew bush outside the front door. "You can't tell me that stringing lights on a palm tree while wearing a skimpy little sunsuit has quite the same nostalgic effect as standing out in a twenty mile an hour gale—"

"And sleet storm," Laurel interjected in the interest of accuracy.

"And sleet storm," Elinor acknowledged, "to do the same thing." Her low, smoky voice took on a singsong quality. "Wet mittens on the radiator..."

"Frostbitten fingers."

"Snow in the moonlight..."

"School delays and no mail delivery."

Elinor shot her younger cousin a dark look. "Spoilsport. Hot chocolate and caroling. That's my idea of Christmas," she finished before Laurel could open her mouth again.

"Mine, too," she conceded, accepting defeat graciously. "And speaking of caroling, old girl, if you don't get over to the church pronto, you're going to be late for choir practice."

"My Lord, what time is it?" Elinor glanced at the dashboard clock. "Six forty-five. I've got to rush." She almost pushed Laurel out of the passenger door. "See you later."

Laurel held her packages close to her chest and turned to look back at Elinor when she heard a slight hesitation in her last words.

"It's good to have you back, even under these circumstances."

Laurel only nodded. Try as hard as she might, she couldn't say she was happy to be back. Not now. Not yet. There was a cold, tight, aching band of anxiety in her chest. Nothing was going as she'd planned eight weeks earlier.

Her worry for her father's health was only slightly more urgent than her fear of meeting Seth Norris again.

Added to that was the growing burden of how she was going to manage an extended leave of absence from her job now, and then have to go to the hospital board once more and ask for maternity leave in the summer. Her father's hospital stay would be at least two weeks, maybe more. His period of recuperation after the surgery would be anywhere from eight to twelve weeks. But how, she'd asked herself over and over during a lot of long, sleepless nights, could she have foreseen any of these events when she'd made her quixotic plans such a short time ago?

Even then, she could have coped with her father's illness and upcoming heart surgery—somehow. She could have arranged her life to accommodate another lengthy stay in Bartlow—somehow. But she was never, never, going to be able to come to terms with Seth Norris's being back in town.

"I'm going to rehearsal, too," Laurel divulged, dragging her protesting thoughts back to the subject at hand.

She'd left only a small crack in the door through which to speak. To Elinor, her cousin looked all of twelve years old, her brown hair peeking out from under a brightly colored knit cap, her small nose pink from the cold, her eyes earnest—and not at all childish. They were even more shadowed with sadness and turmoil than they'd been in October. Laurel was keeping secrets and they weren't all happy ones. She wished her cousin trusted her enough to share the burden of her inner thoughts.

"You are? You didn't say anything about it earlier." Elinor had been cataloging her own purchases by the glow of the dome light in the ceiling while she secretly studied Laurel's pale face. She stopped rearranging sacks and boxes on the back seat and scooted around to watch Laurel more closely. "Need a lift?"

"I have my car here, remember?" Laurel threw the information out almost as though she could read Elinor's thoughts and wanted to give an excuse for her haggard appearance. The weather had been lousy all the way from Arizona: rain, sleet, hail. There were so many people getting an early start on holiday traveling that finding a motel at night had been a real challenge and she'd been in such a hurry to get home.

"Why don't you make an early night of it and catch the Christmas Eve performance?"

So Elinor had noticed her fatigue. The doctor at the clinic had told her it was natural and would probably disappear by the end of the third or fourth month. He'd added that she should be thankful she didn't have morning sickness to complain about, also. She supposed he was right, but Lord, she was tired.

Laurel shook her head. "We can't be sure Kevin got our cable. He always calls on Christmas Eve or Christmas morning. Always. Someone has to be there to take the call if it's Christmas Eve. Since Mom and Dad are both singing in the choir this year, I'm elected."

"Okay." Elinor didn't say anything about the production's second performance the Sunday morning after Christmas. She didn't have to . They both knew Laurel would be with her parents at the Cleveland Clinic. Her father's surgery was scheduled for Monday morning. Elinor looked at her packages one more time.

"Believe it or not, I'm actually finished with my shopping and there are three whole days left until Christmas. I might even be magnanimous and give Jack tomorrow evening off in case he hasn't finished his gift buying." She smiled. "It helps not having to spend hours battling the crowds in the toy departments. Sam did all the shopping for his Mieneke cousins and his half brother."

"Anything for an excuse to get the car," Laurel interjected knowledgeably. Another brief, hurting pang swept across her heart like the cold wind blowing across the yard. She'd sent Penny's gift—a computer game guaranteed to improve spelling skills—off in the mail before she'd left Phoenix. Every day that passed made it apparent that Laurel was less and less important in the little girl's life.

Perhaps that was best. Tom would probably marry again. Penny would have a new mother to learn to love. That thought didn't hurt as badly as it once would have. Laurel would always love Penny, but now she had a child of her own on the way. Her child and Seth's . . . Laurel pulled her thoughts back to the conversation at hand.

"You sound like an expert on teenage boys with that little deduction." Elinor laughed, but the sound held a tinge of unease. "It's almost worth the worry not to have to haul him to basketball practice every night."

She sounded as if she had nearly convinced herself that what she said was true. Laurel raised an eyebrow to show she wasn't fooled.

Elinor shrugged. "I said 'almost,' didn't I? It takes a long time to get used to them being mobile."

"I believe you." Laurel smiled a tiny private smile that never reached her lips but lit her cocoa-brown eyes with a glow from deep within. Someday she would be the mother of a teenage boy—or girl. She didn't care which. But that joyful secret, was hers alone to keep for the time being. "And I also believe I'm freezing to death where I stand. See you later." Laurel slammed the car door and started up the walk, the wind swirling up under the navy wool peacoat she'd unearthed from the back of Kevin's closet and cutting through the soft faded denim of her jeans as though she had nothing on.

Her mother had left lights on all over the house. They beckoned to Laurel with friendly warmth. Brightly colored, twinkling lights shone through a crust of snow on the porch railing and along the roof gables. A huge wreath adorned with pine cones and red ribbons hung on the front door.

The Rafferty boy had helped with their decorations, too. The doctors had advised her father against being out in the cold any more than necessary before the operation, more to avoid overexposure and the chance of getting run down and picking up a bug than because it was bad for his condition.

Not for the first time, Laurel wondered how well her father would accept the long period of recuperation that lay before him. He was an energetic and impatient man. It would take a lot of ingenuity on the part of her and her mother to keep him from overdoing from the moment he got home from the hospital.

Kevin would know how to keep their father occupied. She wondered yet again if he'd received her mother's cable telling him about the heart surgery. They had no way of knowing until they heard from him. "I miss you, big brother." Laurel heard her whispered words caught and carried away by the wind. "I miss you a lot."

She dumped her packages on the hall table and hurried through the hallway and out the kitchen door to the garage. She did miss Kevin. She needed someone to confide in. The temptation to tell Elinor about her pregnancy had been nearly overwhelming as they'd driven home, cozy and snug in her cousin's no-nonsense, midsize sedan. The short December day had been fading into darkness, the wind and cold kept at bay by the steady purr of warmth from the car's heater, but she'd resisted the urge.

She couldn't tell anyone about her baby, not Kevin, not her parents, not Elinor. She couldn't tell anyone as long as Seth Norris remained in Bartlow, recuperating from his brush with death.

THERE WERE ABOUT two dozen other spectators scattered throughout the pews of the Methodist church when Laurel arrived a few minutes later. She slid into a back row and shrugged down into her coat, turning up the collar, tucking her hands deep into the pockets in a vain attempt to get warm.

Her blood was just too thin from living in the desert to cope with a blast of wintry Canadian air, she decided ruefully. Her car had been as cold as a deep freeze, too. Her teeth were chattering, her knees shaking, by the time she'd found a place to park in the lot belonging to the funeral home across the street from the church.

To make matters worse, the lenses of her glasses were fogged up so badly she couldn't see. Laurel slipped them into a coat pocket. That was a phenomenon she couldn't blame entirely on being in Bartlow in the winter. It sometimes happened in reverse in Phoenix after stepping out of an air-conditioned car or building directly into the blistering heat of the Arizona sun.

Pulling her hat off her hair, Laurel squinted enough to bring her parents into focus. About thirty-five singers were milling around the stage set directly in front of the pulpit and altar at the front of the sanctuary. Streetlights outside gave slight illumination to the stained glass windows, pale ghostlike imitations of their bright Sunday morning colors, behind the singers.

Smells of candle wax and pine roping mingled with furniture polish from the shiny oak pews. Laurel inhaled deeply, familiar smells triggering familiar memories of Christmas pageants long past. She relaxed a little farther into her seat.

It was easier to pick out people she knew now that the singers were forming into rows. The participants ranged in age from seventeen to over seventy. Several residents of

Oakfork were in attendance. She recognized two members of her high school graduating class. Sally Benton was expecting again, she noticed. Laurel wondered idly if this made baby number three or four for her old playmate. Sally waved and she waved back, once more pushing down a longing for someone to share her happiness with. She was in this thing alone and she'd get used to the idea if she gave herself enough time.

This was the fourteenth year for the community production, the first year of conducting for the Presbyterian minister. He mounted the podium with a flourish.

"He's something of a martinet but very talented," her mother had said when they'd discussed Laurel's coming to the practice earlier in the day.

"He conducts like a tin soldier on a box," Ralph had added with a grunt. "He's got a tin ear, too."

"Ralph, where's your Christian charity? It's Christmas," Lois had scolded, and that had ended that discussion.

Laurel had to agree with her father about one thing. The Presbyterian minister did look like a toy soldier on a box. He was short and slim, with a head of thinning, blond hair that was pretty long in the back and on the sides by Bartlow standards.

The organist struck a chord, and a low hum, in good eight-part harmony, drifted toward the back of the church. The Methodists had the biggest organ in town, the Lutherans, down the street, the biggest auditorium, so they alternated hosting the event every year. It was a good compromise, compromise being one of the main survival skills necessary for living in a small town.

The Presbyterian minister—Laurel couldn't remember his name, he was new in town, having accepted the call to his flock at the end of September—began counting heads. Obviously someone was missing. He looked out into the dim auditorium as if searching for the missing members of his chorale.

Just then, the heavy, native walnut doors opened behind her and a blast of arctic air swept down the center aisle. Laurel slid a little farther down in the pew to shield herself from the cold currents as two teenage girls, followed shortly by Michael Norris, walked by.

The youngsters mumbled their apologies and took their places in the chorus. Mike stepped into a spot next to her father in the baritone section. Laurel swallowed a grin. Last year, she recalled, he'd been singing with the tenors.

Elinor was standing next to Laurel's mother. They were both altos with lovely voices. Laurel was a soprano with a pretty good range but lousy pitch. She hadn't sung in a church choir in years. She missed it, she found, as the group began a spirited rendition of "God Rest Ye Merry Gentlemen." Laurel hummed along under her breath.

It wasn't until midway through the second verse, whose words she didn't know by heart, that her attention began to wander and she noticed someone standing beside the pew where she was sitting. She looked up, startled, to find her eyes caught and held by Seth Norris's night-blue gaze. The moment she'd been dreading—and, God help her, anticipating—since she'd returned to Bartlow was at hand.

"Hello, Laurel." He'd frightened her. Her eyes were as big as saucers, yet deep in the warm brown depths he thought he detected a leaping spark of welcome. Her hands clamped around the edge of the pew and seemed to be the only thing keeping her from getting up and running past him. That, and the cane he was holding in his left hand. He didn't need it for walking, but for standing it came in awfully handy.

It was coming in handy right now, he discovered. He rested most of his weight on the sturdy oak shaft and tried to get his breathing under control. Only part of the difficulty with his respiration came from the recent exertion of climbing a flight of steps to reach the sanctuary. Most of it came from seeing the woman who'd haunted his feverish dreams for more days and nights than he cared to admit. "May I sit down?"

She didn't answer with words, only scooted away from him as though he were a ghost. Seth took the gesture as an affirmative and levered himself down onto the pew beside her. He was making quite a production of it, he realized, catching sight of several interested observers out of the corner of his eye. The pew was low and he was still so damned stiff that he felt at least a hundred years old.

He also felt slightly light-headed because he'd taken one of the potent little white pain pills the doctors in D.C. had prescribed before they turned him loose last week.

Or was that reaction, too, the dizziness and shortness of breath, due to the woman beside him?

He wasn't altogether sure his physical symptoms were all caused by the medication. Normally he stayed away from the stuff, but this time he was glad he'd taken the precaution. The sniper's bullet had torn up a lot of muscle tissue and cracked a rib. He hurt like hell. He'd had no idea how much effort it took, how much energy it required, just to get from the car into the church, until he'd tried it.

He was exhausted; he couldn't deny it. Yet at the same time he also found himself filled with a strange, jittery, restless energy. He hadn't expected to find Laurel Sauder here, although he knew she was back in town. What was even more obvious was that she hadn't expected to see him. That if she thought she could get away with it, she'd turn and run just as she had that afternoon in October.

Laurel had never felt such confusion in her life. What could she do? What could she say? She wanted to run and hide; she wanted to reach out and trace the hard, beard-shadowed line of his jaw and reassure herself that he was indeed alive and regaining his health; she wanted above all else to thank him for the precious gift of life he'd given her.

But she couldn't do any of those things and the sudden disappointment that realization caused was bewildering in its intensity. *She was so very happy to see him again.* The strength of her emotions frightened her; she didn't want to acknowledge them even in the most private recesses of her own thoughts—of her own heart.

"How are you feeling?" She whispered, not so much because of the ongoing choir practice, but because she couldn't trust herself to get the words out in the right, casually concerned tone she wanted. *I prayed for you,* she added in the privacy of her mind.

"I'm doing okay. Didn't lose anything I can't live without." Physically, that was true, but emotionally, he wasn't so certain.

Laurel had never been *his* in the true sense of the word. But what they'd shared that night in October had meant far more to him than he'd ever thought possible with a woman.

He wasn't even angry with her; at least, he hadn't been for very long, because he'd seen the pain and remorse in her eyes and knew she was hurting. No, he wasn't angry, but he was hurt, and he fully intended to find out why she'd run away rather than face him.

He'd never expected to have an opportunity to do so, but fate had intervened.

"I didn't..." Laurel ran her tongue over her dry lips. "I didn't think they would allow you to travel so soon." She couldn't think of anything else to say. She was afraid to let their conversation get too personal. *She could sense he had no intention of letting go without an explanation for her behavior.* Perhaps he wouldn't demand to be told why she'd acted as she did, here and now, but sooner or later, he would. *She was going to have to lie to him,* and the realization hurt.

Seth gave a snort of rough laughter. "I threatened to walk out of the hospital on my own. Since there were a dozen reporters outside day and night, no one wanted that to happen. My superiors decided to go along with the idea." He looked proud of his perseverance. "I flew into Toledo in an army helicopter, compliments of the White House." He shook his head, his expression rueful. "There was even a damned private ambulance waiting at the airport."

"I heard." Laurel couldn't help smiling at the obvious embarrassment he'd felt. Seth was a private man; he'd never be happy as the center of attention. "I suppose you know that every member of the Bartlow EMS has his nose out of joint because of you."

He stared at her in amazement.

"You would have been the most important 'transfer' they've ever had to transport."

"Knock it off." He groaned and settled back into the hard pew with a grin on his face. He pretended to pay attention to the singing, but every nerve in his body was attuned to the small, alluring woman at his side. He was trying very hard to keep the conversation casual so he wouldn't frighten her off with the intensity of the feelings roiling inside him. It occurred to him that he must already be pretty far gone or he wouldn't be encouraging her to talk about the shooting. He didn't want to be reminded of it any more than necessary.

"You're a hero."

Laurel obviously intended to have her say. Her jaw was set in a soft, stubborn line Seth found so intriguing he couldn't help but stare. His hand itched to reach out and touch her hair, her face, her mouth. He wanted to trace that stubborn set to her jaw with his lips. He folded his hands around the head of his cane, instead.

"I was doing my job, Laurel. And I evidently screwed that up or the guy would never have gotten past our security." He knew there was no softness whatsoever in the line of his jaw.

"The newspapers said he was probably the only person who even remembered there was an air duct big enough for a man to crawl through leading up to that balcony."

Laurel forgot how awkward she'd felt in his company only minutes before. She forgot they'd parted in such an abrupt and hurtful way. She could only concentrate on the deep, pleasant growl of his voice and the intoxicating warmth of his body next to hers. "Why did he do it?"

Seth didn't answer for a long moment and Laurel realized she'd made a mistake. "I shouldn't have asked that, right? You don't have to answer me."

She looked chagrined, like a little girl caught with her hand in the cookie jar. He shook his head. "It isn't that. It isn't classified or anything like that. I don't really know why he did it, Laurel. That's for the doctors and lawyers to decide. I'm afraid I don't know any more than what you've read in the papers. He worked for the hotel for years. He came to this country during the uprising in Hungary in 1956. But he wasn't politically motivated. His wife died recently and he was alone in the world. He evidently felt the President was somehow to blame for his loss. No one knows exactly why."

"On TV they said he was recovering, too, but that he was completely disoriented and didn't understand what he'd done." Laurel's eyes were big and filled with sadness and tiny flecks of golden light reflected from the candelabra on the deep window ledges.

Seth nodded. "I gave them my statement before I left Washington, but there are blanks in my memory for some reason." He managed to keep most of the grimness out of his voice. The look on his face was wry and slightly self-conscious. Downplaying the seriousness of what had happened seemed to be the easiest way for him to deal with it at the moment. "I watched the tapes..."

"You watched the tapes?" Laurel couldn't believe what she heard.

"It's my job."

This time the harsh quality of his words didn't escape her.

"Anyway, it wasn't that bad."

He was lying and she knew it.

Seth shrugged and ended the topic under discussion. "Once was enough."

"I don't doubt that it was."

Laurel shivered in reaction to his words, but Seth took the opportunity to change the subject. "You're chilled. I didn't expect this thing to go on so long."

"Dress rehearsals always seem to last forever."

"This one certainly is. Why don't you let me buy you a coffee?"

Laurel hesitated. What was she going to say to him? How could she spend time with him—as a friend—and still keep her precious secret safe? *Was this where the lies began in earnest?*

"I don't know..." she said truthfully. She shouldn't take the risk of being alone with him even for a moment, even in a public place, but the temptation was too great to resist.

"That's okay, Laurel. I understand. You came to hear your parents and Elinor sing. I'll just sit here for another couple of hours until Mike's ready to take me home. I can't drive yet, you know.''

Seth was aware his behavior was shameless, but what he said wasn't entirely untrue. He *wasn't* looking forward to sitting on the hard oak pew for any extended length of time. And he *wasn't* allowed to drive yet. Not for several more weeks, but that didn't mean he wasn't up to taking advantage of this chance meeting with Laurel.

"I might be overdoing it tonight," he conceded ruefully, "but I was getting stir-crazy sitting around the house with Mom fussing over me and nothing but animated Christmas specials to watch on TV." He sighed and shifted on the seat, watching Laurel covertly from the corner of his eye.

She looked perplexed for a moment, then unconsciously squared her shoulders, as if coming to a decision. "How about a cup of hot chocolate, instead? They're about due for a break here and we'll tell your brother where we're going." She had to learn to act normally around him. They were both going to be in Bartlow for the next few weeks; avoiding him would cause talk. She couldn't afford that.

And if she was honest with herself, she wanted to see him again, no matter how many warning signals went off in her brain. Her pregnancy wouldn't be obvious for some time yet; she could enjoy the bittersweet pleasure of his company and store up memories for the future.

Thirty minutes later they were settled in front of the fireplace in Laurel's parents' living room. Seth was stretched out comfortably on the couch, supported by a mass of pillows. Laurel was curled up on the floor, the slight roundness of her stomach hidden beneath the fleecy bulk of her mint green pullover. She felt warm and comfortable and secure, not at all the way she expected to feel alone with Seth for the first time since the night they'd spent together in this house.

"I can't remember the last time I've been in so many places with live Christmas trees." His voice broke into her thoughts gently and quietly. "You've been staring at that tree for the past ten minutes." He smiled down at her and rested his head against the back of the couch, focusing his gaze on the gilt angel at the top.

"I know. In Phoenix I have an artificial one."

"The past two years I haven't even bothered to put one up at all."

Seth was unprepared for the vehemence of Laurel's reaction. "That's awful. I can't imagine Christmas without some kind of tree."

"My ex-wife was a decorator. She always took care of the tree." They were always color coordinated, always carrying out that year's theme. Country, Victorian. The last, he remembered, had been art deco, all black and silver, a far cry from the multicolored lights and hodgepodge of glass ornaments on the Sauder tree.

"Is that why you haven't had one?" Laurel felt a strange pain twist inside her as she watched a frown darken his brow. "Because it reminds you of your divorce?"

"No," Seth answered before he could stop himself. "I've traveled with the President the past two Christmases. It just didn't seem worth the effort to decorate an empty apartment."

"Oh." Laurel leaned back against the couch, relaxing once more, aware her cheeks were flushed but hoping he'd attribute the added color to the heat of the fire. "I thought..."

"My marriage is over and done with. There were no hard feelings. There weren't many regrets, either."

"Of course." Laurel stood. "Would you like some more hot chocolate?" she asked, changing the subject abruptly.

"No. But I wouldn't object if you wanted to put some Christmas carols on the stereo." He'd strayed too close to forbidden waters again. "Or I can take you on at any board game known to man. Cribbage. Backgammon. Or cards. Canasta? Poker? You name it."

"Is that how you spend your free time?" Laurel half turned away from the stereo, hands on hips.

Seth set his mug of lukewarm cocoa carefully on the marble-top table beside the couch before answering. "Off-duty agents spend a lot of time in dreary hotel rooms. We don't rate a suite along with the President, you know."

"You're playing on my sympathies again, Norris," Laurel warned, replacing album jackets in the stand beside the stereo.

"I'm getting good at it," Seth admitted without a trace of shame. "I figure this cane and a pained grimace now and then are good for at least another couple of weeks or so. I'll know when I'm fully recovered, though . . ." He broke off enticingly and Laurel couldn't help but rise to the bait.

"How will you know?"

She tilted her head slightly to the left, the way he liked her to do.

"One morning Mom will point to a pile of dirty laundry and tell me I'm well enough to do it myself."

Laurel laughed out loud; she couldn't help herself.

"That's the first time I've heard you laugh tonight." His voice was dark and rough, and the sound of it sent pleasant little chills running up and down her spine.

"I'm enjoying myself." Laurel was surprised to find she really meant what she'd said. Their eyes met and held across the room. Seth held out his hand and Laurel moved forward to take it. Slowly, hesitantly, she sank to her knees in front of him. He reached up and cupped the back of her head with his hand.

Seth could feel her tense and knew he must move slowly, with caution, or he'd frighten her away again. The blood was pounding in his lower body and less pleasantly in the still healing scars on his chest. He moved his hand to trace the line of her jaw. Her skin was warm and soft as silk beneath his fingertips.

If she moved closer now, it would be her choice. Her eyes were dark with confusion and something else he chose to believe was need and longing, the same emotions he himself was experiencing.

"Do you have your Christmas shopping done yet?"

His casual, unimportant question caught Laurel off guard just as he'd hoped it would. She didn't pull away but rested her weight on her hands and stared down at him, perplexed. "Yes, I have."

"What did you buy for me?" His voice was as warm and gentle as a lover's touch.

"Nothing..." Laurel said without thinking. "I mean...I'm not quite finished..." She stuttered to a halt.

"Oh." He layered the word with a heavy coating of disappointment. "I was hoping there was a present under the tree for me." He took her left hand from where it was resting and held her lightly by the wrist.

"Well, I'm sorry, but there isn't." Laurel had regained some of her equilibrium. She knew he could feel the racing beat of her pulse beneath his fingers, but she couldn't do anything about that. Oddly enough, she didn't want to. He was teasing her again. She could get used to this bantering very quickly, she realized. "What do you have for me?"

A tiny smile played around the corners of her mouth. She was wearing some kind of pale pink lip gloss and blusher. Her brown eyes were shadowed by the same green as her sweater. Her hair caught the light of the dying fire and stray glints of auburn made it glow with a warmth all its own.

"I'm not in any shape to fight the last-minute crowds shopping," he reminded her without a trace of shame, but the groan he bit back when he shifted against the pillows behind him wasn't all for her benefit. The potent little white pills were beginning to wear off.

"Then how about one of your mother's marvelous coffee cakes?" Laurel hadn't missed the sudden tightening of his jaw, the uncomfortable shift in the long relaxed frame against the cushions. It was time to bring this very pleasant interlude to a close. She didn't want him to leave, but it was almost time to take Seth back to the church to meet his brother.

As if he sensed her resolve to end the evening, Seth tightened his fingers around her wrist. "I think I can manage that. And what will you give me?"

Laurel didn't pull away, as he'd half expected she would. "What do you want, Agent Norris?"

"A kiss?" He didn't try to keep the question out of his words. He had to move slowly, with infinite patience, or he'd scare her away again. That was the last thing he wanted to do. He was playing with fire as it was. He'd made a grave mistake allowing himself to make love to her that night in October. He should have heeded his instincts and stayed away. She wasn't like the others, no matter what she'd told him at the time. Their lovemaking must have meant something to her, or she wouldn't be this uneasy around him. Now all he could hope for was that it was because she cared, whether she was ready to admit it or not.

"A kiss." She spoke the words so softly that if he hadn't seen her lips move, he wouldn't have heard them at all.

"I don't think one small kiss will strain your Christmas budget past its limit, will it?"

"I suppose not." But it might very well bankrupt her emotionally, Laurel thought. "It's a cheap enough gift."

The words came out more roughly than she'd intended. Her heart was beating so hard she found it difficult to breathe. She felt scared and exhilarated all at once. It was a dangerous risk she was taking, but the pleasure of being with Seth again, of listening to him talk, of laughing at his jokes...of touching him again, outweighed all her fears of discovery.

"Not cheap," Seth said, as she leaned closer to brush her lips across his. "More precious than you know." He lifted his hand again to hold her still.

Their lips met and clung. Laurel rested her weight on her hands, her breasts brushing lightly against the soft cotton of his shirt, through which she could feel the bulky thickness of the dressing over his wound. She thought again how close he'd come to death and sent a silent prayer of thanks winging skyward.

"Thank you," Seth said, moving his lips to taste the corners of her mouth. "That's the best present I've ever had."

His breath was soft and moist against her lips. He tasted of chocolate and smelled of some spicy cologne and slightly of wood-smoke from the fire.

"Merry Christmas, Laurel."

She let him kiss her again because she couldn't seem to find a reason to say no. And if she was honest with herself, she'd admit she wanted to kiss him, too. No matter how many warning signals went off in her brain, no matter how worried she might be that he would discover her secret, she couldn't bring herself to leave his side. She let her hands slide up around his neck, let him take some of her weight as she rested against him. She kissed him again.

"Merry Christmas, Seth." She closed her eyes and rested her head on his shoulder. Her mind was no longer in control of her actions. Her heart was. "I'm very glad you're home again."

IT WASN'T SNOWING anymore. Christmas Day dawned bright and sunny and cold. The snow on the ground blew into drifts, but they were small and the roads stayed clear. Laurel found herself looking forward to the holiday. Seth hadn't asked her for anything more than she was willing to give that night after choir practice. Her attraction to him was even more intense than it had been in October. Sometimes she wondered if she was doing the right thing in keeping her secret from everyone. Then she would realize how complicated it all was, how many lies she had already told, and she would become frightened again.

Her thoughts were so fragmented since she'd come home, her loyalties and needs were pulled in so many directions, she didn't know which way to turn. But today was Christmas Day, and she'd made a vow with herself to put all those divergent thoughts and feelings out of her mind and to concentrate only on her family and the joy of the holy season.

So far she'd done pretty well. Dinner was over, the family gathered around the tree. Presents were yet to be exchanged, fudge and cookies to be sampled. For the moment, she was content to let the future take care of itself.

The phone rang as Laurel was walking by the hall extension. She picked it up on the second peal. "Sauders."

"Merry Christmas, Squirt."

Kevin's voice sounded strange and metallic, but very dear. He wasn't in the jungle anymore, Laurel deduced, or he'd have had the call patched through a ham radio operator somewhere here in the States. Was it possible he was already on his way back to civilization?

"Where are you, big brother?" She had to raise her voice to make herself heard. Her parents were still in the kitchen, loading up the dishwasher, but other family members were scattered throughout the big old house. Her father's brother and his wife and assorted offspring, as well as Elinor's parents and Laurel's two living grandparents, were sharing the day with the Sauders.

The house was crowded and warm and full of Christmas happiness. Laurel was filled with a great contentment and awareness of where she had come from as well as hope for the future. "It's so good to hear your voice, Kevin. Where are you?"

"I'm in Manaus, Sis. I got Mom's cable." He hesitated a moment, then went on. "I'm glad you could get home for the holidays. How's Dad doing? I never even suspected there was something wrong with his heart."

"None of us did, Kev." Laurel's tone was gentle but firm. "So don't go blaming yourself. He's going to be fine. Hearing your voice will do him a world of good. He's helping Mom and Grandma Gerschutz load the dishwasher."

Laurel put one hand over her ear to block out the merriment around her. "Aunt Lettie and Uncle Josh are here with their kids and Grandpa Sauder. Uncle Will and Aunt Evelyn are here, too, with their kids and all the grandkids. It's a zoo. The little ones want to open their presents so badly. Grandpa Sauder wants to take his nap first . . . well, you remember how it is." She smiled fondly at Elinor's tall, gangly son as he raced by, two small cousins hanging on his pant legs, one perched ecstatically on his shoulders.

"I remember. Next year I'll be home, Sis. That's a promise."

Laurel could feel a lump rise in her throat that threatened to choke off her words. She swallowed hastily and fought to bring her wayward emotions under control. "This must be costing you a fortune, Kevin. I'll get Mom and Dad on the line."

"No, wait a minute, Laurel. Are you telling me everything? I feel so damned helpless. There's no way I can get home in time for the surgery. I only got the cable three days ago. It's taken me that long to get to a real phone."

"Dad's going to be fine, Kevin." Laurel put every ounce of conviction she could muster into her voice. "Not that Mom and I didn't have our hands full convincing him to go ahead with the operation." She tried for a laugh and almost brought it off. Oh, how she wished her brother were near enough to touch, to reassure with her hands and her eyes, as well as her voice.

"Sure he is. Dad's a tough old bird." Kevin's voice was a shade too hearty; he knew it and Laurel knew it.

"I'll be here with them. I'm going to stay as long as necessary. I've taken a leave of absence from the hospital."

"I'm going to be there for Dad's recovery, too, Squirt. I'm coming home. The rainy season started early this year. If I don't get out of the jungle now, I'll be holed up down here until July."

"But your book." Laurel couldn't keep the elation out of her voice, yet her happiness was tempered with concern.

"I've got just about everything I need. It's going to be a good book, Laurel. But it's time for me to come home. Put Mom and Dad on so I can give them the news."

"I will, Kevin." She paused a moment. "There's so much going on here, so much I have to tell you." She thought of Seth's being shot, of his being back in Bartlow, too. Kevin hadn't heard anything about the assassination attempt, she was sure, or he would have mentioned it. She thought of her own wonderful secret and felt a rush of emotion so strong it caused tears to form. "I'll get Mom and Dad right away. Oh, Kevin, hurry home. I do miss you so."

Chapter Eight

"I hear the Sauder boy, the one that takes the pictures for them fancy books, is comin' back to town." Clint Norris dipped a bolt from the engine he was taking apart in a container of solvent and scoured away at it with the bristled end of a long-handled brush.

"Elinor Mieneke told me the same thing." Seth straightened from his cramped position under the hood of Clint's twenty-year-old farm truck. They were overhauling the engine in hopes of getting one more year of field work out of it. He jumped down off the bumper of the truck and felt only a twinge of pain in his side from still healing muscles. He could see his breath fan out in clouds of steam as he spoke. It was one of those miserable January days that show up at the end of the month, just about the same time as the first of the Christmas bills arrived in the mail. Except today the weather was so bad there hadn't been any mail delivery at all.

"So what's holdin' him up? They say Ralph Sauder's mendin' pretty good from the cuttin' he had done on his ticker. Still, he ain't as young as he used to be. None of us are." Clint studied the worn fitting in his hand thoughtfully for a moment.

"According to Elinor, there's been a lot of hassle with the Brazilian authorities about Kevin taking his film out of the country." Seth stamped his feet. The cement floor was like ice. His feet were like ice, even in heavy-soled work shoes. The closed-off corner of the barn that served as a machine shop was barely above freezing. There was no way two propane space heaters could compete with the below zero conditions outside. He wiped his hands on a greasy rag. He strongly suspected he had grease on his face, as well as his hands, but he didn't care.

"Crazy things go on in that part of the world." Clint's tone was dry as dust.

"Kevin's stuck in Manaus," Seth added as an afterthought. He'd been to a Super Bowl party at Elinor's the Sunday before. He'd gotten the information about his old friend's trials and tribulations from her. Laurel hadn't attended the gathering and Seth was disappointed. And frustrated. She'd been avoiding him since before the holidays and he couldn't understand why, but he intended to find out.

"Manaus? Where in blazes is that?"

"Brazil. On the Amazon somewhere, I think." Seth frowned. World geography had never been his favorite subject. "I'd have to look it up to be sure." He smiled at Clint and shrugged. Already his world was contracting and reshaping itself to the contours of the land around him. He didn't think of it as a narrowing of his vision, only a reordering of his priorities.

"Hell of a long way from Bartlow." Clint gestured at the near blizzard conditions outside the barn. Snow was blowing almost parallel to the ground, piling up in heavy drifts when an obstruction halted its flight.

"Hell of a long way," Seth agreed.

"The government Communist down there in Brazil?" Clint asked.

"It's a republic, Dad. Or supposed to be." Seth couldn't recall if Brazil's current president was part of a military or civilian regime, and at the moment he didn't care.

"Grow a lot of soybeans and corn, though, Commies or not. Knocking the bejesus out of our export trade. Them and Argentina."

"Yeah. Washington's farm policy is for the birds." Seth decided he was even beginning to sound like a farmer again.

"Been going downhill for three administrations, but go on with your story," Clint advised.

Seth obliged. "I guess Kevin had his work cut out for him convincing some of those petty bureaucrats he'd only been taking photos of birds and monkeys for a picture book. They're pretty touchy about being accused of devastating the rain forests."

"The way I hear it from your mother—and she got it from Lois Sauder—that's exactly what the book is about. No good comes of messin' with the environment like that. Hell, the soil under them rain forests ain't fit to farm, anyway. You'd think they'd know that." He shook his head. Clint's main focus in life was the land he worked, but his overview of the world situation wasn't as limited as an outsider might think.

"I hope Kevin doesn't get in over his head."

Clint nodded and picked up another piece of the disassembled motor to clean in the solvent bath. "Kevin Sauder's nobody's fool. He'll make out all right."

"Yeah. When they threatened to x-ray his film, he ended up getting most of it developed down there to prove to them he was on the level. Evidently it took some time to find a lab whose quality satisfied him." Seth couldn't help but smile when he thought about his impatient friend riding herd over a bunch of photographic technicians. "All in all, it's been a pretty frustrating month for him."

Something in his voice must have alerted his father. "And what about you, son?"

Clint changed the subject so suddenly Seth didn't have time to react with anything less than the truth. "Physically it's been damned frustrating."

"Does that mean you're ready to go back to your own life?" Clint stopped brushing at the small part he held in his hand, but his lined and chiseled features gave no hint of what he was thinking.

Seth was quiet for a long moment, too. He watched his breath swirl and eddy in the cold air of the workshop. He listened to the roar of the wind and the creaking of hand-hewn beams in the haymow that had come from trees tall and mature before the Civil War. He thought of the two meetings he'd already had with old Mabel Jackson about the possibility of buying her land.

"I'm not ready to go back." He didn't say anything about his negotiations with the shrewd and feisty old lady. He hadn't told anyone of his dream—yet. But it was time he started paving the way. "I'm not sure I want to go back to the Service."

"Maybe not. Can't blame you there. But you could make a good living for yourself in Washington, anyway. Be one of them high class security consultants that charge five hundred dollars an hour just to talk to people over the phone."

"That's not for me, Dad." Seth took a deep breath and put his hand on Clint's shoulder. They seldom touched, never embraced. But this was no ordinary time, no ordinary conversation. He'd been quietly burning his bridges in D.C. He'd made arrangements to sublet his apartment, extended his medical leave of absence indefinitely and had his car driven to Ohio by a courier service. He was regaining his health and his optimism.

"I want to stay here, Dad. I want to farm with you and Michael," Seth went on speaking, determined to have his say before Clint could turn him down. His relationship with his father was better than it had been in years; still, he wasn't sure what the older man's reaction to his request would be.

"I wondered how long it'd be before you asked." Clint's expression was guarded.

"I know I hurt you a lot when I left home, but that was a long time ago." Seth wasn't apologizing, just explaining, and Clint accepted it as such. "I've learned plenty about myself in the past few months, but even before that I knew deep down that I wanted to come home. If you'll have me."

"It's a big step, son."

Clint didn't bring up the pain of the past. Seth knew he probably wouldn't unless he did so first. Perhaps it was better not to rehash all the old arguments. These days people analyzed everything to death. Maybe faith was a better basis for starting over than logic. He was a man now, tested and not found lacking; his father knew that and seemed to respect his judgment.

"I think it's the right decision, but I need a chance to find out. Will you take me on?"

Clint wiped his hands on the cloth stuck in the back pocket of his insulated coveralls. "I'm not takin' back anything I said to you about this business last fall. It's killin' work. More years than not, it's a losin' proposition. But I'm gettin' on in years, too. And I can use the help when your brother goes off to college in the fall."

Seth opened his mouth to challenge the last statement, then closed it again. It wasn't the best time to plead Michael's case. He wanted to try to get his dad to see Mike's point of view, but he needed to have his facts straight when he did so. He needed to talk to the younger Norris first. He'd give it his best shot; he owed the kid that much.

"If we took on another couple hundred acres, there'd be plenty of work for us all—" Seth broke off. So much for testing the waters. He might as well have been talking to a brick wall. Clint's jaw was set, his face a stony mask.

"You might as well know it from the first if you're determined to come back to the land, son. We aren't in any position to take on new ground. Not without some new equipment. The combine's seen better days and the corn header's damn near shot to pieces. I've got most of my capital tied up in that new tractor and your brother's education. I can't offer you any benefits." He turned and put both hands on the workbench, looking out into the fading daylight and the unrelenting fury of the wind and snow. "I can't even promise you much of a future if things don't start lookin' up prctty soon. Do you still want to stay here and work the land? You've got time to change your mind. Just say so and we'll forget this whole conversation ever happencd." He turned and eyed his son with proud defiance. "We'll just say it was a dizzy spell or somethin'."

Seth held out his hand. "I haven't had a dizzy spell in weeks. No way you're backing out on me already. I'm home to stay."

"You never did have a lot of sense. Just like your old man." Clint's handshake was brief, but his grip was strong as his bony, work-roughened hand closed over Seth's. "I guess we'd better get your mother's approval on this merger." He pointed toward the house, pulling his collar up around his ears before opening the small side door to leave the shelter of the barn. "She's the real boss of this outfit, and don't you forget it or you'll rue the day."

Seth laughed. "I'll remember." He'd passed the first hurdle to building the new life he wanted for himself. He was back home to stay. Now it was time to put the second phase of his master plan into action.

Laurel.

He wanted her, God knew. And he needed her just as badly. Hell, he was more than halfway in love with her already. There was one thing about coming as close to death as he had in that hotel ballroom. It made a lot of things very clear in a big hurry. But she was avoiding him. There was no other word for it. It was time to find out why.

Her father was recovering from his heart surgery. She might not be staying in Bartlow much longer. He had to work fast, but at the same time, he needed to be very careful. He couldn't afford to scare her into running away from him again.

He'd go into town as soon as the snowplows cleared the road. He'd ask her to Mike's next basketball game at the high school. What could be more innocent than that? But the plans he had for the rest of the evening were far from innocent.

Seth was painfully aware he was falling deeply in love with Laurel Sauder. The fact was irrefutable and he accepted it with characteristic forthrightness. What he intended to do about it was also characteristic, straightforward and to the point. He intended to take his best shot at making her fall just as deeply in love with him.

THE STORE WAS QUIET for a Friday afternoon. Overhead a fluorescent light flickered and buzzed. It needed to be changed—and soon. It was driving Laurel crazy. She wondered if Kevin would be home in time to do it before the store opened Monday morning. If not, she'd hire Rudy Sunderson's brother, Malcolm, the town handyman, to do it Monday afternoon for sure. She said as much to Caroline Insenmann, who was hidden from view by a ceiling-high set of shelves.

"He'll probably be tied up till then, anyway," her companion answered, peering around the obstruction. "Lots of folks got caught unprepared for this cold spell. He'll have plenty of busted water pipes to keep him occupied all weekend."

"You're probably right there." Laurel sighed and resigned herself to another day of the buzzing light tube. "At least it's stopped snowing." It was something of a ritual ending to most conversations these days. The weather was better than it had been for over a week, but the temperature was still way below freezing and the wind was raw and cold.

"When you get done there, will you check the inventory of oral antibiotics?" Laurel asked a few moments later as she scrolled through medication records on the computer screen. "Dr. Mitchell called over before you got here this morning. He's seeing a lot of cases of the new strain of flu virus and he says it's a doozy. Lots of upper respiratory problems and secondary infections."

"Just what we need," Caroline said grimly. "It's going to be a stinker of a winter."

Laurel had to agree. It also meant she'd be coming in for her own share of questions from Bartlow's residents about what over-the-counter remedies would be safest and most effective to help alleviate the aches and pains, runny noses and sniffles that accompanied the affliction.

"Better double our order for Tylenol, and let's get another thousand tablets of ASA. Aspirin is still the best thing around for adults when it comes to pain and fever."

It was another of her father's opinions she agreed with wholeheartedly. He was recovering from the coronary surgery so quickly that Laurel and her mother were hard-pressed to keep him occupied at home. In three weeks the doctor had promised him he could come back to work two afternoons a week—if he behaved himself in the interim.

And Laurel, for her part, would be glad for his help. Her father worked long, hard hours and she was doing her best to match them with only the assistance of a pharmacy resident from the University of Toledo who worked on Saturdays until three in the afternoon. She was tired and a little run-down and she was anxious to get back to Arizona before anyone suspected her condition. Especially her baby's father.

Already she could feel the tissue of lies she had thought so innocent at first beginning to tighten into bands of steel around her heart. She'd begun to drop hints about a man in her life back in Phoenix to Elinor and her parents; and each and every word coming from her mouth burned like acid.

How different everything would be if she were free to tell Seth everything. Her baby needed an image of his father as he was growing up. He would resent her eventually for never telling him who the man who had given him life really was. It was all so much more complicated than she'd allowed herself to believe it would be when she'd asked Seth to make love to her that lovely autumn night.

Her feelings for Seth were so much more complicated than she had intended them to be. He excited her; he frightened her; he made her happy; he made her dream impossible dreams. It wasn't fair. She had thought they would come together briefly, beautifully and never see each other again. But reality was a very different thing.

The lovemaking had indeed been beautiful beyond anything she'd ever known with Tom. And it had been all too brief.

But the rest of her dream had been selfish and self-serving; there was no other way to describe it.

What would happen to her child if she had an accident, or contracted a serious, debilitating illness? Who would care for her little one? Her parents? She hadn't taken their wishes and needs into consideration when she'd made her quixotic, momentous decision.

And the financial considerations. Laurel shuddered. Already the savings she'd thought adequate for seeing her through her pregnancy and for a reasonable time after the baby was born were being eroded by travel expenses and time away from her work. After her accumulated sick leave was gone, she'd have to take time off without pay, straining her finances still further.

What if there were complications with the birth?

What if there was a planet-wide famine?

"What if the world ends tomorrow?" Laurel said aloud, and gave herself a shake. Good grief, being pregnant was making her maudlin and pessimistic. None of the books about pregnancy she'd read had said anything about those particular side effects.

She was young and strong and very healthy. She would make it all come out right somehow. She wanted her baby; she loved him already. She would be the best mother she could possibly be.

And tomorrow she would write a letter to Seth, explain everything and place it in her parents' safety deposit box just in case. He would do everything in his power to see that their child was safe and happy and cared for. The thought made her feel content and at peace with the world.

"I think I'll take a quick break," Laurel said to Caroline, a smile playing across her lips. "I need a cup of coffee." One cup a day was all she allowed herself, for the baby's sake.

"Coffee sounds great. Pour me one, too."

The voice she heard wasn't coming from behind her. And it was definitely not Caroline's. It was low and dark and very male. "Seth." Laurel whirled around so quickly she felt a momentary wave of dizziness wash over her. She put a hand on the counter to steady herself. "You startled me."

"Sorry, I didn't mean to. I'd think that bell above the door is loud enough to wake the dead."

He didn't look apologetic. On the contrary, he looked very pleased with himself. And very, very good. He still needed to regain some of the weight he'd lost in the hospital, but the slight sharpening and refining of his features only made him look even more handsome than she remembered. He watched her for a long moment, and then his lips curled into a smile. That marvelous, heart-stopping smile she wanted her baby, whether boy or girl, to inherit.

Leaning both elbows on the counter next to the cash register, he said quietly, "I'm buying."

"I don't know," Laurel responded in all honesty. He was so close all she would have to do was move her hand a few inches and she would be able to touch him. He wasn't wearing a hat and his dark curly hair was tousled and wind-blown. The tips of his ears and nose were red with cold, but his hand on the counter looked hard and strong and warm. She remembered the way those hands had held her, caressed her, how well he had loved her.

"I haven't had a chance to talk to you since the holidays." Seth smiled again, gently, and this time it crinkled the corners of his lake-blue eyes.

Laurel found herself smiling back. She wanted those blue eyes for her baby, too. At least part of her did. The rest of her knew she was flirting with disaster. Deep in her heart a persistent voice kept repeating over and over that she would never be able to forget this man as long as her child's every look and smile reminded her of his father. Especially if the child she carried were a boy.

Dear heaven, please let my baby be a girl, Laurel prayed silently.

"I was planning on having my coffee up here. I'm really swamped." She defended herself by pointing to an array of amber pill bottles needing to be priced and bagged for Dr. Mitchell's morning patients to pick up in the next few hours.

"I'll finish them up, Laurel. You go get your coffee."

Caroline came out from behind the shelves and smiled broadly at Seth. He smiled back. Being the town hero had its advantages, Laurel decided, giving up her solitary battle of wills. She was playing with fire and she knew it, but there would be even more talk around town if she continued avoiding the man for no apparent reason.

"I'll only be a few minutes." Laurel spoke over her shoulder to Caroline because she found herself unable to detach her gaze from the dangerous, mesmerizing warmth in Seth's blue eyes.

"Take your time." Caroline was still checking off ampules of penicillin against the list on the clipboard she held in her hand. "I'll holler good and loud if I need anything."

"When are you expecting Kevin to get into town?" Seth asked, as he stepped aside so she could open the half door and move down the three shallow steps to floor level.

"This weekend, we think. Sunday, most likely." Her heart was in her throat, beating a light, rapid cadence that sent blood singing through her veins.

Seth unzipped his heavy, golden-brown parka. Underneath he was wearing a bright green plaid shirt, open at the throat to reveal a triangle of dazzling white T-shirt.

"Great."

He laughed, and Laurel allowed herself a moment to savor the sound. He sounded happy now, not strained and serious as he had in the fall. She was so thankful he hadn't died in that Washington hotel, so very glad.

"Dad's really excited," she said, rushing her words to hide the catch in her voice. "He's actually quit complaining about being cooped up in the house. He's cut his phone calls to the store down to six a day so the line won't be busy when Kevin calls through his flight information." She laughed to show she was teasing. "Actually, I'm always calling him for advice."

"Your dad's a good man."

"I know." Laurel didn't do anything to hide the pride in her voice.

"I'm looking forward to spending some time with Kevin. How long is he staying this time?"

Warning signals danced like live current all the way to her fingertips. He didn't sound like a man on the verge of returning to the dangerous, yet exciting world of the Secret Service. "I have no idea." Laurel regretted the stiffness of her words, but she'd been too close to relaxing her guard and forgetting why she couldn't let Seth close to her again.

Could he discern the very slight thickening of her waistline, the new fullness of her breasts beneath the heavy white linen of her lab coat? She didn't think so, but she couldn't be certain of anything with a man as observant as Seth Norris. She balled her hands into fists and stuffed them into her pockets, holding the jacket a little away from her body as she walked.

"Kevin's the proverbial rolling stone," Seth said with another smile.

Laurel tried to relax when she stepped behind the soda fountain. The waist-high counter gave her an illusion of safety from the probing directness of Seth's disturbing blue gaze. "How long are you staying?" Her words were blunt, but she was too distracted to be coy.

"Awhile yet." Seth lifted one shoulder in a lazy shrug. He wasn't certain why he was prevaricating about his plans for the future. It was a gut reaction to the haunted look in Laurel's big brown eyes, the tenseness of her shoulders and the soft, yet stubborn line of her jaw. It wasn't that she was frightened of him, at least not exactly frightened, but nervous and wary.

He knew she was remembering what had happened between them in the fall. There was a slight flush of color along her cheekbones and she avoided meeting his eyes whenever possible. He was equally as certain she didn't want to discuss their night together.

Seth leaned his elbows on the marble top of the soda fountain. *Lord, the memories this place brought back.* But he didn't want to think about the past, at least the far distant past, right now. He wanted to work on bringing Laurel into his present and his future.

He laid his hand over hers. Her fingers were chilled from the marble. He could feel its coldness even through the heavy sleeve of his coat. He kept his voice low and quiet, as though he were dealing with a frightened fawn. "Laurel, I'm not going to ask you why you left town without even saying goodbye last fall. I understand how...alien...our spending that night together must have seemed to you in retrospect. I'm sorry I caused you distress. I never meant to pressure you into seeing me again. I can understand that you might regret making love with me at all."

Laurel's eyes were like the fawn he'd compared her to moments before, dark and liquid and filled with golden lights.

She turned her hand suddenly so that his fingers were imprisoned within the softness of hers. She squeezed his hand as though trying to convey through her touch the sincerity of her words. "Oh, no, Seth. I don't regret anything about that night." Her smile was a little tremulous, her eyes brilliant with unshed tears. "But . . ."

"Our having a past makes you uncomfortable around me now."

"A little." Laurel almost choked on the words. Having him around terrified her and fascinated her at the same time. She couldn't believe how badly she wanted him to take her in his arms, hold her, kiss her, as he had that night before Christmas...love her...as he'd done that magic night in the fall.

"Were you frightened that evening at your parents'?" He asked as though reading her thoughts.

"No."

"I promise never to bring up the subject again unless you're willing to talk about it. Give me a chance. We'll start all over, Laurel. As friends." He smiled wryly. "Very close friends." She was going to say no, refusal was written all over her face. Seth felt his stomach tighten into knots as he forced himself to speak quietly and rationally. Passion would scare her into flight; he knew that as surely as he knew his own name. "I'll always believe we shared something very special that night. I think we should give ourselves a chance to find it again."

"I'm going back to Phoenix very soon, Seth." Laurel's thoughts were chaotic. "My life is there. My future is there."

"Give me a chance, Laurel. That's all I ask, a chance." He gave her another smile, slightly crooked and a little rueful. "Come with me to Mike's basketball game tomorrow night. Surely you can't feel threatened by such an innocent request? We won't even call it a date. Just two old friends—"he emphasized the word very slightly "—spending a typical Saturday night in Bartlow."

"Just a typical Saturday night in Bartlow, accompanied by the town hero?" Laurel felt her traitorous heart and body responding to him with an intensity that no other man had ever come close to arousing in her. She wanted to be with him. Surely she could see him as a friend without exposing her heart and soul—and her secret—to undue risk. She heard herself speak and knew she was lost.

"Being seen in my company does have a certain cachet." He didn't smile, but his eyes were laughing with her.

Laurel sighed. She couldn't help it; she loved it when he teased her. "I'm aware of the honor." She marveled that her voice sounded so normal. "I'd like very much to go to Mike's basketball game with you tomorrow night."

Chapter Nine

"I'd appreciate it if you'd get my brother in by his curfew, Ms. Sauder." Michael Norris looked down the length of his nose and shook his head gravely. "He's not a well man." He was already taller than Seth by over an inch, but slender, with narrow shoulders and hips, unfinished looking, as only a seventeen-year-old boy can be. "Our mother put me in charge of him tonight. I don't want him getting into any trouble."

He grinned, and Laurel's heart did a little flip. It was Seth's smile—and every bit as potent.

Mike would be her baby's uncle. The thought had never occurred to her before this moment.

The youngster faked a punch in the general direction of Seth's left shoulder. "I'm not going to get my chimes rung because he's out painting the town red with a very lovely lady."

Laurel ignored the compliment in his last words, although she couldn't help being pleased by it. "I thought you were completely recovered..." She faltered and shut her mouth with a snap, chagrined that her concern for Seth's well-being should surface so easily. He was staring at her intently, his eyes darkly brilliant in the cold glare of fluorescent lighting above them.

"I'm fine and this bozo knows it," he assured her before giving Mike a long hard look. The youngster was going to blow this evening for him yet.

Mike returned his stare with gray eyes innocent as a baby's.

The wide hallway outside the gym was crowded with people laughing and calling out to one another. Seth had had his hand shaken so often, his back pounded in greeting so many times, his shoulders ached. Half an hour earlier the Bartlow Pirates had defeated their arch rivals and were well on their way to clinching the league championship for the second year in a row.

Mike had made sixteen points and pulled down seven rebounds. He was coming in for his share of back pounding, too. Everyone was in a festive mood, and even though Seth didn't like being the center of attention, he was content to be where he was. He never wanted to return to the life of loneliness and danger he'd known in Washington.

"I only have your best interests at heart." Mike placed his hand over the organ in question, or at least over the big orange *B* emblazoned on his letter jacket.

Seth snorted. "Kids these days." He looked at Laurel for support of his statement.

"Hey," Mike accused, laughing, "you sound just like Dad, and you don't even have a kid of your own."

Seth glanced over at Laurel again, laughter in his eyes. It was harder than hell to stay mad at the youngster, no matter how outrageously he behaved.

Laurel wasn't laughing. Her face had suddenly gone white; her big brown eyes looked stunned, bruised with anxiety. Mike kept right on talking, oblivious to the tension that suddenly filled the air around them like cold fog on a sunny day.

Laurel closed her eyes against a rush of guilt. *Seth did have a child.* Only he didn't know it; he could never know it. *Was she doing the right thing in not telling him?* Suddenly she was no longer sure of her chosen path.

"Tell Mom not to lock up. I'll be home when I get there, understand?"

Seth's voice seemed to come from far away, although moments ago less than a foot of space separated them. Laurel took a deep breath, willing herself to be calm. She opened her eyes just as Mike looked down at his size eleven high-tops. The movement drew her eyes, as well. The tongues were hanging out, she noted, the shoelaces dragging on the floor. How did he walk without tripping over them?

"Yes, sir." Mike snapped a salute. "But seriously, Laurel. Don't let him overexert himself, okay?"

At the sound of her name Laurel looked up. Michael's gray eyes were solemn, the levity wiped from his face. She hesitated, trying to still the confusion of her thoughts. She made herself look at Seth. "Are you sure you're feeling all right?" He looked rested and fit, but Mike seemed so certain.

"He has dizzy spells," Seth's brother whispered in a lugubrious tone, shaking his head mournfully.

Laurel felt a distinct tug on her leg, and made an effort to join in Mike's teasing. "My goodness, you don't say? And I never thought to bring my smelling salts with me. Perhaps I should drive back into town?" She tilted her head slightly, her expression serious, as though waiting for Mike's opinion of the suggestion.

"Knock it off." Seth grabbed Mike around the shoulders and put his hand over his mouth. He was laughing and Laurel relaxed enough to laugh, too. "This show of brotherly concern is strictly in his own interests."

"I don't understand."

Laurel was still looking concerned and slightly wary. Seth liked the concern; he didn't like the wariness that was always lurking just behind her smile.

Mike dragged Seth's hand away from his mouth. "I'm not letting him out of my sight until we have lunch with the President. Didn't he tell you about it?" Released from Seth's grip, he bent over to pick up the canvas gym bag he'd dropped during the scuffle. "He's getting a medal of valor from the Treasury Department and everything."

"Seth, how wonderful. Have you released the news to the *Bartlow Flag* yet?"

"No!"

Several nearby conversations had halted and heads turned to listen.

"I'll tell you later." Seth put his hand under Laurel's elbow and attempted to steer her toward the big glass doors leading to the parking lot.

She resisted. "I think under the circumstances it would be best if you take me straight home so you can get your rest." She winked at Mike and he winked back. *Maybe her baby would have gray eyes instead of blue, and Mike's dark red hair. Or would he look like her side of the family?*

"Oh, no, you don't. We're meeting Elinor and Wade Armstrong for pizza at the Station. Take a hike, kid."

"You will take care of him, won't you, Laurel?"

It was the second time Mike had called her by her given name and Laurel was secretly pleased. "I promise."

"Mike." Seth let his tone become serious. "You guys take it easy out there yourselves tonight." Times had changed, but not that much. Drugs weren't as big a problem in Bartlow as they were elsewhere, but there was always alcohol to deal with. Most of the kids had cars, and more than a few had an older brother or sister, or friend, willing to buy beer for Saturday nights. Seth had done the same thing seventeen years ago. Sitting on a back road drinking beer and smoking cigarettes had made them all seem like real men. It was grown-up and exciting. Now it only scared the hell out of him to imagine Mike doing the same thing.

"Don't bother to start your sermon." Mike lifted his hand and signaled to his friends that he was ready to leave. "I'm not going to blow my chance to be First Team All League by getting tanked up during the season." He grinned and pulled on his gloves.

He wasn't wearing a hat, even though his thick, dark red hair was still wet from the shower. Laurel bit her tongue to keep from saying something about it—something very motherly.

"Smart kid." Seth was far more pleased, and relieved, than his offhand words revealed.

"Pick of the litter," Mike agreed smugly. "Besides, Coach has a spy network like you wouldn't believe. I'll be home and sound asleep long before you hit the sheets, old buddy. And don't wake me up banging around getting ready for bed. I'm a growing boy. I need my rest."

"Don't wake me up at the crack of dawn playing that god-awful new Bon Jovi tape you got for Christmas and it's a deal." Seth held out his hand.

Mike took it. "Deal. No Bon Jovi on Sunday morning, anyway. That's Dad's rule."

Seth searched his heart for the old familiar surge of antagonism against their father for all the rules and regulations he'd set down when Seth was a boy. There was nothing there; it had all disappeared years before. Even his anger at being made to quit the football team had faded away to nothingness. Kids needed rules and parents had to be tough enough to make them and enforce them. Seth understood now, a little bit at least, how hard it was to be a parent.

"Goodbye, Laurel."

"'Bye, Mike, take care." Laurel echoed Seth's words and, unknowingly, his thoughts. Children were so vulnerable at Mike's age, yet so eager for their independence. How did parents ever find the wisdom and courage to let them go when the time was right? How would she know, raising her child alone, what would be the best path to choose for him as he was growing up? The thought was a sobering one. God had intended children to be raised by two parents. She was depriving her baby of that right. She was depriving a good and caring man of even the knowledge of his son or daughter.

"You take care, too." Mike gave her a knowing leer so comically exaggerated that Laurel couldn't help laughing out loud.

"Take off, big mouth," Seth ordered with a growl. "Let's get out of here before he says something I have to punch his lights out for."

Laurel couldn't be sure, but she thought she detected a faint tinge of dark red along Seth's cheekbones. He'd promised her a relationship based on friendship alone. Mike's good-natured innuendos must be as embarrassing to Seth as they were upsetting to her. Her mind was pleased by the deduction; her heart was not.

"Oh, yeah, you and who else?" Mike moved off down the hall, tossing the last comment over his shoulder.

Seth didn't bother to reply, only shook his head. "Come on." He hustled Laurel outside before she could analyze her feelings any further. "Elinor and Wade will wonder what happened to us. They left twenty minutes ago."

"IT'S BEEN FUN, Seth. Thanks for asking me." Laurel was pleased her words hit just the right light note of friendly thanks. She turned her head toward him to gauge his reaction. His profile was sharp in the light from the streetlamp on the corner.

They'd decided to walk home from the Station, declining an offer of a lift from Elinor and Wade Armstrong. Seth had left his car in Laurel's parents' driveway to avoid having to find two empty parking spaces on Main Street. The night was quiet and still, the sky luminescent with the pale glow of low-hanging snow clouds. Here and there a few heavy flakes drifted to the ground.

It had snowed yesterday and the day before that. The ground was covered in a thick blanket of snowy white. They angled off to take the path through City Park. Only a block square, it was filled with big old trees, swings and teeter-totters and a Spanish-American War cannon. Tonight they had the park to themselves, with only the creaking of bare branches above them and the crunch of new snow under their feet.

"I enjoyed it myself. I can't remember the last time I went to a high school basketball game. It must have been my senior year in college, though." Seth shook his head, wondering how so many years could have passed so quickly.

It had been a good evening. He needed the comfort and companionship of small town living. Wade Armstrong felt the same way; he knew it instinctively. They'd both been out there in the world, nearly lost their souls and their lives, and they wanted in out of the darkness.

Seth couldn't speak for the new town marshal, but he knew he himself wanted the light and warmth of a woman in his life. He wanted a friend and lover to share things with.

He wanted Laurel.

"Your nose is red," he said, trying to come up with a less volatile subject of conversation.

"So's yours." Laurel reached up a mittened hand and tapped his nose. "That's a far more serious condition in your case." She looked at him sideways and burst out laughing. "Sorry, I couldn't resist it."

"We Norrises are proud of our noses," he said with a great deal of offended dignity. "They're bold...they're noble..."

"They're big," Laurel said with another ill-concealed giggle.

"Hey." Seth stopped walking and turned her to face him. "Them's fightin' words, woman."

"Are they?" Laurel countered mischievously. She stooped and came up with a handful of snow, already packing it into a ball as she rose.

"Oh, no, you don't," Seth warned, holding up a restraining hand. "I hate cold wet snow down my neck."

"I remember," Laurel said, backing up a couple of steps to improve her aim. She ignored all the warnings of her heart once more, pushed aside all the unanswered questions. She never felt so alive, so happy, as when she was with Seth. That was a fact; there was no explaining it. There was certainly no denying it.

"I'm practically a tourist attraction in these parts," Seth reminded her piously. "People won't take kindly to the assault on my person."

"Too bad," Laurel said without a hint of remorse. "Maybe some cold wet snow down your neck will bring your head back down to its normal size." She weighed the snowball thoughtfully in her hand. "Ahhh," she continued, shaking her head wisely. "Now the truth is coming out. Mr. Upright Secret Service Agent has some very kinky ideas when it comes to man-woman relationships." With a quick overhead toss she let the snowball fly and had the momentary satisfaction of seeing it land squarely in the middle of his chest. Snow splattered Seth from waist to eyebrows.

"You're going to pay for that." He took a step forward, and Laurel turned to sprint down the dimly lit path in the direction of home.

"Laurel." Seth was after her in the blink of an eye. The cold winter air seared his lungs, but except for an occasional twinge from still healing muscle and tissue, he didn't feel any pain. He felt good, exhilarated, like a man with the woman he loved. "Laurel, wait." She'd disappeared into the shadows of the Garden Club's rose arbor near the northwest corner of the park.

"You'll never catch me, Norris," she called back, laughter in her breathless words.

"I know." He stopped running and leaned against the snow-covered lattice of the arch leading into the arbor.

Laurel was already halfway through, but she paused at the rough, strained tone of his voice. "Seth? Seth, are you all right?" She walked back toward him, the ends of the red plaid muffler she'd wrapped around her throat trailing behind her as she walked.

"Laurel?" He was on his knees beside the barren rose trellis.

Lord, he'd hurt himself roughhousing with her. Laurel felt a stab of panic that nearly took her breath away. "I'm here, Seth." She dropped to her knees beside him. She couldn't see his face in the shadow of the trellis. His breath came in quick, hard gasps. "What's wrong?"

He moved quick as lightning. "Nothing," he growled with a laugh. "Gotcha." He pulled her into his arms as they both tumbled backward into the soft drifts of new snow.

"You tricked me," she accused, her slightly arched brows drawn together in a frown. "I've been had!" She rested her mittened hands on the warm bulk of his golden-brown corduroy coat. "That was sneaky and underhanded—"

"Resourceful," Seth corrected complacently.

His arms tightened around her when she tried to get up. Her legs were tangled with his; the white mist of their breath met and mingled between them. She looked down at him, only slightly worried that he might discern the new roundness of her figure through the thick layers of their clothes. As always, the pleasure of his touch outweighed her fear of discovery.

"Very resourceful," she admitted with a sigh. "Seth . . ."

"Shhh. I haven't played in the snow for years. Don't spoil it."

"I won't." Surprising herself, Laurel leaned forward and touched her lips to his. His skin was cold, but his lips were warm, his touch as exciting as ever. "We'd better go. I . . . I promised your brother to have you home by midnight."

Seth tightened his grip as she moved to raise herself from beside him. "Why did you kiss me, Laurel?"

"I don't know," Laurel answered truthfully. "It seemed the right thing to do at the moment."

"It was the right thing to do."

Holding himself ruthlessly in check, Seth stood and helped Laurel to her feet. She brushed at the snow on Kevin's old navy peacoat she still insisted on wearing and refused to meet his eyes. Seth took off his glove and held out his hand. Laurel let him remove her mitten and fold her small hand inside the warm confines of his own.

They walked quietly for the rest of the short trip home. It was snowing harder. Laurel's brown hair beneath her red knit cap was frosted with crystal flakes that twinkled like tiny fragile stars every time they passed under a streetlamp.

His car was parked in the driveway. They stopped behind it. "Thank you for a very nice evening," she said formally, tugging to free her hand from his grip.

"Don't go inside just yet. I want to talk to you." Her eyes were big and dark in the reflected light of the lamp her mother had left burning in the front window.

"It's late, Seth." He could hear the uncertainty in her voice.

"Sit in the car with me for a minute. Please. I want to see you again, Laurel. I think we should talk about it, and it's too damn cold to stand out here."

Laurel got into the car, her mind in a whirl. *What should she say? What could she do?* He didn't say anything else for several minutes. The sound of the engine and the heater's purr were loud in the darkness. Warm air rushed over her legs and warmed the small car quickly.

"Comfortable?" Seth asked, ending the silence that had fallen between them.

"Yes." His voice was low and rough in her ears, soothing and exciting at the same time. It turned her bones to liquid and set her nerves on fire.

"Laurel, would you rather not see me again?"

Tell him yes, a small cowardly part of her brain urged.

"I want us to be friends," she replied, sidestepping his question.

No, Seth thought, *I don't want you as a friend. I want you as my lover, as the woman I love.* "I want us to be friends, too," is what he said aloud. It was a beginning, even though his instincts clamored at him to make her his quickly, before she could slip away again.

Laurel relaxed slightly. Being with him tonight had been a very pleasant torment, the basis for memories she could store up for the lonely times ahead. "It is nice having someone to talk with in a place where you don't quite belong anymore, isn't it?"

"Don't you feel as if you belong here anymore, Laurel?" Her face was in shadow; there was a tenseness in the way she held her head, sudden strain in the slope of her shoulders. He longed to take her in his arms and soothe away that tension, learn its cause, banish its hold on her. He wanted to make love to her, feel her respond with the hidden passion he'd tasted so briefly that special night they'd shared.

"I'm not sure where I belong." They were skirting the edges of a subject that had been touched upon while sharing a large deluxe pizza with Elinor and Wade Armstrong. Yet now there wasn't any banter, no noisy background music and laughing voices to disguise the emotion underlying the words. "My life is in Phoenix now, but sometimes that's hard to remember when I'm back here. Being here makes me feel torn and uncertain. It's not a comfortable feeling. When it gets too strong, I know it's time for me to go back."

"Is that feeling very strong tonight?"

Laurel sighed. "I don't know." She asked a question of her own. "When are you going back to Washington, Seth?"

"I'm not going back." He spoke softly, afraid he might startle her otherwise. Her eyes gleamed with reflected light, golden flecks dancing on a surface of velvety brown.

"You're not going back?" She lifted her hand to her throat as though the red plaid muffler were suddenly too tight. Her heart gave a furious lurch, then beat to a faster cadence. *He wasn't going back to Washington. He was going to stay here in Bartlow, safe from danger and death. Stay in Bartlow.* The realization brought her up short.

"Not permanently, anyway." Seth rested his forearm on the steering wheel. "There are congressional hearings on the assassination attempt scheduled in the spring. And the damned award ceremony Mike's so excited about." He shrugged it off as if medals of valor were given out with every paycheck.

"You're planning on living in Bartlow for the rest of your life?" Laurel repeated the words as if she hadn't heard them right.

"I'm going to start looking for a place of my own as soon as possible."

Seth let a smile curl the edges of his mouth. She loved to see him smile. She wanted her baby to have that smile. In spite of her uncertainty, Laurel smiled back. "I'm happy for you, Seth."

He laid his arm along the back of the seat. His coat sleeve brushed her hair where it hung loose over the collar of her coat. His knee brushed against her thigh. She was happy for him, even if it meant she would have to alter her dream of single parenthood yet again. *How could she keep him from learning about her child if he came back to Bartlow?*

"You could come back, too." Seth held his breath. Would she consider such a request?

"I don't know." Laurel clamped her mouth shut on the traitorous words. "I mean, no. I can't...." She couldn't be more adamant, though God knew she needed to be. He was too near. She wanted to tell him not to touch her hair, to move his leg away from hers, but she couldn't get the words out. Instead, almost against her will, she turned her head a fraction of an inch so that the palm of his hand brushed her cheek.

"I think you could be happy living here." *We could be happy living here.*

"Yes." Her pleasure at seeing him safe and well, content, knowing he wouldn't be going back to the Secret Service to risk his life again and again, momentarily overpowered the worry of keeping her pregnancy a secret. She spoke the truth.

"Then why don't you come back?" He couldn't keep himself from asking the question, although from the haunted look in her eyes he knew she wasn't going to give him the answer he wanted to hear.

"That's impossible. I have . . . obligations." This was the perfect opportunity to relate her carefully constructed fantasy about the man she'd left behind in Phoenix, the shadowy, nonexistent father of her baby. But she couldn't. Not now, not yet. It was madness to be torn this way between wanting to be with him and wanting to be far, far away. It was madness to succumb to this urgent need to be close to him, to touch him, to love him, if only for a little while.

Why couldn't her feelings for him be easily labeled and categorized: gratitude for the marvelous gift of life he'd given her, remorse for being less than honest with him. Unfortunately, her emotions where Seth was concerned had never been that simple, that uncomplicated.

What she felt for this man wasn't simply passion or friendship. She was very much afraid it was love.

Seth's fingers tangled more deeply in her hair. His hands pulled her closer and she went willingly. The warm air of the car carried his scent to her nostrils. He smelled of wool and snow and smoke from the tavern, but mostly he smelled like Seth.

His breath was moist against her skin. She found herself leaning into his strength, the rock hardness of his chest. She found herself anticipating the glory of his kisses, the pleasure of his caresses. Their lips met briefly, for no more than a heartbeat, then separated, leaving Laurel bereft and craving more.

Seth leaned his forehead against hers; her arms moved to circle his neck and he held her close. God, she smelled good, sweet and spicy at the same time. Her mouth was as soft and sexy as he remembered. He wanted to crush her close, to thrust his tongue deep into the satiny softness of her mouth, sheath himself even more intimately in the liquid satin of her body. He held his breath to slow his careering heartbeat. They were silent for several seconds.

"Life is very strange, isn't it?" Seth asked when his breathing slowed and steadied. He felt shaken by the fleeting touch of her lips in a way he'd never experienced before, as if he had indeed possessed her completely in the split second of that kiss. His voice was a low possessive growl he hardly recognized as his own.

"Yes, very strange," Laurel agreed in a whisper.

He shifted position a little so that he could watch the play of emotions across her face. "It's made up of a whole series of separate strands. They weave in and out of each other, but you can't seem to find a pattern in them, no matter how hard you try."

He couldn't seem to keep his thumbs from brushing across the velvet softness of her cheeks, lingering at the sensitive corners of her mouth. She was quiet under the touch of his hands; she scarcely seemed to breathe at all.

Seth went on talking, as much to make sense of his thoughts as anything else. "Then suddenly something happens and the individual pieces start to come together—the whistle-stop assignment, your vacation, that poor bastard with a rifle in the hotel, your dad's surgery. Each strand drawing us closer, drawing us here together."

"Do you think there was a reason for it all?"

Her lips were very close; her hands rested on his shoulders. He wanted desperately to know what she was thinking, but her eyes were guarded, her thoughts hidden from his view.

"Yes, I believe there are reasons for whatever happens in this life." His hands were lost in the silky mass of her hair; his heart was lost in the brown depths of her eyes. *I don't want to be just your friend, Laurel Sauder. I want to be your lover. I want to be the man you love.*

His words were never spoken; their lips didn't touch. The pounding in his ears wasn't the thunder of his own heartbeat. Someone was banging on the steamed-over window of the car. Seth straightened abruptly, smacking his hand on the steering wheel in frustration. Laurel stiffened, pulling out of his arms, throwing open the car door before he could stop her. With a laugh that was almost a sob she launched herself into her brother's arms.

THREE HOURS LATER, Kevin Sauder sprawled in the corner of the living room couch and contemplated life. Laurel was curled up against his shoulder, sound asleep. She looked worn to a frazzle, poor kid. Lord, he wished he could have gotten home sooner. He couldn't have taken the burden of running the pharmacy off her hands, but he could have kept his father entertained and his mother from worrying herself to pieces over his recovery.

He downed the last bit of warm, bitter beer from the glass he was holding, then lowered it to the floor by the corner of the couch. His parents had gone to bed a couple of hours ago, even before Seth Norris left.

Now there was a strange turn of events. Seth Norris coming back to town, to live and to farm.

Kevin closed his eyes and leaned forward to brush aside several of the two or three dozen black-and-white and color prints of various birds and animals that were scattered over the low oak table. He stretched out long denim-clad legs and stared at his feet in grungy white socks with the same abstract expression he'd worn moments earlier.

Maybe his old friend wasn't crazy. Maybe he was smart, a lot smarter than he himself was. It was good to be home again with a comfortable bed, hot water, good food. The big old house he'd grown up in was welcoming and solid, quiet now except for the rumble of the furnace in the basement and the howl of a rising west wind outside. It was going to snow again. He hadn't seen it snow in a long time.

Maybe he would stick around for a while this time. At least until that old restless longing, the desire to capture on film the essence of some new land, some strange and exotic flora and fauna, started to gnaw at him until he couldn't ignore it any longer. Then he'd be gone again. But not now, not yet. For a while he'd bask in the warmth of his mother's fussing and his dad's undemanding companionship. And he'd play big brother.

Kevin looked down at Laurel's face, unguarded as she slept. There were dark shadows under her eyes and the faint crease of a frown between them. Her hands were curled into fists, as if even in sleep she was afraid to let go of something. Is that what being in love did to a person?

If it was, he was glad he'd escaped the ravages of the affliction.

Or was he? He was thirty-four, almost thirty-five years old, and he'd never been in love in his life. At least not the kind of love that counted, the kind his parents seemed to have found and hung on to. Maybe someday he'd find the right woman and quit worrying about settling down.

Anyway, he wasn't going to be in any hurry, if what was going on between Seth Norris and his little sister was any indication of what was in store for him. Hell, Seth looked just about as miserable as Laurel did.

He was a little surprised Seth had accepted his invitation to come into the house after he'd inadvertently broken up their clinch in the car. From what his parents had said, it was the first time Laurel and Seth had gone anyplace together, and then only to the high school basketball game. How the hell was he supposed to have known there was something more than that between them?

It had been a little awkward at first, but after a couple of beers it had been like old times. Seth had been properly impressed by his shots. Kevin had been equally impressed by the way his old friend had handled his brush with death and the notoriety that accompanied it. Laurel, on the other hand, had sat quietly between them, adding little to the conversation. After Seth left Kevin tried to talk to her about the plans Seth had revealed.

"Coming back to farm with his dad. Hell, he spent the first half of his life trying to keep from doing just that."

Laurel had said "I know" in a funny, toneless little voice. She kept on sifting through some of his best prints as if they were blank pieces of paper. Kevin lifted the photographs out of her grasp and put them on the table. He took both her hands in his and made her face him.

"He's pretty far gone on you, I think." He'd said it more to tease her into a reply than anything else. She'd looked up from their clasped hands and fixed him with those big brown eyes and started to cry.

Not big, gulping sobs or anything like that, just silent heartbroken tears that tore at his insides. He sat beside her for a moment, stunned, while the tears continued to run down her face, turned the end of her nose red and made big dark splotches on the front of her sweater. It was pink with enormous sleeves and so big it hung almost to her knees, making her look younger and smaller than ever.

Kevin hadn't been able to think of a word to say that would make any sense, so he took her in his arms. He almost couldn't find her in the folds of pink wool. After a while she'd stopped crying. He turned up her chin with the tip of his finger.

"Come on, Squirt. What the devil's going on between you two?" Had Seth changed into some kind of monster rapist or something in the years he'd been away? Kevin felt an instant's uncontrollable rage against any man who would hurt his sister. "Was he making a pass at you? Is that why you flew out of that car like a guided missile?"

Laurel pushed his finger away and buried her face in his shirt. She spoke so quietly he couldn't be certain he'd heard her correctly, but she was shaking her head at the same time, so he proceeded on the assumption that Seth had not. He relaxed a little.

"I wanted him to kiss me, but it didn't mean anything more."

"Don't try and con me. Seth looked like a poleaxed steer. He's about as far gone as a man can be." He might not have been certain of the fact when he first brought the subject up, but now he was.

"You haven't seen the man for seventeen years. How do you know he's in love with me?"

Kevin smiled, resting his cheek against the top of Laurel's head. Even that small show of her usual spirit made him feel better. "A blind man could see."

She'd started crying again after that and cried herself to sleep. Once she'd mumbled something about a very nice man she was seeing in Phoenix, but when he pressed her for details, she contradicted herself more than once and Kevin got the crazy feeling she was lying through her teeth.

"You aren't still hung up on that louse you divorced, are you?"

"No."

"What about Penny?"

"I love her, but I can't have her. It's not that, Kevin. Please, let's just drop it."

"I wish you'd tell me what's really bothering you."

She'd laughed then, but it was a funny little laugh, strained and somehow sad, and it had sent shivers up and down his spine.

"I just want to go back to Phoenix, but I can't leave Mom and Dad. It worries me."

Another lame excuse if he'd ever heard one. He ought to tell Laurel she was the world's worst liar and always had been. But why was she in such a hurry to get back to Phoenix?

Once, when he'd been visiting her and Tom there before the divorce, they'd gone out to eat. After two margaritas Laurel had confessed that living in Arizona gave her the strangest feeling. As if the whole city weren't quite real, shouldn't even be there, like Oz. All those swimming pools and fountains, waterslides and lakes in the middle of the desert. He'd felt the same way and he didn't think Laurel had changed her mind. With her qualifications she could get a job anywhere she wanted. Tom had taken Penny away, so it wasn't being near her stepdaughter that had prompted this strange behavior. Maybe there was a man, but he couldn't be very important in her life or she wouldn't have spent the past two hours staring at Seth as if he were the only man on earth, then crying herself to sleep when he left. Why in hell was she in such a hurry to get away?

It never occurred to him that she didn't want to see Seth again. If Seth had it bad, then so did his baby sister. Kevin wondered if Elinor knew what was going on between them.

He'd never played matchmaker in his life, but what better time or place to start than here and now, with his best friend and his one and only sister?

Chapter Ten

"Hello, favorite cousin. Got time for a little chat?" Kevin draped himself over the high narrow counter surrounding the nurses' station and smiled disarmingly.

"I'm busy, Kevin." Elinor didn't even look up from the chart she was reading. She was wearing a one-piece jumpsuit-style uniform with a bright blue long-sleeved cover-up over it. She put down the chart and pushed up her sleeves. "I really am swamped with work, Kevin." Her ash blond hair was pulled up on top of her head in a soft twist. She wasn't wearing her nurse's cap and Kevin was disappointed. He liked her in the starched white headgear with it's big winglike flaps and wide black band of ribbon.

"This is important, Ellie. I wouldn't bother you at work otherwise. It's about Seth and Laurel." He lowered his voice on the last sentence and tried to look suitably mysterious.

Elinor sat up straighter, intrigued in spite of herself. "Are you sure it isn't just another ploy to get me to go off snowmobiling with you, or out for a 'little drive' that ends up taking us all the way up to Lake Erie to watch the ice break up? I have a job to do, as I've pointed out to you more than once."

"I get the point. This won't take long. And while I'm thinking about it—" he produced a single long-stemmed red rose from beneath his coat "—Happy Valentine's Day, sweet lady."

Elinor's throat tightened at the thoughtful gesture. She hadn't gotten flowers on Valentine's Day in ages, since long before her marriage to Sam's father had ended. How like Kevin to have realized she wouldn't be receiving any tokens of the day, and how equally like him to present it in such a casual way. "Why, thank you, Kevin. It's lovely."

"So are you," Kevin replied with a negligent dismissal of her gratitude. "You're wasting away here in this old folks' home, you know?"

"No, I'm not." Her voice was sharper than she'd meant it to be because sometimes she thought the same thing. "I like my work." She changed the subject. "Let's go get a vase for this." She stood and motioned him toward the kitchen at the end of the long hall.

Kevin was more than ready to leave the reception area of the big old house on Main Street. Bartlow's one claim to anything approaching a mansion, it had been built just before the turn of the century by an oil tycoon from Pennsylvania who'd guessed—wrongly, as it turned out—that the oil boom would make it this far west. It hadn't, but he sold his land to the railroad when it came through and made a bundle, anyway.

Even though Oakfork was a retirement home, not a nursing home, it made Kevin nervous. Probably, he decided astutely, because it made him more aware than he wanted to be of the way time was passing. He'd been home only a couple of weeks, but already he found himself with too little to do and too many hours to consider his future.

"Want some coffee?" Elinor nodded toward the big institutional-size pot on the countertop.

Kevin poured two cups, taking the heavy mugs from a nearby stack, still warm from the dishwasher, while Elinor dealt with the rose and conferred with the head cook about changing that night's dessert.

Preparations for the evening meal were in full swing, but Elinor led the way to a quiet corner of the big sunny room set apart for the staff's breaks. There were lace curtains at the windows and geraniums blooming in pots on the sills. A couch and two rocking chairs that had seen better days, as well as an oval-shaped table and chairs, small TV and refrigerator, completed the grouping. The three big windows that housed the geraniums looked out on a wintry backyard.

"Okay," Elinor began without preamble, "what's going on in that devious mind of yours?" She set the small bud vase containing her rose on the table and accepted the second cup of coffee as her own.

"I think my sister and Seth Norris are in love. Or they should be, if they had the sense God gave a duck."

"You're taking a lot on yourself assuming that, Kevin." Elinor tried to look stern and disapproving of his meddling, but for the most part she agreed with him. Her hesitation must have shown on her face, because Kevin waved aside her reservations and went right on talking.

"What they need is some time alone together to get this romance off dead center." He ticked off points on his fingers. "Seth's still living at home, sharing a room with his brother, as far as I know. Laurel's cooped up with Mom and Dad and me."

Elinor didn't hesitate to interrupt. "In other words, they'd have more time alone together if they were teenagers." Teenage boys and girls and what they did when they were alone together had begun to exercise Elinor's thoughts with more and more frequency since Sam had gotten his driver's license and acquired a following of giggly freshmen and sophomore girls.

Kevin nodded, hiding a smile. He had a pretty good idea what Elinor was thinking. "Something like that. It's no wonder Laurel's dragging her feet about it."

"She was hurt very badly by her divorce, Kevin. It's only natural she should be wary of another relationship." Elinor had spent some time with Seth and Laurel the past few weeks. She really wasn't certain how Laurel felt, but Seth's feelings, occasionally, if only for a fleeting second, reached his eyes. Elinor knew love when she saw it, and Seth Norris was in love.

"Don't you think I've already figured that out?" Kevin's green eyes darkened almost to jade. He looked stern and formidable, a man it would be better not to cross. "Sometimes I'd still like to get my hands on that jackass ex-brother-in-law of mine."

"What sort of plan do you have in mind?" Elinor found herself wanting to bring back the happy smile that was so much a part of him.

"I want to get them off by themselves for a few days, let nature take its course."

"How are you going to manage that?" Elinor leaned both elbows on the walnut tabletop and laid her chin on her hands.

"I've got a friend with a houseboat. He's out of the country for a while. He left the key with a real estate agent and told me to use the place whenever I wanted."

"That's nice, Kevin." Elinor was puzzled. "But this is hardly the time of year for houseboating." She looked out the window at the winter-bare trees and bushes in the garden, the drained goldfish pond with its messy blanket of dead leaves, and shivered.

"It's the perfect time of year in Key West."

"Key West? Florida?" Elinor's mouth was hanging open. Kevin reached over and touched his finger to her chin. She closed it with a snap.

"The one and only. Margaritaville. Easy living, easy money, easy women... Well, you know what I mean."

"It would be fabulous, but I simply can't get away. Sam's got a science project due in ten days and he hasn't even picked a subject yet. Jack and half the residents are down with this blasted flu." Elinor let the disappointment show in her eyes and on her expressive face for a moment before she banished it with her usual sunny smile. "Oh, well, that's life."

"That's also the devious part of my plan." Kevin had the grace to look a bit sheepish. "We wouldn't actually be going along."

"I wondered when you'd get to the hook. Come on, Kevin, out with it. What nefarious scheme have you concocted for those two innocents?" She held up an admonishing finger. "I'll warn you right now, I won't go along with it if it's too bizarre."

"Oh, yes, you will." Kevin leaned forward, his eyes gleaming. "You never could say no to me and you're not about to start now."

Elinor laughed. "I suppose you're right." She smiled and shook her head. "I came within ten minutes of being with you and Seth the night you 'borrowed' old Henry Jackson's pickup."

"We wouldn't have taken you along. You were a girl." Kevin grinned wickedly.

Elinor didn't grin back. "I'm a woman now. Let's hear this master plan of yours."

Kevin had enough sense to conceal his elation. "It's simple. I invite you and Seth and Laurel to join me for a long weekend. Dad's getting along real well. He's working two afternoons a week now, so the store's covered.''

Elinor nodded. Ralph's recovery had been quick and so far uneventful.

"Then you back out gracefully a day or two before we leave, citing the very good reasons you just gave me for not going in the first place.''

"And then . . .'' Elinor couldn't keep a smile from lightening her hazel eyes. So far his cockamamy scheme had its points.

"And then I miss the plane," Kevin finished triumphantly. "I know I have to go along with it at least as far as the airport, probably the boarding gate, but once Laurel's on the plane, she won't get back off for fear of making a spectacle of herself." He leaned back in the chair, looking smug.

"And what about Seth?" Elinor had to agree with him about Laurel not making a fuss and getting off the plane. If Kevin timed it right, and she had no doubt he would have things worked out to the split second, it just might work.

"Seth will probably name his firstborn son after the boy's old Uncle Kevin out of pure unadulterated gratitude.''

"Good grief." Elinor set her coffee mug down with a snap. "You are full of yourself today, aren't you?" She threw up her hands in defeat. "Okay. I'll go along with your idea since it's no skin off my nose. And since, for once in your life, I think you're right. I'd swear those two are falling in love with each other, but Laurel's fighting him every inch of the way and I don't know why.''

"Exactly," Kevin said with a hoot.

"Not so fast, cousin. If this thing blows up in your face, I had nothing to do with it. Understand?"

"You'd leave me to take the rap all alone?" Kevin's look of betrayal was worthy of an Academy Award.

Unmoved by the performance, Elinor snapped her fingers. "Like that."

"Jeez, thanks a bunch." Kevin shook his head. "The things I do for love."

"GOODBYE KIDS, have a great time."

Kevin ground his teeth as Laurel hesitated on the snowy top step of the porch. It was pitch dark, not yet six o'clock in the morning and as cold as only the end of February in Bartlow could be. His parents were already shivering in the draft from the open door. If they didn't get the goodbyes over with in a hurry she'd start talking about backing out on him again.

"Dad, are you sure?" She'd asked that same question at least a hundred times since he'd first proposed the trip two weeks ago.

"I'll be fine unless I get pneumonia standing here in my pajamas. Get going, you two. You have to pick Seth up yet."

"Have fun, but don't get too much sun," Lois cautioned with a wave of her hand, already shutting the door partway against the icy draft rushing over her slippered feet.

Bless you, Mom, Kevin said to himself, *now shut the door.*

"Mom, I live in Arizona. Key West in February can't possibly compete with what I'm used to."

Kevin put his hand under Laurel's elbow and began urging her down the steps.

"You haven't been in Arizona for two months." Ralph Sauder always liked to have the last word if he could get it. "The sun hasn't gotten out from behind the clouds here for thirteen days. Son—" He directed his next remark to Kevin.

Reluctantly Kevin stopped and turned to face their father. "Yes, Dad?"

"Are you positive you got Elinor's ticket canceled in time? I could sure use a dose of sun and sand myself."

"I got it canceled in time." He picked up Laurel's small carryon bag and made it halfway down the walk.

"It was worth a try." Ralph grinned at his offspring.

"Getting back to work will be just as good as a vacation for you, old man," Lois said, tugging her husband back out of the cold. "Have fun, you two."

"We will, Mom," Kevin answered for both of them, lying without compunction. "Let's go, Laurel."

"I THINK WE'VE BEEN HAD." Seth's voice was tight, his words clipped.

Laurel felt a surge of anxiety wash over her skin. She twisted around in her seat, taking her eyes off the forward cabin door of the airplane for the first time in the past ten minutes. "I don't understand." The roar of the engines increased in pitch and intensity. "Oh, Seth, this damn plane's starting to move. Where's Kevin?"

"Right there." Seth pointed out the window. His features were grim. Laurel couldn't see anything past the intimidating width of his shoulders beneath a navy corduroy jacket.

He was sitting in the middle seat; she was on the aisle. Flying made her nervous, so she'd opted out of the window seat, saving it for Kevin after he'd rushed back to the car to retrieve his precious Mirachi lens. Laurel couldn't understand how he'd managed to leave it behind, but she was about to find out.

"Well, I'll be damned." Seth unsnapped his seat belt and moved into the vacant seat as the plane taxied slowly from the covered entryway.

Laurel undid her seat belt and moved into the middle seat. "I can't find my glasses in this darn bag," she muttered, digging through her belongings. "Seth, what's going on? Is Kevin all right?"

"He's fine. Or he will be until I get my hands on him," he vowed under his breath. "He's standing in front of the window of the boarding area, holding a sign in big black letters. It reads—"

"Never mind, I found my glasses. I can see it for myself. 'HAVE A GREAT TIME! SEE YOU ON MONDAY!'" The plane was moving faster now and Kevin's waving figure was lost from view. Laurel flopped back in her seat. "He missed the plane on purpose. That's why he insisted I carry everything with me—the rental car reservation, directions on how to get in touch with the real estate agent about the houseboat. Everything. Seth, I'm so sorry." Laurel closed her eyes in distress and embarrassment at being so easily taken in by her brother's scheme. "Elinor must have been in on it, too."

"Do you think so?" Seth leaned over to refasten her seat belt in response to the steward's request. "She sounded as if Sam's science project was really giving her fits."

"And Jack and some of the residents at Oakfork have been down with the flu." Laurel looked over at him. "I filled all the prescriptions." She looked half frightened, half wary, like a child at the top of the first big hill on the roller coaster.

"We'll give Elinor the benefit of the doubt." Seth took her hand as the plane gathered speed heading down the runway. When he touched her all thoughts of her resembling a child shriveled in the heat of desire that coursed through his veins.

"Kevin has always been able to talk Elinor into anything."

She didn't pull away from him, though for a second he thought she might. At least, so far, she hadn't seen fit to question his part in what was obviously a well-planned scheme.

Laurel held her breath until the plane was off the ground. "Kevin knows I really don't like to fly. I'm going to get even with him for this."

Seth laughed for the first time. Maybe Kevin had done him a favor throwing them together like this. God knows he'd tried often enough and failed often enough on his own. Apart from an occasional evening with Elinor and Wade, a movie, or another one of Michael's basketball games, she always found an excuse not to be alone with him. Had Kevin seen he was striking out and moved in to help in his own unique fashion?

"I was ready to rush forward and beg them to hold this flight for him, while all the time he must have been sitting in there, making that ridiculous sign." They were off the ground now and the terminal was in sight below them. Seth sketched an imaginary salute to his friend. *Thanks, old buddy, I think.*

"I was even contemplating asking you to stage one of your award-winning relapses," Laurel said seriously, but she couldn't keep her lips from curling into a smile. "You're so good at it." She looked over Seth's shoulder at the rapidly diminishing view of the terminal.

"That was a low blow," Seth said, pretending to be hurt by her teasing.

"I'm going to strangle that man with my bare hands when we get back," Laurel promised, sitting back in her seat.

"We might have some trouble getting straight back." Seth's eyes were dark, his expression hard to read in the low cabin lights.

"Oh, Lord, you're right." It had never occurred to her to question Seth's role in the affair. The plan had all the hallmarks of one of Kevin's brainstorms. Her brother had decided to play matchmaker with no idea how complicated her relationship with Seth actually was. *Four days and nights alone with him.* The danger was very real, but so was the attraction.

"I'll get us back somehow if that's what you want, Laurel."

She pulled her thoughts away from her quandary and studied the man beside her. "You've been looking forward to this trip, haven't you?" It was one of the reasons she hadn't found the resolve to veto the idea from its very inception. He needed some time to relax before the demands of the upcoming assassination hearings in Washington began.

"Yes. But I swear I had no idea Kevin would pull a stunt like this." His voice dropped in a low sensuous slide that raised gooseflesh on Laurel's arms. "You do believe me, don't you?"

"Yes." Laurel smiled, and for Seth it was more brilliant than the sun coming up on the horizon. "What should we do, Seth?"

He considered for a moment, knowing that even though Kevin had been responsible for giving him the opportunity to be alone with Laurel, it was up to him to keep her from taking the first available plane back home. "This flight goes straight through to Miami. Even if we can get seats on a flight back today, our luggage won't make it. It's routed through to Key West." He tried very hard not to stack the deck against her by looking tired or dejected, but the temptation was almost overwhelming.

"It will be a terrible hassle getting the tickets changed, I imagine." Laurel bit her lip, her face a study in indecision.

"Probably."

Seth shifted his position and immediately Laurel looked concerned. "Is your side bothering you?"

"No, but I could manage a dizzy spell if you think it would get them to set down at Dayton or Cincinnati."

"No." She laughed again. "We'll probably end up having to spend the night in Miami with no luggage." Laurel shook her head slowly, expressing her confusion.

"Could be." Seth continued to look thoughtful, as though he were weighing the possibilities, but inside elation drove his heart into his throat. She was so close to agreeing to stay with him.

"I've never been to Key West." Laurel couldn't keep a hint of wistfulness out of her voice.

"Neither have I," Seth answered with total honesty.

"I like Jimmy Buffet songs."

"So do I."

"I don't know." Momentary panic replaced the whimsy in her voice.

"It's a three hour flight to Miami, Laurel. We have all that time to make up our minds." Seth lifted the armrest between the seats. "Why don't you consider our options until then?"

He pulled her head down onto his shoulder with such gentle force that Laurel couldn't have refused if she'd wanted to. "I am tired." She sighed. "I really would like to lie in the sun and do nothing at all, think of nothing at all."

"That doesn't sound like too difficult an order to fill." Seth kissed the top of her head so lightly that Laurel wasn't even sure he had.

"Just lie in the sun and let the rest of the world take care of itself. Would you like that, Seth?"

"I can't think of anything I'd rather do. As long as you're with me."

Laurel didn't say anything more, but from that moment on she knew she was lost to the forbidden, dangerous pleasure of his company.

Chapter Eleven

Laurel stepped out of the small terminal building at the Key West airport and into another world. The air was as thick and humid as a late spring day back in Ohio. The temperature was in the middle seventies. There were palm trees everywhere, but that didn't make the almost tropical atmosphere of the island any more like Phoenix than it did Bartlow.

"Whew!" Seth shrugged off his corduroy jacket and hooked it over his shoulder with one finger. He unbuttoned the collar of his shirt and sighed in relief.

Laurel caught herself looking at the bronzed triangle of skin and dark hair at his throat and hastily turned her eyes back to the view.

"What's Dorothy's line in *The Wizard of Oz*?" he asked with a grin. "'I don't think we're in Kansas anymore'?"

"Something like that." Laurel smiled and ran her hand through her hair. She was wearing it loose and the warm trade wind kept lifting stray wisps across her face and mouth. "I'm glad I decided not to go back in Miami."

Seth gave her a long measuring glance that brought more color to her cheeks. "Me, too."

Laurel didn't know how to respond to his last remark, so she avoided an answer by fishing in her tote for her glasses.

The sun was high and bright even this early in the year. She waited a moment for the lenses to darken.

"There's the car," he pointed out, accepting her silence.

Laurel followed Seth's broad back toward the rental car Kevin had made arrangements for. Had she been wise in coming here with Seth? Probably not. How could it possibly be wise to spend the next four days alone with a man she was on the verge of falling in love with—but could never have?

She realized her feelings for Seth were growing stronger every day, even though they had spent so little time alone together. But the quandary still remained to torment her. Was she falling in love with Seth for his own sake? Or because he was the father of her child?

Laurel just couldn't be sure, and the pain of not being able to understand her own heart was agonizing. Only the joy of feeling her baby grow and move inside her kept her from breaking down at times.

Twice she'd gone to a women's clinic in Toledo for routine checkups. Not because she didn't trust Dr. Mitchell to know her secret, but because it would have been almost impossible to explain regular visits to his office on Maple Street to her parents or anyone else. The facilities at the clinic were adequate, the doctor competent, if impersonal, and a few days earlier he had confirmed what she'd suspected. The small fluttering movements she felt were indeed her baby moving inside her.

A baby, whole and complete, God willing. No longer just a mass of tissues, but a recognizable being with arms and legs, fingers and toes, a heart beating on its own.

A baby with genes already imprinted for brown hair like her own, or perhaps blond like Kevin's shaggy mane. Or red like Michael's. Or black and curly like his father's. And his nose. Laurel smiled to herself. It would be such fun to tease

Seth about how unfair it was to saddle a tiny baby with a Norris nose. Especially if it was a girl. Her daughter. Her son. Her child.

And Seth's.

Was she doing the right thing? It had all seemed so simple that night in October. Now it was complicated far beyond her worst imaginings. Laurel climbed into the front seat of the rental car automatically. So complicated. Still, she couldn't give in to the promptings of her heart. It was better that Seth didn't know, just as she'd planned from the beginning. Laurel clung to that conviction.

Everything she was doing was for the best.

After this weekend with Seth, she had only to get through the next few weeks and then she would be safely back in Phoenix, where she could get on with the life she'd planned. Alone. Suddenly that word sounded even more hollow and lonely than ever. Yet in Phoenix—alone—her elaborate network of lies, most of them still unspoken, but no less bitter, would certainly be in less danger of exposure.

She didn't really want to be alone, she acknowledged honestly to herself. But in Arizona her heart would be out of danger, also. Seth would go on with the new life he'd chosen for himself in Bartlow, and he would never know of the wonderful gift he'd given her. He would be content and healthy and out of danger. That's what she wanted for him. Love, happiness, a good life. The same things she wanted for herself and their child.

Their child.

She knew she was very close to being in love with him. That was the one variable she'd never factored into her equation of single parenthood. It was the biggest complication of all. If she did indeed love him, she could probably learn to hate him. Those two emotions, each so strong in itself, were opposite sides of the same coin. What she longed for were no feelings for him at all. But innate honesty made her admit that degree of uninvolvement would be impossible to achieve. She could never be indifferent to Seth Norris, and that was the most frightening prospect of all.

THEY DIDN'T HAVE any trouble finding the houseboat. It was anchored directly off Roosevelt Boulevard, in the lee of a shallow cove, not far from a public beach on the Atlantic side of the island. Motor homes lined the roadway. Vendors hawked T-shirts and hot dogs. Two or three windsurfers, the colored sails of their crafts outlined sharply against the blue-green water, whizzed along the beach, dodging sunbathers and joggers with consummate ease. Laurel was entranced by the sounds and color and movement of an island that knew only perpetual summer. Her darker thoughts retreated momentarily to the back of her mind.

The radio announcer relayed the latest forecast from the weather service: highs in the seventies and a chance of thunderstorms morning and evening. He gave the temperatures for Key Largo, Key West and the Dry Tortugas. Laurel laughed and shook her head. "You're right, Toto. We *aren't* in Kansas anymore."

The houseboat was charming, white clapboard with red trim. A miniature house, complete with shutters on the windows and plants hanging from the porch. There were two minuscule bedrooms, an even smaller bathroom—or head—Laurel wasn't sure which term to apply, and one fairly good-sized living room-kitchen combination. Laurel had guessed wrong; there was an air conditioner, but they didn't turn it on. Instead she threw open all the windows and sank gratefully into a wicker rocking chair.

A few minutes later Seth walked out of the bedroom he'd taken as his own. "What would you like to do for the rest of the afternoon?"

He seemed to fill the small room and Laurel had to tilt her head against the back of her chair to see his face.

"Would you like to rest until dinnertime?"

"No." She stood and he moved back a step. "Let's explore. There's the treasure hunter's exhibit and Ernest Hemingway's house. Even I know that much about Key West. And Kevin said not to miss the Conch Houses."

She sounded like a kid on vacation. A sparkle of whimsy and something like magic shone in her eyes. The unease he so often glimpsed there seemed to have vanished and he wanted to keep it at bay. "Okay," he agreed. "According to the guidebook, Duval Street is the best place to start."

"And I'll stay close by to protect you if anybody makes a pass," she promised. She looked at him altogether too innocently. She was wearing some kind of frothy tunic top over a slim white skirt. It had a scooped neck and tiny sleeves. It was light and airy and floated around her, shimmering with the color of aquamarine or turquoise, or the waters of the Gulf.

"Who's gonna make a pass at me?"

Laurel smiled wickedly and her brown eyes gleamed with mischief. She lifted her hand to smooth the collar of his shirt. He'd changed into gray cotton slacks and a short-sleeved, light green polo shirt, which for some reason made his eyes darker and bluer than ever. "Kevin said his friend told him there were an awful lot of gay men down here."

Seth sighed and looked down at himself in mock alarm. "Are you telling me I look like the type most of them would like to take home and ravish?"

Laurel giggled and he hurriedly buttoned the placket of his shirt. He was certainly the type she wanted to take home and ravish.

"Actually..." She brushed his hand aside and boldly undid the shirt once again. Their quiet bantering was charged with sensual excitement that sparked along her nerve endings like live current. Could he feel it, too? She stopped smoothing the material of his shirt and swallowed, fighting to keep her voice steady and light. "I was thinking more along the lines of some nubile college coed. They make up a significant portion of the population down here this time of year."

"I'd probably have as much trouble handling a pass from one of them." Seth wasn't kidding, although he pretended to be. There wasn't a woman on earth who interested him except the one standing in front of him, smiling up at him.

Laurel's smile faded slightly. Her fingers still rested lightly against his chest. He covered her hand with his own and her fingers fluttered like butterflies caught in a net. He tightened his grip. A pulse beat swiftly at the base of her throat. She sucked in her breath and swayed toward him slightly. Seth felt his body tighten in response to the unconscious sexuality in the movement and sound.

She wanted him.

Lord, he was glad. He'd tried so hard to keep their relationship on an even keel, to keep his emotions reined in enough to make her feel at ease with him, that sometimes he wondered if he'd succeeded too well.

Seth was aware as he'd never been before of the strength of a woman's desire and how it was communicated to the man she wanted. He could kiss her now and she wouldn't object. He could go on kissing her again and again until she surrendered completely. It was the stuff that dreams were made of—his dreams, at least. But he wasn't going to do anything at all except be her friend—at least for one more day.

The teasing light had left her eyes. They were already darkened, dulled by the familiar veil of wariness he dreaded seeing. What was she hiding from him? If there was another man in her life, she would have told him. Laurel was far too honest to play sexual games. Whatever it was that troubled her, it was eating her alive. He wanted her to confide in him. They would work through the difficulty together and then he would be free to make her his again. And this time it would be forever.

Seth let go of her hand, although she no longer struggled to be free. For the time being he was her buddy, her friend, nothing more, and he'd go right on being her friend—even if he lost his mind doing it. "Come on, Laurel. The Conch Republic awaits."

He saw to it they did all the appropriate tourist things, including observing the sunset from Mallory Square, abbreviated by towering thunderclouds off in the west, and having a drink at Sloppy Joe's bar before the band and college kids came out of the woodwork. They were both ready to call it a day long before midnight.

"Good night, Seth," Laurel said at the doorway of her bedroom.

"Good night, Laurel. Tomorrow the beach, okay?"

"If it doesn't rain."

She reached up on tiptoe to give him a good-night kiss. If it hadn't been for the trembling of her lips against his mouth, Seth would have figured she'd kiss Kevin in exactly the same way.

"Pleasant dreams, Seth."

He almost laughed out loud at that. He'd be lucky if he got to sleep at all.

Seth went to bed wondering how many points toward sainthood that day had garnered him.

As IT TURNED OUT, they spent only the afternoon on the beach. The morning was too overcast. Laurel did some shopping; they strolled along the narrow shaded streets before they became filled with tourists, and Seth let the sweet stinging tension build between them.

Lunch was Mexican, with the best margarita he'd ever tasted. Laurel had lemonade, claiming tequila gave her a headache. The food was adequate, Laurel decided, but if he wanted authentic Mexican food, he had to come to Phoenix. He said he would and then couldn't understand why she retreated into her shell as quickly as one of the sea turtles in the aquarium.

They spent the afternoon at the beach, Laurel in a voluminous white cover-up because she didn't intend to go back red as a beet. She looked happy and relaxed, and he wished she'd stay that way forever. For dinner he made reservations at the Pier House and began his seduction in earnest.

The sunset was fantastic and he said so.

"It's going to storm tonight," Laurel predicted, gazing out at the steep bank of clouds backlit by the setting sun in a glory of orange and mauve.

"I think you're right." Seth finished off the last of his key lime pie and made a face.

"Didn't you like it?" Laurel asked. She'd declined dessert.

"Too sweet. I like my mom's lemon meringue a lot better." Seth motioned the waiter over and used his credit card to pay the tab.

"I'll settle up with you back at the houseboat," Laurel said firmly as she gathered up her purse.

Seth decided not to argue about who was paying the bill at that particular moment. It was almost dark by the time they got to the car. Twilight didn't linger here as it did farther north.

The beach was deserted. "Let's take a walk," he suggested because the moon was high and bright and he wanted to watch the way her silky hair caught its shifting light. He held out his hand and Laurel placed hers on his palm. They walked and he slipped his arm around her shoulders, inhaling the fragrance of her shampoo and the light floral scent she wore.

Laurel couldn't decide if the tide was coming in or going out. It didn't really matter; she was only trying to concentrate on anything that might blot out the mental images of Seth's hands on her body. The full skirt of her gauzy pink sundress floated around her knees, brushing against his pant leg in the wind picking up off the Gulf.

She told him, haltingly, and as much to remind herself as anything else, that she was going back to Phoenix very soon.

Seth stopped walking and pulled her around to face him. His hands were hard on the soft flesh of her bare arms. She winced and he loosened his hold immediately, rubbing her arms with soothing circular motions of his thumbs. "I'm sorry, Laurel. I didn't mean to hurt you. It's just that I don't want you to go back to Arizona. I think you already know that. What you might not realize is the reason I don't want you to go back is that I'm in love with you."

Laurel jerked away as though she'd been slapped. "Seth, please, don't say anything more."

The panic was back in her eyes, fear so intense it brought an answering surge of terror rushing through his veins in primitive response. He refused to let her turn and run, as she seemed poised to do. He held her with his eyes as well as his hands. "I want you to stay in Bartlow with me. Come home with me, Laurel."

Tears crowded her eyes, stinging and burning, nearly blinding her. Laurel wanted desperately to brush them away, but her arms were pinned to her sides. "Seth, please, let go." He did, but the power of his dark blue gaze kept her at his side.

"I'm buying Mabel Jackson's farm, Laurel. You're the first to know. I haven't even told my dad yet. The house goes with the place. Mabel's thinking of moving into town. It needs a lot of fixing up. We could do that together." She didn't say a word and Seth was getting desperate. "I'm asking you to marry me, Laurel. I want you to be my wife, the mother of my children."

"I can't." Her voice was only a whisper. All the color had drained out of her face. He thought for a moment she might faint. The moon rode free of the clouds, high and remote, bathing the sea in a pearly luminescent brightness that reflected in her dazed eyes.

"Laurel?" She seemed to pull herself together with an effort that was heartrending to see.

"I have a life in Phoenix, Seth. My career." She put her fingers to her mouth to stifle a sob. Her career was an obstacle to throw up between them that at least didn't involve a lie.

"I'm not asking you to give up your career." Seth put all the love and sincerity he could command into his words. "But you could find work near Bartlow, couldn't you? Maybe even your dad's store?"

Laurel stepped back so quickly she nearly stumbled in the soft sand. Seth moved to steady her, but she held him off. "I don't want to be a small town pharmacist, Seth. It's almost as big a commitment as being a small town doctor. I wouldn't have anything left of myself to give to a husband or family."

"I understand that."

Seth raked his hands through the dark waves of his hair, already curling wildly from the humidity. Laurel balled her hand into a fist in an effort not to reach out and touch it.

"I love you, Laurel. I'm asking you to marry me. Is your position at the medical center more important to you than what we could share together?"

"No." She couldn't speak the lie, even if her heart told her it was the expedient thing to do.

"I'm taking a big chance in my life right now." Seth shoved his hands in his pockets in an effort to say exactly the right words. "I'm making big changes. I may be getting a slow start as a farmer, but it's what I want to do . . . need to do with my life. The bottom line is that I can't do it anywhere but Bartlow."

Laurel held up her hand to stop him and to keep some small distance between them. "I know. You aren't denigrating my career. And you're right. I can be a pharmacist anywhere I choose. My bottom line is that I choose to be in Phoenix." Her voice was harsh, but it was rough with swallowed tears, nothing more.

Seth ignored her upraised hand, pulling her so close she could feel her breasts push against his chest with each and every breath she took. "I'll accept that." His voice was distant, a low growl that echoed the surf beating along the shoreline. It sent ripples of fear and an equally insistent longing skimming along her nerve endings. "All you have to do is stand there and tell me you don't love me."

Laurel closed her eyes and lied. "I don't love you."

Seth shook her hard and angrily. "Open your eyes, damn it, Laurel," he commanded, and it was the voice of a man accustomed to being obeyed. "Look at me and say you don't love me."

Laurel opened her eyes. They were bright with tears. She focused on his dark blue gaze and found his eyes filled with an anguish as terrible as her own. She spoke the truth. "I . . . don't . . . know."

"I'll show you the truth." His mouth lowered to cover hers, and Laurel was lost. He parted her lips with his own; his tongue slipped inside her mouth. He swallowed her inarticulate little cries of protest and began a slow deliberate stroking that left her clinging to him as though the earth had crumbled from beneath her feet.

"Seth, please."

Please what? Stop loving her? Or not stop loving her? Laurel was so confused she couldn't think straight. How could what she was feeling this moment be anything but love? If this singing excitement coursing through her body was merely lust she might have given in to its siren call and let Seth make love to her, here on the beach, with no regrets. But it was not lust. There was pain beneath the glory and the knowledge of betrayal. Laurel started to cry. Silent tears running down her cheeks, seeping between their still fused mouths to mingle with the taste of salt spray on their lips.

"Don't cry, please." Seth scooped her into his arms and carried her back to the houseboat. He set her down on the wicker settee that matched the rocker and let her cry for a few minutes. He knelt beside her and took her hands between his own. "Tell me what's making you so sad."

The gentleness in his voice was almost her undoing. "I can't marry you, Seth. I made a mess of my first marriage. Tom left me. He took his daughter away from me." Laurel's voice died away. Seth might take his baby, too. "I tried to make him keep loving me, but I failed, so I lost Penny, as well. I can't go through that again."

"I'll never stop loving you." His words only made her cry harder. He began to worry she might become hysterical.

Then suddenly the tears stopped. Laurel sat up straight and folded her hands in her lap. "I can't marry you, Seth. I'm going to have a baby."

"A baby?" He sounded an awful lot like the parrot at the Mexican restaurant where they'd had lunch and he didn't care.

Laurel looked right through him. She closed her eyes. "I'm pregnant. And you're not the father."

Chapter Twelve

"Are you in love with him?"

Laurel's eyes flew open. She twisted her hands together so tightly her fingers hurt. "I ... *God, it was all so much harder than she thought it would be.* Seth looked as if she'd kicked him—he looked as if he'd been shot. Laurel shook her head, willing away with the physical gesture the memories of that terrible night. Seth stood with the lean lithe grace of an athlete and moved away from her. She had to force herself not to reach out and pull him back.

"You don't look pregnant." She never heard quite that tone in his voice before, hard, metallic. Unforgiving? It sent chills down her spine.

"I am."

"When is the baby due?" He spun around but didn't look directly at her.

"The middle of...August." *Not July.* Another small lie. Her mother always complained of being two weeks late, even with Laurel. She might be lucky that way, too. And for once she had to bless the lush fullness of her hips for masking her condition. But if the baby came early... *Not now.* She'd worry about that possibility later.

"I see." Seth was mentally calculating the date of conception, the way everyone else would when they learned she was pregnant. Her face flamed and a small ripple of pain slipped across her heart. "Does the baby's father know?"

At least that question was easier to answer. She didn't have to lie. And she didn't have to look at him. He'd turned his back to her again.

"No. He isn't going to know. Ever." Her voice was stronger, but inside she felt as if she might fly into a million pieces at any moment. All it would take from this man, suddenly so aloof and distant, was one word, one gesture, and she would shatter. There was a dull ache behind her eyes. Her throat hurt with the effort to keep from crying. "This is my baby, Seth. Mine."

"It's usually a joint effort."

Each and every word struck her like a hammer blow. Chills ran up and down her spine. He would be a formidable enemy. She started shaking and couldn't stop. Laurel crossed her hands over her stomach in an unconscious protective gesture.

"I told you I wasn't very good at relationships. It was over almost before it started. I . . . I was careless." Maybe if she kept skating the edges of the truth she could get through the nightmare. She found herself rocking silently to and fro, and, by a sheer effort of will, folded her hands in her lap and sat up straight.

Seth turned to face her once more. He snorted. "It must have been some whirlwind romance, all right. Or was it just a one-night stand like ours?"

She deserved that, she supposed, but it didn't make it any easier to hear. "Seth, please." Laurel stood. Her face was pale and pinched looking.

He hated himself for the way he was behaving but it didn't do any good. She walked through the sliding glass doors to the covered deck masquerading as a country porch. It had started to rain. He could see drops hitting the surface of the water, hear the patter of raindrops on the roof.

"Hell, Laurel, I'm sorry I said that. It's none of my business." He came up close behind her but didn't touch her. She might have been made of crystal she looked so fragile.

"I never wanted you to know." An impossible dream, she knew now, but the truth nonetheless. It was very important to her to speak the truth whenever she could. It was a little easier to breathe outside, but the humidity was so high it seemed to be stealing the oxygen out of the air. "I want this baby very much."

"Do you plan to see the baby's father again after you get back to Phoenix?"

"After I get back to Phoenix? No."

Seth put his hand on her shoulder. Her hair brushed across the back of his fingers like ribbons of silk. He turned her to face him. "Do you still love him?"

Please don't keep asking me questions I have to answer with lies. She looked at the bruised disbelief in his eyes. "No." *Was that a lie? How could you love a man who didn't exist?*

"Do you love me?" His touch was so gentle she barely felt it. He tipped her chin up so that she had to keep looking at him. His eyes held her more firmly than his hands. "Answer me, Laurel. Do you love me?"

"I want to." Her voice was a whisper as soft as the patter of raindrops on the sea. She remembered the happy hours they'd shared. She started to cry again and her tears were crystal bright. "I want to."

"Shhh." He drew her close. "It's all right. No more questions tonight. The past is over and done with. We can't change it. We can look to the future, though."

He kissed her slowly, lingeringly. Laurel felt a slow bloom of warmth steal inside her heart. Hope and longing and desire unfolded inside her like the petals of some exquisite flower.

"Let's live for the moment, at least for a little while." His smile was tinged with sadness when he lifted his lips from hers. "Give me tonight, Laurel, to share as we did last fall. I don't want to be alone. I want you with me. Tomorrow we'll face the real world again."

"Tonight will be just for the two of us?" Laurel could no longer deny she wanted to have him with her for one more magic night.

"The two of us." He bent his head and kissed her again. He lifted her slight frame in his arms and carried her into his room. The only illumination came from a string of colored lights outside the window, giving the tiny space an aura of unreality, a sense of timelessness. He looked down into her huge bewildered eyes and kissed her again. "We'll make tonight last forever."

HOURS LATER, Seth lay in the dark, listening to the rain and the sound of Laurel's breathing. The bed was narrow and hard, but the physical discomfort was small compared to the pain in his heart and soul.

Laurel was going to have a baby. Another man's child. Some stranger had known the same pleasure in loving her he had been privileged to feel. And this man had given her a child. A child she obviously wanted very much. For a few moments he'd hoped she would say he was the father. But in the span of time it had taken him to figure out when the child had been conceived, that hope had died to ashes.

Laurel wouldn't lie to him. If she loved him she wouldn't want to lie. It wasn't his child. He would have to accept that fact. But God help him, no matter whom the child belonged to he was still hopelessly in love with its mother.

Could Laurel accept that? Would she believe he would be the best father he could to another man's child? That he would accept the baby as his own, love it as if it were indeed his flesh and blood? In her present fragile state he even doubted he could convince her of that.

He was acquiring the patience of Job. He hadn't made love to her yet. One look at her face when they'd gone into the bedroom had been enough to put any thought of it out of his mind. He'd seen strong men collapse in shock before, and Laurel, small and delicate as a flower, was so close to the edge it frightened him.

He'd pulled off her clothes and tugged a T-shirt over her head. The sleeves hung below her elbows and the hem came halfway down her thighs. She looked like a kid, followed his orders like a little girl, except for her eyes. They were huge, the pupils enlarged and filled with a thousand sorrows. He'd kicked off his shoes and socks and lain down beside her on the bed. "Go to sleep, Laurel. It's a long, long time until tomorrow."

She'd curled trustingly against his side and dropped off to sleep in a matter of moments. Maybe being pregnant did that to a woman. Overrode mental stress to give her body the rest it needed for the baby's sake.

The thought was intriguing. He'd have to read up on pregnancy and find out for sure. He'd never been that interested in the condition before. Certainly not when he'd been married to Gina. Children had been the last thing on their minds. And when the marriage came apart at the seams he'd been glad there was only the two of them to call it quits.

But now it was different, because he was different. And because Laurel was . . . Laurel.

She stirred in her sleep. Her arm snaked across his chest. Her leg moved to tangle with his. Seth groaned and turned his lips into the fragrant silkiness of her hair.

"Seth?" Her voice was small and airy in the darkness of the bedroom, a firefly of sound in the night. "Are you asleep?"

He chuckled. "No. Is anything wrong?"

"No." She sighed and her hand traced a light pattern over his ribs. "It's very right. I didn't mean to fall asleep on you, though." He could hear the thread of embarrassment in her voice.

"You were worn out."

"I'm not worn out anymore." This time she slipped her hand under the soft cotton of his shirt. She rubbed her palm across his chest. Her fingers faltered as they traced the outline of the scar below his ribs. "I'm glad you're not going back to Washington," was all she said.

"Me, too." He laid his hand against her cheek. It was warm and dry. "Are you going to go right back to sleep?"

"Why?"

She sounded puzzled in the darkness. Her breath was sweet as rainwater against his lips. "Because I want to make love with you, but only if you're wide-awake."

"I'm wide-awake and I thought you'd never ask."

She laughed delightedly, and once again the image of fireflies dancing through the yard on a summer's night invaded his mind.

He slipped the T-shirt over her head and pulled his own shirt away from his body. He held her close for a long moment, then lowered his head to her breasts. He tasted the soft skin of her throat and teased the soft peaks of her breasts. She moaned and pressed close to him and for the first time he noticed the soft new roundness of her belly.

It felt so good to be with him again. She didn't need to keep her body shielded from his gaze or his touch. Great spiraling tendrils of tension unwound themselves from the edges of her soul to be replaced by growing passion.

The touch of her, soft, warm and pliant against his own rough length, the knowledge of the new life she carried within her, did something to Seth. He wanted to ask her to be his wife again, to tell her he would love the child she carried as if it were his own, but he did not. Instead he showed her with his hands and lips and body all the things his heart was too full to say.

He rolled her on her back and did away with the cotton panties she still wore, as well as the rest of his own clothing.

Laurel saw his body was sleek and long, his chest covered with a light dusting of hair as dark as that on his head. It arrowed down over his lean, flat stomach, interrupted only by the obscene slash of the scar below his ribs.

He had come so close to death. She closed her eyes against the stab of anguish that thinking of what might have happened always caused her. He leaned down, resting his weight on his elbows; their lower bodies tangled together and thoughts of death were sent winging into oblivion.

He was very much alive, and very male. The thrust of his lower body against her soft curves proclaimed the continuation of life in age-old rhythms. He moved over her and she opened to him, welcoming him into the heated mysteries of her woman's body, rejoicing with him in their coming together.

Seth entered her slowly, their eyes locked as intimately as their bodies. He pressed deeper in long silky strokes that left her gasping for breath. Laurel wrapped her legs tightly around him in an effort to be closer still. For Seth, possessing her so completely meant he could somehow, by some means of magic or prayer, make the child within her his, as well. He couldn't explain the feeling, but Laurel seemed to understand and accept his need. Their coupling went on and on, slowly, tenderly, endlessly. It was a time for love, for acts of love, if not words of love, the melding of their bodies the only communication necessary in the quiet of a rainy tropical night.

Laurel moved beneath him in languorous contentment that held an edge of fiery excitement. She pulled his head down so that her lips found his as the heat built between them. He rested his weight on his elbows and began to speed the slow sensuous dance that had brought her to fulfillment that special night.

"I don't want to hurt you, Laurel." There was a rough edge to his words that spoke of iron control.

"You won't."

She moaned against his mouth and the sound sent jolts of pleasure streaking through his blood. Seth didn't think of anything else after that; he couldn't. He became a creature of sensation and emotion, as did Laurel. Her desire matched his. She was with him; she was his. She gave as well as accepted. Together they rode the gathering storm; together they felt its fury break over them. Spent, they rested in each other's arms as it faded away.

THE PHONE'S INSISTENT JANGLE woke Seth from a very pleasant dream.

"Seth, wake up." Laurel was shaking his shoulder. Her voice carried a tinge of anxiety that banished the fuzzy edges of sleep. "I don't like answering phones in strange places," she said, and a tint of rosy color stained her cheeks.

"I'll get it." He sat up and pulled on his briefs. He was out of the bedroom, picking up the receiver on the sixth peal. "Norris."

"Seth, old buddy, it's me, Kevin. I got the phone number from the realtor. How's the weather down there?"

Laurel's brother sounded as close as next door. Seth glanced at the clock on the galley stove. Ten-thirty. He hadn't slept this late in years. "It's raining."

"Too bad. Beats the weather we've got up here, though. Snow," Kevin added unnecessarily. "And cold as a witch's...well, it's cold."

"What do you want, Kevin?" He wasn't about to stand there all day in his underwear, trading pleasantries with the man who'd landed him and Laurel in what could have been a damned awkward situation.

"Just wanted to let you know I'm driving your car up to the airport this afternoon so you'll have a way home tomorrow night. Got the keys from your folks after church this morning."

"Thanks." Seth let his tone soften a little. After all, everything was turning out fine. Better than fine, great.

"Don't mention it. Elinor, Sam and I are going up there to take in a movie, anyway." Kevin cleared his throat. "Is Laurel enjoying herself?" His tone was just a bit too casual to hide his uneasiness.

"She's in the shower," Seth fibbed. "Do you want to talk to her?"

"No." Kevin took the hint. "Thought it might be a good idea to find out what kind of mood she was in before you get home. You know, give myself a few hours to get out of town if I have to. Is she having a good time?"

Seth decided to set Kevin's mind at rest as far as he could. "It's great down here, even if it is raining. Thanks, old buddy. We'll see you tomorrow night."

"Watch the roads when you get back home. Wind's supposed to pick up. Probably be drifting pretty bad by then."

"I'll keep that in mind." He said goodbye and hung up. "It was Kevin," he reported, going back into the bedroom. "He's taking my car to the airport so we have a way home."

"How thoughtful." Laurel's tone was dry. She sneezed.

"Bless you. Catching cold?" Seth asked, sitting down at the side of the bed to rest his hand on her forehead. Her cheeks were pink, but the color suited her. "You are a little warm." He frowned down at her slight form on the bed.

"I'm okay," Laurel insisted.

She looked tired, he noticed. There were shadows under her eyes and tiny lines alongside her mouth that he'd never seen before. She was tense again and he wanted to be the one to soothe that tension away.

Seth decided to prolong the illusion of their being the only two people in the world a little while longer. Laurel seemed so fragile, so vulnerable there beneath the green-and-white sheet that he wanted to keep her safe in his arms for the rest of their lives. "I'm not ready to get up and face the day, are you?"

The look of relief on her face was plain to see. "If you've seen one recovered Spanish treasure trove, you've seen them all." She tried to be flip but winced in pain as she said the words.

"Headache?"

Heartache. "A little." Laurel scooted up against the pillows, pulling the sheet up with her. She was a weak woman. They couldn't stay in this fantasy and she knew it, but her need to be near him, to touch him, love him, was far more insistent than her common sense.

"The only sight-seeing I want to do this morning is right here in this bed."

Laurel sighed and surrendered to her emotions, as well as to the man beside her. "Me, too."

She hugged the sheet tightly under her chin. Seth twitched it away and took her in his arms. Laurel sighed and snuggled down into the softness beneath her. She curled her arms around his neck, savoring the scent of him as he nuzzled her throat and the curve of her ear. She held him tighter, relishing the contact of his broad hard chest as his weight pressed her back among the pillows.

Laurel was well aware her happiness was a crystal illusion based on the fantasy of time standing still. This wonderful interlude couldn't last; indeed, it was slipping away like sand through an hourglass. Her head was fuzzy with desire and the beginning of a fever, but she wasn't so lost in daydreams that she believed reality had changed overnight.

Seth had told her he loved her in the dark quiet hours they'd shared. From the way he cherished her body she knew he would love the child she carried, too. A baby he would accept and love, although he believed it wasn't his. He was a good man, a person of integrity—honest, caring, the way she'd thought herself to be.

But she wasn't honest and caring. She had used him, taken from him the gift of life that was his alone to give. He would never forgive her for that betrayal. For that reason, she couldn't tell him the truth.

Even if he believed her, he'd never trust her again. Would he take his disillusionment out on an innocent child? She didn't think so, but the knowledge gave her little comfort.

She loved him, but even that earthshaking discovery didn't matter anymore. She'd lied to him and intended to go on lying to him because she had no other choice. She would cherish their time together, hold him close and be safe for one more day. Tomorrow she would go on into the future. Alone. Just as she'd planned from the beginning.

LAUREL STOOD JUST INSIDE the automatic doors of the airport terminal and waited for Seth to bring the car around. She stared unblinkingly at the snow swirling pinkish yellow beneath the glow of the parking lot lights.

The glass doors opened with a whoosh and a blast of arctic air started her shivering again. It was such an unpleasant contrast to the steamy, sunny weather she'd left behind in Key West that afternoon. Poles apart, wasn't that the old saying? The extremes in climate were almost as big a contrast as the sweet passion she'd shared with Seth these past two days and nights and the certain harsh reality of the future.

She had changed her mind again, deciding to tell him the truth—something she should have done as soon as she'd learned he was coming back into her life—so that she could find some measure of peace within herself.

Laurel rubbed the back of her neck with her hand. She ached all over, partly from tension, partly from illness. Her fever was climbing steadily, although she wasn't aware of it; the inner misery she was experiencing blocked out even the physical discomfort of coming down with the flu. She couldn't go on deceiving him this way regardless of the consequences of her confession.

She closed her eyes against a stabbing pain and kept them closed until another blast of cold air made her open them again to find Seth towering over her, holding out her coat for her to slip into.

"Kevin left these on the front seat of the car," he explained, indicating his own gold-brown corduroy parka.

There was little traffic so late at night and they soon found themselves out on the highway and heading south toward Bartlow. The wind was already piling up new drifts for the snowplows to break through before morning. Laurel found herself glad Kevin had brought Seth's car to the airport and not her own. Her head ached so badly she couldn't see straight.

Leaning back against the seat, she tried not to think of anything at all. The blue-white patterns of snow skimming across the roadway were hypnotic. She closed her eyes and must have dozed off, because the next thing she was aware of was Seth shaking her shoulder and telling her they were home. He switched off the engine and got her bag out of the trunk while she fumbled in her purse for the door key. Setting her bag on the porch, Seth took her in his arms.

"Don't go in yet, Laurel."

"It's cold, Seth." Her heart seemed to rise into her throat, increasing the painful pressure there. Time was running out on her selfish, unrealistic fantasy of single parenthood.

"I don't want to let you go."

His voice was low and husky with desire. She wanted to mold herself against him and let him hold her like that forever.

"I keep thinking of you sleeping up there in the room where we first made love."

He laughed softly and Laurel soaked up the warmth of the low rumbling sound.

"It keeps me awake at night remembering."

Laurel didn't say anything, just stared at him with fever-bright eyes and waited for the moment when her world would come crashing down around her.

"We didn't talk any more, at least not with words, about the baby, Laurel."

"Oh, Seth." She was afraid if she tried to say anything she would start crying again. He lifted his hand and brushed a strand of hair away from her face. She wondered if it was the last time he'd ever touch her with such tenderness.

"I love you. I want to marry you. I want to be a father to your baby."

His kiss was soft and gentle but filled with passion so explosive that when it ended Laurel was dizzier than ever. She put out a hand to steady herself against the beveled glass oval in the front door. "I can't marry you."

The words were so low and hoarse that Seth had to strain to hear them. "Why not?" He smiled in puzzlement, but when he saw the desperate seriousness in her eyes, the smile disappeared. His face hardened into a wary mask.

Laurel saw the change in his features and her heartbeat stumbled with the pain. "Because I've lied to you. From the very beginning." She lifted her fingers to her lips to still the trembling and hold back a sob. "And I don't want to lie anymore. Oh, Seth. Why did you have to come back into my life and spoil all my plans?"

"Laurel, what the hell are you talking about?" He was starting to feel as if he'd been transported back to that Washington hotel. Danger was lurking in the shadows and he couldn't pinpoint the source. Only this time the threat was to his dreams of the future, not his physical well-being.

Laurel took a deep breath that seared her lungs with cold air. She squared her shoulders and looked up into the frightening effigy that seconds before had been a caring, passionate man. "There isn't any other man—there never was. I planned it that way. I...seduced you because I wanted to get pregnant."

"Seduced me?"

Seth laughed, and the sound was so lifeless, so frightening, that Laurel pressed herself against the door to escape the jagged sound.

"You're trying to say you used me to get yourself pregnant?"

"Yes." Laurel nodded, stubborn pride forcing her head up to meet his chilling gaze.

"You lied that night, too?"

"About it being safe not to use any birth control, yes. I wanted a baby so much. You promised me we'd be together for only that one night." She looked past him then, into the darkness and her memories. *So much left unsaid, but he wasn't going to listen to her little bits and pieces of hopes and dreams.* "I thought I'd never see you again. You were never going to know."

She crossed her hands over her stomach and looked at him with such fear and misery in her eyes that Seth took a step forward, wanting to hold her despite the wrenching pain in his gut and heart.

"You're carrying my child?" Her eyes grew wider. He knew he was frightening her but couldn't seem to help himself. Had she been lying to him in Florida? Or was she lying to him now? Nothing she said was making sense to him at the moment. "My child?" The words were half curse, half prayer.

Laurel shook her head, then nodded, looking scared and mutinous at the same time.

He reached for her as though to shake the truth out of her. "For God's sake, make up your mind." His voice was a snarl of pain and rage.

Laurel's voice rose alarmingly and he realized then how close to the edge of hysteria she really was. "It's my baby. Mine. No one is going to take my baby away. Not again.... No one. Not even you."

She swayed against the doorframe and Seth reached out for her, already regretting his outburst. The door opened from within and Laurel stumbled backward into warmth and light and the safe haven of Kevin's arms. She was crying all of a sudden, noisy gusty sobs that left her gasping for breath.

"Laurel?" Kevin's arms closed around her slender form. "What's going on?" he asked, bewildered. He laid his hand against his sister's cheek. "She's burning up with fever. Answer me, Seth, what's going on here?"

Laurel was crying as though her heart would break. Seth stared at her, dumbfounded. "She said it was only a cold." It was a stupid, inane comment and the only words he could dredge up out of his reeling brain.

"Kevin." Laurel's voice was a thin thread of sound. "Make him go away. I don't want to see him again. Ever." She cried harder.

"Laurel, wait. We have to talk." Seth didn't know what else to say that wouldn't make matters worse. He'd known Laurel wasn't feeling well, but he'd had no idea she was so ill. "Kevin." He appealed to his friend and met with nothing but a stony glare.

"What the hell did you do to my sister, Norris?"

Seth nearly laughed out loud at that. "Stud service, evidently."

Laurel wanted to sink into the floor. It sounded so crass and clinical, nothing like the loving exchange that had actually taken place. Seth really did hate her now. His words proved it.

He was the enemy. She would have to get away from Bartlow quickly, or he would take her baby just as Tom had taken Penny. She couldn't live through the hurt of losing a child again. If only her head didn't hurt so; she couldn't think clearly.

She looked up at her brother, seeking his help. Kevin had always been there for her. He would keep her and the baby safe. "Kevin, don't let him take my baby away." She swayed again and Kevin scooped her up into his arms.

"Baby?" His eyes narrowed dangerously. "You'd better explain pronto, Norris."

Seth ran his hand through his hair. "I'm as mixed up as you are, Kevin. If she's ill, hadn't we better call Doc Mitchell?" He moved to step into the foyer.

Kevin blocked his way, still holding Laurel securely in his arms. Her sobs were quieter now but no less wrenching. "Get out of here, Seth, or so help me God, I'll call Wade Armstrong to have you dragged off the property. I'd do it myself but I'm liable to break your neck if I do."

The door slammed shut in his face. Seth stood on the porch a long time before he got back into his car and started home. He'd never really believed it was possible to love and hate someone at the same time, but he was finding out it could happen. It was happening to him, now, at this very moment. He loved Laurel and he hated her for what she'd done to him. Worst of all, he couldn't honestly predict which emotion was going to be the lasting one.

Chapter Thirteen

With the possible exception of the day he'd walked into that Washington hotel ballroom, the next seventy-two hours were the worst Seth Norris had ever spent in his life. He was worried sick about Laurel. She refused to speak with him, although her parents assured him, stiffly but politely over the telephone, that she was going to be fine. And so was the baby; there was nothing to worry about on that account. But he did, constantly, day and night.

Seth was learning that spiritual pain could be every bit as agonizing as physical pain. In his case, he decided morosely, it was notably worse. In the hospital after the shooting, at least they'd pumped him so full of analgesics that half the time he wasn't sure of his own name. Oblivion would suit him just fine right now; anything to get that last scene with Laurel to quit replaying in his brain. But the only cure he could think of for what ailed him was to get roaring drunk.

That age-old remedy was out of the question, though. Helen Norris, staunch Methodist that she was, didn't approve of drinking in the middle of the day—at least not without a damn good excuse. He had a good excuse, all right, but he didn't feel like unburdening his soul to anyone right now, even his mother. He wanted to hole up somewhere like a wounded animal and lick his wounds. His lacerated heart needed time to heal, just as his body had after the shooting.

The trouble was, broken hearts didn't rate sick leave. He had to go on living each day as if nothing had happened in Key West to turn his world upside down. The questions circling through his thoughts were equally adamant about not being shuffled off into limbo. Was there a future for him with Laurel and their child? Or was he destined to be forever a shadowy stranger on the fringes of his child's life? A child he would know as little as he or she would know him? Could he give Laurel the freedom she evidently wanted so desperately to prove that he loved her more than anything else?

He did love her. One decision that had taken only as long to be sure of as his first panicked call to the Sauder house early Tuesday morning. There was nothing like a sleepless night of worry and soul-searching to convince a man what love really was. But there were other, equally important decisions pending in his life and they weren't about to wait around for him to make a bigger fool of himself over Laurel Sauder than he already had.

Yesterday he'd given Mabel Jackson his answer about the farm. He had enough money to swing the deal—barely. And with the future of a son or daughter of his own to think about, he was more determined than ever to come back to the land. This time next week he'd be the proud owner of three hundred sixty acres of prime farmland—at least as long as he could keep making the payments to the Bartlow State Bank.

And he had a schism within the Norris clan to deal with. The tension in the big cozy kitchen was thick enough to cut with a knife. He should have known he and Mabel couldn't keep their transaction a secret in a town the size of Bartlow

Rumors had been flying for quite a while that an out-of-town buyer was dealing with the old lady for her property. Seth had seen no reason to tell anyone he was the out-of-town buyer. Mabel hadn't squelched the rumors, either, enjoying the stir she was creating. But last night Michael had picked up the story, coming home in a scowling rage to shut himself in their room. He pretended to be asleep when Seth came to bed. Fresh from yet another stilted and unsatisfactory conversation with Laurel's mother, Seth was eager to avoid an acrimonious discussion, as well. This morning Mike had still been snoring away when Seth left the room a long time before the early March sun had peeped over the horizon.

That was over two hours ago and now all four Norrises were assembled around the big oak table. There was some sort of teachers' meeting going on at the county seat, so Mike was home from school, his head bent over a bowl of cold cereal. Clint had just come into the kitchen in his stocking feet. He sat down at his accustomed place with a nod for Seth, who was lounging against the counter near the coffee maker.

"How about a couple of soft-boiled eggs this morning?" Helen asked from where she was standing at the sink, cold sunlight picking out the multiplying gray streaks in her dark hair. Clint nodded absently, his eyes on his youngest son. In a gesture of defiance, Mike hunched his shoulders and cupped his arm around the cereal bowl like a furious young hawk mantling its prey. There was a heavy dusting of dark red hair catching rays of sunlight on his arm. He was lean and muscled and no longer just a boy but a man, Seth thought with a quick flicker of pride in how well his little brother had turned out. If only he would give in and go to college as Clint wanted. Seth figured Mabel Jackson's land coming into the family would be just the ticket to accomplish the feat.

"You can't go on fussin' about Mabel Jackson's farm, Mike. It's sold. That's all there is to it." Clint's voice held its usual dry note, but his eyes were fixed on Mike's averted profile intently.

"Why didn't you at least bid on it, Dad? We could have swung the deal. Especially with Seth coming home to help out around here." Mike glanced up at Seth as though for someone to second his plan.

Seth leaned back against the counter, cradling his coffee cup in both hands. It would be better for the other two Norris men to work this through for themselves. No one knew better than he did how long hurt feelings could fester inside a man.

"I'm not takin' on any more land, boy. You know we need the money for your college tuition." Clint set his stubborn Norris jaw and stared out the kitchen window at the melting snowdrift cutting through the driveway. "Student loans aren't as easy to come by as they used to be. I don't have capital to spare for more land."

"And I told you, I don't want to go to school and end up stuck behind a goddamn desk for the rest of my life."

"Michael, you'll watch your language in my house." Helen spun around from the stove so quickly all three men were startled.

Mike's spoon clattered back into the bowl, splashing milk onto the table. "Sorry, Mom." He apologized with a little duck of his head and shoulder that pointed out how much a boy he was, despite the physical signs of maturity Seth had noticed a few minutes earlier. "I meant what I said, though. I'm not going to college. I want to farm."

"You can't."

Seth half expected their father to explode in a rage, as he'd often done twenty years ago, but he did not. Clint spoke as quietly as before, but his voice was rough with contained emotion.

"You leave the farmin' to me and your brother for as long as he can stick it out. That's an end to it." He clamped his teeth shut on the last word.

Mike stood, shoving back his chair so quickly it toppled over and hit the linoleum with a crack. "No, it isn't the end. I'm going to find a job working for someone else as soon as spring planting starts." Mike looked mulish, his hands clenched into fists at his sides. "I can work full-time after graduation. Butch Thompson's looking for help since his dad retired. He'll take me on. I'm going to be a farmer, Dad, whether you want me to be or not."

Twin sets of gray eyes clashed and held across the width of the scarred oak table.

"You're going to school first." Seth pulled a chair out from the table and straddled it, still holding his coffee cup. "Pick up that chair, Mike, and sit down. You, too, Mom. Let the eggs go. We'll have egg salad for lunch, okay? I've got something to tell you that involves us all."

Still stiff with anger, Mike hesitated, then obeyed, curiosity winning out over his temper. Helen lowered the flame under the rapidly boiling pot of eggs and did likewise.

"I bought Mabel Jackson's farm yesterday." Seth let his little bombshell explode into the silence.

Mike let out a whoop that could be heard across the county line. He reached across the table and grasped Seth's forearm halfway to his elbow. "You didn't?"

Seth nodded.

Mike laughed again and pumped his fist in the air in a victory salute. "All right. Way to go! Three hundred sixty of the best acres in the township. All right!"

"Seth, are you sure you can afford it?" was all his mother said, her fingers twisting a cotton dish towel into tight spirals.

"Damn fool," Clint sputtered. "You'll be bankrupt within two years." But his eyes held a glint of pride and a smile twitched at the corner of his mouth.

"I can afford it, Mom," Seth assured her. He managed a grin for his dad, knowing the emotion that underlay the gruff statements. "I won't go broke if I have your help, Dad."

"And mine," Mike broke in, still grinning.

"When you've graduated from college," Seth said, qualifying the statement.

Mike looked severe but held his peace.

"Come on, Dad, what do you say?" Seth found he was holding his breath, and let it out slowly on an almost soundless whistle.

"I suppose I can't leave my firstborn dangling out there to twist in the wind for all the neighbors to see, right, Mother?"

"That's not the Norris way," Helen agreed placidly. "We stick together."

Seth squeezed her plump, work-roughened hand. "We stick together."

"And you want me in the business, too." Michael had been quiet for the past few moments. He looked at his father. "I told you I want to be a farmer, Dad." All the intensity of his seventeen years lay behind the words.

Clint opened his mouth to say something, then closed it again. "Don't suppose I can complain too much. It's in the blood, after all. But..."

"After you get your degree we'll form a partnership and buy Dad out so he and Mom can retire to Florida for the winters like everyone else in the county." Seth was more teasing than serious. He kept his voice light as he waited to see how his parents would respond to the suggestion.

"That don't sound half bad. Your sisters won't ever want anything to do with the place."

Clint was thoughtful. Seth realized how far they had come from that first tentative conversation in the fall. Then his father had been set on selling off the Norris homestead, land that had passed from father to son for a hundred years. Now he was looking ahead to the next generation of family working the acreage.

"How about if I apply to the Agri-Science program at the tech school at the University of Toledo? It's a great program. I can commute, be here when you need me." Mike's voice cracked with excitement. "I don't have to go to Ohio State for four years to learn to be a good farmer. I've got a hell of a teacher right here. Oops, sorry, Mom."

He shot her a grin that was going to be a very potent weapon on campus, Seth thought with some amusement.

"I don't see why that wouldn't work, do you, Clint?" Helen watched her husband thoughtfully from across the table.

The older man stared down at his hands for a long minute. "No, I think that just might work out okay." He held up an admonishing hand. "If you promise to add an accounting minor to your studies. The bookkeeping for this operation is goin' to keep someone mighty busy. Might as well save the money it'd cost to hire an outsider to do it."

"I'd already thought of that," Mike admitted with another grin, although this time he had the grace to look a bit sheepish, too. "I've been listening to what you say, Dad, even if I don't act like it. I may even go to night school when I'm finished. Might even manage to make CPA by the time I'm as old as Seth." Mike sounded as if he considered being thirty-four an impossibility.

"You do that." Heaven knows Seth felt as old as Methuselah right now.

"It would be nice to be able to spend a few weeks in Florida," Helen said wistfully. "I'd feel safe leaving the house empty if both you boys are going to settle around here. You can keep an eye on things. Clint, could we afford that?" There was a glint of teasing humor in Helen's eyes.

Her husband pretended to ponder the matter for a minute. "We might, Mother. If you're willin' to pitch a tent somewhere down there in an orange grove. Farm economy ain't gonna turn rosy overnight just 'cause the Norrises are goin' into business together."

"I'll be happy anywhere as long as I'm with you."

Seth watched the display of affection between his parents with envy. He wanted to have a woman to love and cherish that way after forty years together. Damn it, he would have, if he could manage it at all. He might as well get the news out in the open.

"I have something else to tell you all. It isn't going to be a secret much longer." Three sets of eyes homed in on him. Seth could feel his ears getting red at the tips. *Hell, it was going to be harder than he thought.* He wished he could be more certain of the outcome of his campaign to win Laurel's heart and trust. "Laurel Sauder is going to have my baby."

THIRTY-SIX HOURS after his disclosure of Laurel's condition, Seth stood on the porch of Ralph Sauder's house, pounding on the beveled glass door with slightly more force than was polite or necessary. He wasn't going to be put off any longer. He wanted to see Laurel, make sure she was all right, and he meant to do it now.

Lois Sauder opened the door and stood there for a moment, blocking his way, looking uncertain. "Laurel doesn't want to see you yet, Seth. I'm sorry."

She didn't look sorry. Her face was set in a noncommittal mask, but her shoulders were drawn back as if to do battle for her wronged offspring.

"Is she too ill to see me?" Seth asked between clenched teeth, determined to keep his temper, no matter what the provocation. He knew Lois felt as awkward as he did about the situation between her daughter and him, but, damn it, it wasn't his fault. He wanted to make things right; it was Laurel who was dragging her feet.

"No." Her expression softened a little as she saw the deep lines around his mouth from worry and sleeplessness. "She's much better actually, just weak and tired...and very vulnerable, Seth." Lois hesitated, as if debating whether to allow him into the house.

"We have to talk sometime, Mrs. Sauder."

"I know." She seemed to have come to a decision within herself.

Laurel looked a lot like her mother, Seth decided. She had the same warm brown eyes and hair, which likely would fade only slightly over the years. "I think it would be best if you're gone before Ralph and Kevin get home, though," she warned with a small tight smile. "I'm expecting them in an hour or so."

"I understand." Seth nodded and stepped inside.

"She's upstairs in her room. I think you know which one it is."

Seth felt his neck redden, and surprisingly, Laurel's mother smiled more broadly this time.

"You're going to need the patience of a saint, Seth Norris."

"I'm aware of that, Mrs. Sauder."

"You might as well start calling me 'Lois.' I hope you're going to be my son-in-law in the not too distant future. I'm not as forward thinking as my daughter."

"I've never been too keen on being an unwed father myself." Seth hazarded a smile of his own.

Lois only snorted and waved him toward the stairs. "Good luck."

He didn't even bother to take off his coat before starting up the stairs. It was a raw March night, with a hint of snow lingering in the air, though most of the winter's accumulation had melted from the ground.

Laurel was seated in a big old wing chair by the window, half dozing, half dreaming. Kevin and Ralph must have come back from the boat show in Toledo earlier than they'd planned, she mused sleepily. She would never have turned her head to greet the man silhouetted by the hall light with a dreamy welcoming smile if she'd known it was going to be Seth.

"How did you get in here?" she asked in a startled voice that threatened to break with the effort to keep it steady.

"Your mother."

"I should have known." Laurel let out a long slow breath, trying not to cough. Her mother was a pushover when it came to a crooked, engaging grin and a sexy, sincere voice and manner of speaking. And to be truthful, Lois only wanted what was best for Laurel and her baby. It's just that for her mother it meant a husband for her stubborn daughter and a father for her grandchild. The older woman was very lucky, Laurel thought with a stab of envy. She didn't know the pain of trying and failing, of loving and losing, as her daughter did. Laurel just didn't feel strong enough to risk her heart again, even with Seth.

"Laurel?" She'd been quiet for a long time. Her expression was hidden in the shadows of twilight. The only light in the room came from a small reading lamp beside the bed. The covers on the bed were turned back, waiting for her. There was an assortment of bottles and glasses on the bedside table as well as a book and a couple of magazines. The room was cozy and warm and it smelled of Laurel.

"I don't want to talk to you just yet, Seth." What was she going to say? Her recollections of the night they'd returned from Key West were hazy at best and frightening at their worst. She should never have told him the truth, but she'd been too sick to realize just what an irrevocable step she'd been taking.

At the time she'd only been able to act on the overwhelming urge to gain some peace of mind. Now, with the suffocating effects of pain and fever dissipating, she was faced with the ruins of her dream and the reality of Seth's new permanent place in her future.

"You don't have much choice, Laurel. I'm here and I intend to come to some kind of arrangement with you, tonight. You ran away from me once. You're not going to have the chance to do that again."

The words speared new agony through her soul. He was still angry, even if he didn't realize it himself. How could she honestly expect any other emotion? He moved a few steps closer and sat down on the edge of her bed, filling the room with his presence and with the smell of cold winter air and the exciting warmth of his body. He stuck his hands in the pockets of his parka and returned her scrutiny.

She was wearing a fuzzy robe in a soft rosy color that accented the paleness of her skin and the dark shadows under her eyes. There was a slight hectic flush high on her cheeks, as if she still carried a fever. She appeared as small and fragile as a child sitting in the big wing chair, the protective veneer of steely resilience he usually detected within her peeled away by the rigors of her illness. She looked young

and alone and frighteningly vulnerable. His anger, so ruthlessly controlled, so carefully nurtured, melted away like ice
in the sunlight. He wanted only to take her in his arms and
hold her close, tell her everything would be all right from
that moment on.

"I won't run away from you...tonight."

She hesitated over the last word and Seth knew instinctively she didn't intend to lie to him any more. She did it so
badly, anyway, he thought with bittersweet amusement that
tugged at his heart.

"The deal I told you I was working on when we were in
Florida went through. I bought Mabel Jackson's farm," he
said, changing the subject abruptly.

She nodded. "Dad told me this morning. He heard it in
the store."

She smiled and Seth felt the warmth of it all the way to the
base of his spine.

"Congratulations. I know it's what you wanted."

"I want you, Laurel." Seth surprised himself with the
words. He watched as she seemed to curl even farther into
the depths of the big chair. She shifted position, tucking her
feet up under her as though to make herself even smaller, as
though she might disappear altogether if she wished for it
hard enough. Seth cursed himself for the baldness of his
declaration but couldn't seem to stop himself from speaking. "I want us to be together. I want us to be a family."

"Stop."

"Not until I've said what I came to say."

He got up from the bed and knelt beside her chair. He
lifted her hands from where she'd folded them over her
waist. He laid one big hand gently on the rise of her stomach and spoke so softly she almost didn't hear him.

"I love you both."

His head was bent toward her, and try as hard as she might, Laurel couldn't keep her hand from raising to brush over the soft waves of dark hair. "Don't, Seth." A sob escaped her throat and she lifted her fingers to her lips to stop their trembling. She was so very tired and confused. "You're just making this harder for me."

"Why is it hard, Laurel?"

He looked genuinely perplexed, and another wave of sweet longing washed over her skin. She shivered in response to the stimulus.

"I'm so confused." Longing was an enervating emotion, she was discovering to her dismay. She rolled her head against the back of the chair, almost too weary to speak. "Everything seemed so simple, like a fairy tale. You were the knight who went after the moon for his princess, do you remember? You were going to give me the one thing I wanted most in the world, and then you would gallop off on your white charger and I'd never see you again. Only I'd be transformed into the superwoman of the eighties. I'd be mother, breadwinner, sister, everything my child needed, with no reliance on any man."

"Life doesn't work that way." Seth took her face between his hands, forcing her to look directly at him. He longed to kiss her, to hold her and cherish her, but she felt brittle and tightly strung beneath his fingers. He let his hands slide down her shoulders to her twisting fingers, warming them between his palms to still their trembling.

"No, it doesn't. Happily ever after doesn't work that way, either. I'm still afraid of sharing the future with you, with anyone. I won't share my baby, either, and risk having him taken away like Tom took Penny." She squeezed her eyes shut and refused to look at him.

"I can't do anything about Tom taking his daughter away from you."

"I know that."

Her eyes flew open and Seth ached for her misery.

"I was her mother, Seth, from the time she was just a little thing. Now she doesn't even remember to call me 'Mommy.' "

"I love you, Laurel." He was getting desperate to get through to her. She had sealed herself inside a crystal barrier that was thin as November ice but strong as steel. She was as far away from him as the princess on the moon. Worst of all, she wasn't listening to his words, only to her heart's memories. "You said you loved me, Laurel."

"I want to." She'd been so sure in Florida, but her illness had left her confused and uncertain of her feelings once again. She was so tired and so needy. Was it truly love, the kind that would last forever, that she felt for the man with her, or was it only need and desire? She couldn't trust her own unreliable emotions, and that frightened her most of all. She couldn't afford to risk her soul; she couldn't afford to fail at love again.

"You don't trust me, do you, Laurel?" His voice had lost that tender cajoling lilt she craved hearing. He sounded as weary as she felt.

"I want to." His coat was only halfway zipped and the brown-and-gold plaid of his shirt looked soft and inviting to the touch. She raised her eyes from the comforting expanse of the broad flannel-covered chest to meet his enigmatic blue gaze. His expression was unreadable, his eyes shuttered, the blue depths impossible to fathom. "I'm not sure I know how to trust in relationships anymore."

"I failed at marriage, too. We can both learn from our mistakes. I don't want the kind of marriage that falls apart at the first hint of trouble any more than you do. I want the kind of loving partnership my parents and yours have found."

"My baby..." Her dreams sounded so selfish when he talked to her this way. *It wasn't only her baby. It was theirs.* Seth would never steal her baby away. *Our baby.* So simple, so easy to say. She couldn't make herself speak the words aloud however, and the moment to do so passed, leaving empty silence behind.

"If you're determined to go back to Phoenix, I won't stop you."

Seth reached over and smoothed a strand of hair behind her ear. His eyes held her captive, his hands brushed over her shoulders, his fingers lifted to trace the curve of her lip, lingering for a moment in a caress as gentle as a kiss. But when he spoke his voice wasn't gentle and Laurel flinched at the steel embedded in the quiet words.

"Be warned, Laurel. Your baby is also my baby. I won't be shut out of his life because you can't come to terms with Tom's defection."

"You aren't going to insist we get married?" Laurel was surprised and amazed to feel a sharp jab of disappointment around her heart. *This was what she wanted, wasn't it? No interference from the man who'd fathered her child?* He wasn't going to force her to do anything she didn't want to do. A chill swept over her that had nothing to do with her illness. Seth wasn't going to make up her mind for her. If she wanted to carry out her dream of single parenthood, he wouldn't stand in her way.

"I love you, Laurel. I don't want to make you a prisoner of a marriage you're not ready for." He stood, towering over her like a statue in the park. He turned away without another word and started toward the door. "You'll keep me informed about your pregnancy? I'd like to be there when your baby's born, if that doesn't make you too uncomfortable."

He sounded like a polite stranger, the stranger she'd always tried to keep him, and Laurel shivered again. He was giving her the freedom she wanted and all she could think about was how sorry she was to see him go.

"Seth . . ." He paused in the doorway and turned to face her. The awful stillness in his face tore at her heart.

"Yes, Laurel?"

"Have you made up with Kevin yet?" She was clutching at straws to keep him with her, but still she couldn't say the three words that would shatter the barriers between them.

"I don't have anything to be angry with Kevin for. It's up to you how your brother feels about me." He put a hand on the doorframe. "Goodbye, Laurel."

"Seth . . ." She couldn't let him just walk away like that, could she? "I'm sorry I can't be sure." Her voice was barely a whisper. Night sounds came from the street outside, filtering through the lace curtains and the insulating storm windows like faint ghosts of their summer counterparts. The whir of the electric clock on her bedside table sounded overly loud in the silence left by her words.

Seth straightened his shoulders and stepped into the hall. He looked much farther away all at once; miles away, almost as far as the moon in the sky. "But if you change your mind, you'll have to come back here and find me. I won't come to you."

Chapter Fourteen

March was by far the longest month Laurel had ever lived through. The weather in Phoenix was unusually hot and the sun shone with relentless regularity, but nothing could lighten her sadness. She hadn't felt any sense of relief, of homecoming, when she'd returned to her courtyard apartment. Quite the contrary, it seemed even more empty and lifeless than before she'd gone home to Bartlow.

She tried hard to settle back into her routine at the medical center, but it wasn't the same, either. She still didn't want to dedicate her life to a small town pharmacy as her dad had, but she missed the hustle and bustle of the store, the intimacy of working with people, as never before.

Laurel had to admit she no longer found great contentment in being cut off from the main stream of hospital activity. The patients whose medications she dispensed were a source of curiosity and interest to her now. She felt frustrated in not being able to communicate with them in person. She yearned to know something more about them than their room number, diagnosis and drug of choice the doctors had prescribed for their treatment.

She was learning a lot about herself, too, and some of the new knowledge she wasn't comfortable with. When Kevin invited himself out for a visit, Laurel had been more than happy to have his company. It kept her mind off other things; it kept her mind off Seth, at least until the dark quiet hours of the night.

As March waned, even Kevin's presence wasn't strong enough to banish Seth's ghost completely from her thoughts, if she gave him more than half a chance to intrude on her musings. Laurel sighed, crossing her legs to stare at her toes over the growing swell of her stomach. Had she made the right decision in leaving Bartlow again? Was this the life she truly wanted for her baby and her? She was becoming more unsure of her choices and her reasoning with each day she spent away from her family—and Seth.

"What did you say?" Kevin asked without much interest from the matching chaise lounge he occupied on the other side of the glass-topped patio table. It was after ten o'clock at night and the temperature had finally dropped below eighty. Kevin had pulled his chaise close to the fountain and was dangling his fingers in the water as it spilled into the tiled depression in the flagstone patio.

"I said I'm glad it's April." She took a sip of her lemonade and made a face. The ice cubes had melted and the drink was so watered down it had almost no taste left.

"You must be getting a refund on your taxes then," Kevin commented morosely. "Anyway, out here April only means the highs will be in the upper nineties instead of the lower nineties."

"I have the feeling you're going to have to cough up some money to the government in the next two weeks." Laurel chuckled.

"Right. And I have to be heading back to Ohio by then, too. Sure you're going to be all right out here alone?"

"Of course I'll be all right." Laurel sniffed in disdain, but deep inside she wondered the same thing. Would she ever be happy and content living so far away from everyone she loved?

"Hey, look." Kevin sat up straighter on the chaise. "There's some kind of special report on the TV. Wonder who tried to blow up who this time?"

"Shouldn't that be 'who tried to blow up whom'?" Laurel felt the baby kick hard as her stomach clenched nervously. She couldn't keep from associating any news bulletins with the assassination attempt that had so nearly cost Seth his life.

"Beats me. Those guys usually don't speak English, anyway." Kevin shrugged off her feeble attempt at a joke and started toward the patio doors leading into the living room, where the TV was located.

"See what it's about," she said with a strange little catch in her voice.

Kevin halted and looked back at her. "Sure, Sis," he said in a gentler tone than he'd been using. He moved across the warm flagstones with his usual careless grace. He was superbly coordinated for such a tall man, lean and graceful and far too handsome for his own good.

Laurel sat tensely in the chaise, her face turned toward the little fountain that was a source of so much pleasure to her. She didn't look away from the splash of falling water until Kevin stuck his head out the door a few minutes later. "The guy that shot Seth. He keeled over dead of a heart attack a couple of hours ago. They just released the news to the press. Looks like Seth won't be tied up in a long drawn-out legal trial this summer, after all."

"What?" Laurel forgot her uneasy reaction to the bulletin. She pushed herself up off the chaise, moving awkwardly, still not entirely comfortable with the changes in her body. She was glad to hear Kevin mention his old friend's name so casually. They hadn't discussed it, but she had the feeling the two men were working to regain their old friendship and she was glad. Knowing she'd caused such a serious rift between her brother and Seth had been another cause for sleepless nights.

"Poor old coot." Kevin was shaking his head at the photograph displayed on the screen.

Laurel had to agree when she saw the haunted countenance of the accused man's face. "I'm glad it's over," she said softly, just as the still photo dissolved into a replay of the assassination attempt she'd hoped never to have to witness again.

Horrified, fascinated, unable to look away, Laurel relived the first terrible moments of fear and terror that had assailed her that night in December.

"Laurel, let me shut off the damn thing—" Kevin stopped talking when he saw the stricken look on her face.

Suddenly all the niggling doubts and fears she'd harbored within herself for so long were seared away in the flash of certainty that sped through her brain.

This is the man I love more than life itself.

She looked away from the image of Seth's crumpled body on the TV screen to meet Kevin's sympathetic gaze. He reached out and pulled her into his arms. "It's okay, Sis. That's all over and done with. He's fine. I saw him just before I came out here, when he got back from that medal ceremony in Washington. He's fine," he repeated in a gruff soothing voice.

Laurel couldn't stop trembling. "I know. It's just . . . so awful . . . I'd forgotten all the . . . blood . . ." She pulled herself out of his arms. "Turn it off, will you, please? We can listen to the radio if you want to know what's happening."

"Nah. How about a little music, instead?"

"Fine," Laurel answered automatically. She hadn't really heard what he'd said. Other words, in another man's voice, were echoing through her brain. *If you change your mind, you'll have to come back here. I won't come to you.*

Was that what she wanted now? Was that why she found herself so restless and at loose ends here in Phoenix, because she didn't belong here anymore? Did she truly belong in Bartlow, with Seth? She glanced at the dark TV screen one more time, her mind's eye replaying the film of the assassination attempt in vivid detail.

Seth's pain was her own. If she was brave enough to make the attempt, his joys could be hers, also.

"Kevin." She looked up at her brother with a sparkle of tears in her eyes. "I've made up my mind. Let's go home."

"LAUREL'S BACK, Seth," Helen reported, as he was sitting at the kitchen table, scowling down at the tax forms he'd collected from the accountant that day. The screen door was open to a soft warm April night. Sounds of voices, not always in agreement, were counterpointed by the clanging of metal on metal. Mike and Clint were getting the corn planter ready for spring planting. Seth caught his mother's eye and they both smiled. The silent exchange didn't take her mind off the subject of Laurel Sauder as he'd half hoped it might.

"Mabel Jackson told me tonight at the Altar Society meeting that she saw Laurel and Kevin drive into town with a U-Haul truck. It looks like she's coming back to stay," Helen added hopefully.

"I wouldn't know, Mom. I haven't spoken to her or heard from her for seven weeks." He scrawled his name at the bottom of the tax return and stuck it into the envelope. His refund was small, but it would come in handy when the time came to refurbish Mabel's old wood-frame house and barn.

"Are you going to see her?"

Remembering his last words to Laurel that night in her room, Seth knew he couldn't make the first move. If she didn't come to him, then he would never be sure she loved him as much for his sake as their child's. He wasn't proud of himself for having doubts, but it didn't change the fact that they were there, winging their way above his head like a flight of stinging insects—and about as welcome—in the middle of the night.

"I don't have any claim on her, Mom," he said at last, slapping a stamp on the envelope and surveying his handiwork with a scowl.

"Haven't you ever heard of a father's rights?" Helen scowled back.

"You watch too much *Donahue*, Mom."

"It's my grandchild you're whistling down the pike, you know."

"Mom, you're not making this any easier. I'm trying my damnedest not to scare her off. It's more than I hoped for just to hear she's back in town."

"Well, if you ask me, she's showing a decided lack of brains. If she had any sense at all, she'd be out here tomorrow morning bright and early, begging you to marry her and make an honest woman out of her."

"Mom, you sound like a puritan."

Helen laughed a little self-consciously. "I'm just being selfish, that's all. I'd really like a grandchild I can cuddle and watch grow up, not another one that's two thousand miles away like your sisters' babies. Even if I do have to share him with Lois Sauder," she added tartly.

Seth laughed in genuine amusement and headed out the door. "I'm going to put this in the mailbox and then I'd better mosey on out to the barn and referee that shouting match between Dad and Mike. All I need is a couple of partners who can't exchange two words without starting an argument."

"Aren't you glad you take after my side of the family?"

As usual, his mother had the last word.

THUNDER RUMBLED off in the distance as Laurel parked her car along the rutted lane leading back to the field where Seth was planting corn. She could see the big green tractor, moving slowly away from her along the arrow-straight rows, a long time before she got close enough to be sure of the identity of the man in the cab.

It would take him another fifteen or twenty minutes to get back to where she was parked. Laurel looked on the delay as something of a reprieve. Her palms were sweaty and not just with the heat and humidity of the early May day. She scooted out of the car and pulled the big wicker basket from the back seat along with the plaid blanket she kept there for winter emergencies.

She'd put this meeting off too long as it was, Laurel realized as she spread the blanket in the shade of a huge old sycamore tree along the fence row. She couldn't make excuses any longer because she was afraid he might turn her down. She'd procrastinated for over two weeks by making a production of finding a suitable place to store her furniture. She'd arranged her room to accommodate the crib her mother had made Kevin bring down from the attic, check over and—not without some grumbling on her elder brother's part—assist in refinishing in pastel yellow. She'd dawdled away one whole day by showing up for her appointment with Dr. Mitchell almost forty minutes early, only to find he was still at the hospital and would be at least an hour later than scheduled. She'd spent the time exchanging gossip with his nurse.

All that activity was nothing but a smoke screen for her fear. Twice she'd gathered up her courage and called the Norris farm, only to find that Seth was gone the first time and out in the fields the second. Failing to reach him hadn't helped her faltering resolve. His mother had been polite and helpful, but Laurel couldn't make small talk with Helen. She was too nervous and wound up to be anything but stilted and overly polite.

Maybe that's why this morning Helen Norris had taken matters into her own hands and called Laurel. "I won't beat around the bush," she said in her brisk, no-nonsense voice. "If you want to see my son, you're going to have to come after him."

"I know that," Laurel had responded rather meekly, twirling the spiral phone cord between nervous fingers. "Is he...avoiding me?"

Helen answered with a question of her own. "Do you love him?"

"Yes." Laurel's voice was no longer meek or uncertain. "I'm just afraid I've held him off for so long that he's fallen out of love with me."

Helen snorted. "You'll never know if you don't ask him."

Laurel detected a distinct lack of sympathy for her indecision in the older woman's tone.

"I'm not afraid to tell you," Mrs. Norris went on in the same headlong manner. "I'd prefer not to be the mother of a thirty-four-year-old unwed father."

"I'm sorry," Laurel heard herself apologizing, and had to hold back an embarrassed giggle. She felt about fifteen again. Helen Norris was going to be a formidable mother-in-law.

"You could do me a favor."

Helen had surprised her again by voicing a request. "Of course," Laurel stumbled over the polite response.

"Stop by the house in an hour or so and take Seth's lunch out to him. Clint's working ground across the section here, and Seth's over at the Jackson farm. I can't be both places at once."

Laurel knew she had to talk to Seth sooner or later. In her own brusque way, Helen was offering her an opportunity to be alone with her son. Laurel accepted the friendly overture and made a small gesture in return. "I could come now and help you pack the lunches, if that would be convenient."

"I'd love some help." There was a smile in Helen's words that found an echo in the sudden glimmer of excitement and hope in Laurel's brown eyes.

Now she almost wished she hadn't come. She lowered herself to the blanket a little awkwardly, wondering if she'd ever become comfortable with the new unwieldy state of her figure. She wasn't comfortable, either, with being the object of polite attention whenever she went out on the street, but she was getting used to it. What she hadn't come to terms with yet was what Seth would think of her ballooning figure. She wouldn't have much longer to wait to find out.

He had made the turn at the far end of the field and was headed back toward her, a light cloud of dust drifting along behind the tractor like smoke from a bonfire. The field was flat and level, having been plowed under in the fall and cultivated just that morning, she guessed, into a smooth flat surface ready to accept and nurture a new crop.

The sun appeared from behind towering cumulus clouds just as Seth pulled to a halt a few yards away. Laurel used the sudden brightness of the spring afternoon as an excuse not to look at him right away.

Instead she watched him from the corner of her eye. He swung down out of the cab and hopped to the ground all in one swift, lithe movement. He was wearing faded denim jeans streaked with dust, a soft blue cotton shirt open at the throat, with the sleeves pushed up above his elbows, and a dark blue cap with a seed company logo emblazoned across the front. He looked tan and fit and so very, very dear.

"Hi." Laurel didn't trust her voice to utter a more lengthy greeting.

"Hi." Seth could feel his heart pounding in his chest like a trip-hammer gone wild. It had been acting like that ever since he'd spotted her car driving up the lane.

"You look like a farmer," she teased because her heart was so very full of love it threatened to overflow in tears of longing and fear.

"That's what I am, you know." He took off his cap and slapped it against his pants, stirring up a very small cloud of dust that wafted away just like the larger one following the tractor.

"It looks good on you. I've been watching the news. I'm glad that poor man in Washington is at peace, no matter how terribly he acted." She blurted out the statement with no conscious knowledge she was going to do so. She looked down at her hands. Had she blundered so quickly? Perhaps he wasn't ready to talk about the incident yet. He was wearing sunglasses so darkly tinted she couldn't see his eyes at all. It made her even edgier to talk to a reflection of her own strained white face. "Now you won't have to be in Washington all summer, waiting to be called as a witness at his trial."

"I'm glad it's over." Seth bent his head to kick at a clod of dirt with the steel toe of his heavy work shoe.

"I . . . I saw the videotape of the shooting again on TV." She was almost whispering, but her voice still carried to him as softly as the breeze stirring her hair with teasing, invisible fingers.

"So did I." She obviously needed to talk through this trauma. He tried to make it as easy for her as he could. "I looked like a two-bit gangster in an old George Raft movie."

He squatted on his heels so he could be close enough to catch a whiff of her light, sweet scent. He plucked a tall blade of new grass from a tuft at his feet and twirled it absently between his fingers.

"You looked like a hero," Laurel said with a little more spirit.

Seth held back a smile. *She was back in his life. She'd come to him just as he'd wanted, but now what did they say to each other to make it all right?* Damn, this was no place to take her in his arms and kiss away all the questions that still had to be answered between them, although some other spring day he'd have no objection at all to making love to her under the sun and the new leaves of a big old sycamore like the one towering over their heads.

"Storm's coming." He changed the subject abruptly; his life in Washington, in the Secret Service, was over and done with. His resignation was official at the end of the month. His future was here before him and he was anxious to get on with it, but not quite certain where to begin.

"I'm afraid so," Laurel agreed, clutching at the subject of the weather as though it were a lifeline. Maybe it wouldn't be such an adjustment being a farmer's wife, she decided all of a sudden. She was already attuned to the ebb and flow of the seasons and the cycle of life and harvest and winter's rest that would be the focal point of their lives. She fidgeted with the clasp on the wicker picnic basket beside her. "There's a thunderstorm watch out for this afternoon."

"Hope the storm holds off a few more hours and I'll have this field planted." He looked out over the fertile black land with undisguised pride.

"I brought your lunch," Laurel pointed out unnecessarily, indicating the basket and thermos she'd already unpacked. "Your mother asked me to bring it out to you."

Seth flipped his hat onto the grass. The fitful breeze chose that moment to return and ruffle the thick dark waves of his hair. Laurel watched the play of light and shadow in the inky mass with something akin to fascination. Seth moved onto the blanket and stretched out beside her, his back against the smooth gray bark of the old sycamore.

Only his hands, curled into fists at his sides, betrayed the agitation he felt inside. "Is that the only reason you're here, Laurel? Because my mother asked a favor of you?" He needed to hear her say she was here because she wanted to be with him and nothing else.

"No. I'm here because I want to be."

She smiled and the sun came out from behind the cloud, but Seth didn't notice; his eyes were already dazzled.

"You said I'd have to come back to you and I have."

Thunder rolled off in the distance.

Seth waited for her to say more, and when she didn't he frowned. Laurel caught the expression when she lifted her eyes from the sandwich she was unwrapping for him and hurried into speech. "Do you want some lemonade?"

"Yes." She handed him a paper cup full of liquid the same color as her loose gauzy sundress and slender rope-soled shoes.

Laurel tried again. "I'm home to stay, Seth." It was impossible to read his expression behind the aviator sunglasses he was wearing. Her hand itched to reach up and take them off his face so that she could see his eyes, judge his reaction to what she had to say.

"I'm glad, Laurel." Without taking a bite, he laid the sandwich down on the wax paper it had been wrapped in. "You're growing very round." He reached out and placed his hand on her burgeoning stomach with gentle reverence. "I guess I hadn't expected such a change in your figure." At the sound of his voice and the touch of his hand the baby inside her moved strongly and obviously. Seth jerked his hand back as if he'd been burned.

Laurel laughed and leaned over, trailing her fingers across the back of his hand, curling them under his palm, lifting it back to rest on her stomach again. "It's all right. He does that all the time."

"What if it's a girl?" Seth asked, his eyes still hidden, his expression carefully noncommittal, but he left his hand where she'd placed it and his voice was a low enticing rumble.

"Will you be disappointed if it's a girl?" The tension within her was growing stronger with each passing minute, lurking in the background of her thoughts like the storm off in the distance.

"No way," he said, and smiled suddenly, sending Laurel's heart into a stuttering series of kicks just like the baby's movements within her. "Little girls can grow up to drive tractors, too."

"Yes, they can." Laurel smiled in return despite her unease.

"Are you feeling well?" he asked politely, removing his hand from her stomach before turning back to his sandwich and lemonade.

"I'm fine. I saw Doc Mitchell a couple of days ago. He said I was healthy as a horse." She laughed. "I think healthy as a contented cow would be more accurate."

"Are you content, Laurel?" She wasn't certain how he wanted her to answer.

"I'm growing more so every day."

"Your due date is in the middle of July." It was just less than a question.

Laurel felt a wash of color stain her cheeks. "Yes." She didn't want to think about the lies she'd told him in the past.

"Hope you don't decide to go into labor right in the middle of wheat harvest." Seth's tone was dry, but Laurel had the distinct impression he was pulling her leg.

"I hadn't thought of that," she said with total honesty. "It could be a problem, but I'll do my best."

"We'll work something out." He leaned his head back against the tree, suddenly serious once again. "Are you going to be working for your dad?"

Laurel hadn't been able to swallow a bite of sandwich, so she gave up pretending. She laid it carefully back in its wrapping, while her heart beat frantically, high in her throat. He was treating her like a stranger, keeping her at a distance, just as she'd always tried to do with him. She had no idea it could hurt so much. No, that wasn't true. She'd had every suspicion it could hurt like this. That was why she'd avoided him for so long.

She took a deep breath. "Part-time. I haven't made any decision beyond that." It was impossible to say she'd rather be a full-time wife and mother, at least for a while. Her career was important to her—it always would be—but there were other things in life far more important than work. "I still don't think I want to take on Dad's job as my life's work. But later, after the baby's older, I might apply at the county hospital . . . or something. . . ."

The sun went behind another cloud. It was a big one, Laurel noted, dark, with rain around the edges. The breeze was slightly more rambunctious and cooler than it had been a little while earlier. The scent of rain settled down to mingle with the rich smell of newly turned ground and the freshness of spring-bright grass and leaves. It would be heaven for Seth to make love to her in such a place as this.

"I see . . ." He appeared to be very interested in the crust of his sandwich.

Laurel ground her teeth and felt like crying. He finished off the sandwich and brushed at the crumbs on the legs of his jeans. Laurel decided not to cry.

She leaned over and plucked the concealing sunglasses from his face, letting them drop onto the blanket, while she captured the rough, strong angle of his chin between her thumb and finger.

"Will you marry me, Seth Norris?"

"For your sake or the baby's, Laurel?"

His expression was still sober, but she could lose herself in the blue, blue depths of his eyes and absurdly that gave her newfound courage.

"For our baby's sake, yes. Some women make excellent single parents, whether by choice or necessity." A fleeting image of Elinor's pretty smiling face crossed her thoughts. "I would, too, except that I've changed my mind. I want us to be a family, Seth. But most of all, I want to be with you. I want to be your wife, your partner, your friend. I want to be the woman you love for the rest of your life."

Seth sighed and the sound came from the depths of his being. He pulled her head a little closer. She smelled like sunshine and dewdrops and lilacs. "That's what I want, too. That's what I've wanted all along."

She leaned into his embrace as his tongue slipped between her parted lips and tasted the honey within. He smelled like warm skin and black earth and hard work. His kisses tasted of lemonade and hot fiery passion. "I love you, Seth. With all my heart and soul. I'll love you till the end of time."

With roughly tender hands Seth pushed her down onto the blanket and stretched out beside her, nuzzling the softness at the juncture of her throat and the upward swell of her breasts. His finger traced the low scoop neckline of her dress and she felt her body stretch and tighten with longing so fierce it took her breath away. She pulled his head down to hers, their lips meeting and clinging in sweet reunion, their bodies straining closer until they were separated only by the clothing they wore. She'd waited so long to feel him against her once again that she thought she might possibly never be able to let him go.

"God, I've missed you, Laurel. You don't know how often I started to pick up the phone and make a plane reservation to come out to Phoenix and get you and bring you home, but I had to be sure being together was what you wanted as much as I do. The only way to do that was to wait for you to come to me. Does that make any sense to you at all?"

"All the sense in the world." She laughed up into his glittering, passion-darkened eyes and wrapped her arms more firmly about the strong tanned column of his neck. "We've just fallen in love all topsy-turvy."

"Putting the cart before the horse, so to speak."

Seth chuckled and the low sexy sound heightened Laurel's awareness of their intimate embrace even further. "So to speak." She giggled then and let the giggle melt away into a sigh as Seth bent his head to kiss her once more. She wondered if Seth would object to making love here and now under the stormy blue sky, behind the screen of the fence row and the big tractor.

"We have to get married right away." Desire roughened his voice.

She kissed him back. "For propriety's sake?" she asked when she could get her breathing back under control.

"For my sake," Seth said lightly. "I don't think I can wait much longer to have you all to myself."

"I never thought of that. We don't even have a place to live."

"Oh, yes, we do. Mabel Jackson's moving into a room at Oakfork after Memorial Day."

"We'll get married on Tuesday then." Laurel laughed as Seth flopped onto his back, pulling her with him.

"You sure are getting bossy, Mother."

"Nope. Just being a good farm wife. We know how to manage our time and our men. I think I can even guarantee not to have the baby until the last wagon of wheat's in the barn."

"A man can't ask for more than that."

"Oh, yes, he can." Laurel caught and held his lake-blue gaze as she slowly, seductively worked the buttons below the open collar of his shirt from their buttonholes.

"Woman, I have a crop to get in the fields," Seth said sternly, but he didn't do anything to stop her questing fingers.

"Ummmm," Laurel said, kissing his collarbone as he opened his legs to settle her more intimately atop him. The bright full circle of her skirt covered them like a blanket of sunshine.

"I've got everything I own—we own—tied up in this farm, Laurel Sauder." His words were breathless as Laurel worked her way toward the snap of his jeans. "We'll go hungry next winter."

"We'll live on love." Laurel smiled, sliding up the length of his bare chest to whisper in his ear. "I won't keep you long." She slid her hand boldly along his body to rest at the juncture of his thighs, pleased with an ancient feminine awareness by the blatant evidence of his desire for her.

"I'll keep you forever," Seth whispered back as he covered her mouth with his own. "Maybe I can manage to free up some time." He kissed her then and the rest of the world dropped away; nothing existed beyond the edges of their blanket and the canopy of new green leaves above their heads.

The sound of a pickup truck bouncing along the rutted land brought an end to their bantering and their embrace.

"Someone's coming." Laurel sat up, craning her neck to see past the planter at the back of the tractor. "I'm a mess," she wailed, trying to finger-comb her hair into some kind of order.

"You look great," Seth said, grabbing her and pulling her back into the curve of his body.

"Button your shirt," Laurel hissed, but she didn't try to move away from the solid comfort of his broad hard chest against her back.

"Too late. Anyway, it's only Mike. I wonder what he's doing out of school at this time of day?"

Laurel prayed she wasn't blushing but didn't hold out much hope about it. The teenager drove up and leaned out of the window of the cab, taking in their disheveled appearance without blinking an eye.

"Hi, Laurel," he said, flashing a wicked grin that was just as devastating to the female nervous system as Seth's.

"What are you doing out of school, boy?" Seth growled.

Mike ignored the lack of enthusiasm in his brother's greeting. "Early dismissal. Some kind of teachers' in-service meeting or something. I think they're just tired of us. Dad sent me over here to see if you need any help. Looks like you've got your hands full, all right."

The two brothers' gazes met over Laurel's head. She got the distinct impression it was Seth who looked away first when Michael grinned and opened the door to jump down from the truck. He was wearing a red mesh football jersey with his name emblazoned across the back and jeans so old and worn they had holes at the knees.

"Laurel and I are discussing wedding plans," Seth replied, and steel edged his words.

"'Bout time," Mike said with a grin, unimpressed by the show of brotherly intimidation. "When do I get to kiss the bride?"

Laurel was regaining her composure. "Right now." She held out her hand and Mike pulled her up from the blanket. He was very strong, despite his slender build.

"Happy ever after, Sis," Michael offered with touching dignity as he kissed her on the cheek. He held out his hand to Seth as the older Norris rose to his feet. "You're one lucky guy, big brother."

"Don't think I don't know it." The two brothers shook hands.

Mike nodded toward the tractor. "I'd better get at this field or we're going to get rained out. You two get back to your...planning session...only remember, don't get too carried away. I'm just a kid. You wouldn't want to hinder my emotional development."

"Get on that tractor or I just might hinder your physical development even more," Seth ordered with a grin.

"I'm petrified." Mike put his hand over his heart and staggered backward toward the tractor in mock terror.

Laurel laughed and leaned back into the welcoming circle of Seth's arms. "We could be courting disaster, you know," he said, turning her to face him, his hands warm and strong and loving on her shoulders.

"In what way?" Laurel tilted her head a little to better read the fascinating play of sunlight in the depths of his eyes.

"Our son could grow up to look and act just like that one." He jerked his head toward the youngster climbing into the cab of the big green tractor.

"Nothing would make me happier." Laurel turned in his arms to watch Michael maneuver the machine with skill and ability. He was born to the land, just as Seth was. Just as their baby would be. She was proud to think that someday it might be her son tilling the soil, another link in a long unbroken chain of commitment to working the land and feeding the world.

Laurel snuggled into the curve of Seth's shoulder, suddenly impatient for that future to be upon her, yet at the same time content with the present—secure in the knowledge that with Seth and their child to love and care for, her life would be filled with happiness and pride. For as long as the earth drew life from the sun, there would be dedicated men and women who would work the soil and give nature's bounty to mankind.

Epilogue

Laurel stood at the window of the small yellow-and-green room they'd picked as the nursery. Lightning danced across the midnight blackness of the July sky, briefly illuminating the pale green carpet and wallpaper dotted with circus clowns and merry-go-rounds. She liked living in Mabel Jackson's house. *Their house now.* She smiled to herself. There were three big bedrooms upstairs plus a huge drafty old bathroom and the little room under the eaves, where she was standing.

Downstairs there were four big rooms. A kitchen with walnut cabinets under half a dozen coats of paint, which she itched to start refinishing, and a corner full of windows, double hung and multipaned, that would someday be a charming, sunny breakfast nook. It would take time and hard work, but she was filled with excitement and enthusiasm for the project. But first things first. Pain tightened across the small of her back and moved around to her stomach. The baby kicked in protest and Laurel knew he was anxious to be born.

The contraction passed and she relaxed against the window frame. They were stronger now and more evenly spaced. It was time to wake her husband. She promised Seth she wouldn't have the baby until the wheat harvest had been completed. She'd kept her promise. Barely.

For the past two days and nights the Norris family had raced the weather to combine and store the rich golden acres of grain. Today at dusk, just hours ago, they'd finished. All week thunderstorms had rolled across the sky in the afternoon and evening, promising moisture for the earth and relief from the oppressive heat, but with the threat of damaging winds and hail to ruin the crop, as well. Through luck and prayer the storms had all gone a few miles to the north or south and the farmers around Bartlow kept up their relentless pace of harvesting.

But tonight the storm had not veered off. It was coming straight for them, full of sound and fury. Their baby didn't seem to care that the weather wasn't cooperating. He wanted to be born. A few minutes ago she'd called Dr. Mitchell. He'd promised to meet them at the County Hospital. Laurel turned and left the small cheerful room next to their bedroom. Seth was so tired she hated to disturb his sleep, but she didn't think the newest Norris was going to wait until a decent hour of the morning to make his appearance into the world.

"Seth?"

He came awake instantly, but not, thank God, any longer with that stinging jolt of adrenaline that had marked his waking moments when he was in the Service. "Can't you sleep, honey?" he asked, reaching out to take her hand in his. Her fingers were cold. He blinked, adjusting to the darkness after a brilliant flash of lightning. Laurel wasn't wearing the ridiculous tent of a nightgown she'd bought, mostly as a joke, just after they were married last spring. She was dressed, fully dressed.

She smiled and held out the car keys. "I think it's time to go."

His heart started pounding harder in his chest. Seth took a deep steadying breath. He'd read all the books, attended the classes. He was supposed to be the calm one, the supportive one. "Are you sure?" Sometimes first-time mothers tended to panic. All the articles said it was up to him to make sure this wasn't a false alarm. He tried to smile reassuringly and swallowed hard.

Laurel smiled again, calm, superior and loving. "Yes, I'm sure. Get dressed. I'll fix you some breakfast."

"Breakfast? Are you crazy? I'll be ready to leave in fifteen minutes." He swung his feet over the side of the bed. Laurel held out her hand, touching him lightly on the shoulder, but as usual for Seth, the merest touch of her fingers held the impact of an electric shock. He stood and folded her into his arms, feeling the taut fullness of her stomach press against him.

"Don't be silly. We've got time for something to eat." Then another contraction caught her unaware.

Seth held her close, tried to breathe with her, steady her, support her. *God, he was scared.*

The contraction passed and Laurel looked up at him, surprise and elation written plainly on her face. "Maybe we'd better just make that juice and coffee. I think this Norris is in as big a hurry as all the rest of you."

Seth curled her fingers over his and lifted them to his lips. "I'll be ready in five minutes." He didn't release her hands but bent to kiss her lightly on the mouth.

"I love you, Seth Norris. Picking you to be the father of my baby was the smartest thing I ever did." She grinned up at him impishly. It was amazing how quickly the painful defeating memories of the past faded away like wisps of summer mist when you were happy and content and in love.

"I'm going to be the father of all your babies," Seth said with mock severity. They kissed again long and lingeringly.

"And lucky for me this fatherhood deal is going to turn out to be a job with lifetime seniority." This time he wasn't kidding at all.

EARLY ARRIVALS on Main Street that morning were treated to the sight of Kevin Sauder arguing amiably with his father. What made the occurrence unusual was that Kevin was balanced precariously on the top rung of a ten-foot extension ladder. Ralph, beaming from ear to ear, was directing operations from the ground. If you looked closely you could see several of what appeared to be cigars protruding from his shirt pocket. At least that was Earl Conklin's opinion as he picked up two cinnamon rolls and black coffee at the Family Kitchen bakery, just as he'd done every morning for the past fifteen years. The other patrons nodded in agreement.

Kevin unfurled the sign he'd been tacking into place. It hung limply while the ladder was moved, its wording obscured. Conversation languished while the banner was pulled into place above the door of Sauder's Pharmacy. Deputy Rudy Sunderson, holding the bakery door politely for the mayor's wife, had the best vantage point.

"I see Seth and Laurel Norris must have had their baby last night," he announced to the room in general. He broke into a grin. Necks craned toward the window, more grins spread across sun-bronzed, work-lined faces. The message was simple, only three words, but they held a lifetime promise of love and care and hope for the future.

!!IT'S A BOY!!

ATTRACTIVE, SPACE SAVING BOOK RACK

Display your most prized novels on this handsome and sturdy book rack. The hand-rubbed walnut finish will blend into your library decor with quiet elegance, providing a practical organizer for your favorite hard-or-soft-covered books.

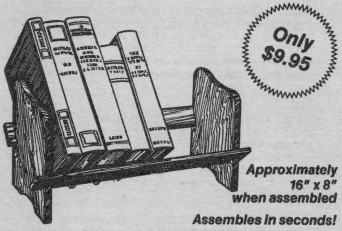

Only $9.95

Approximately 16" x 8" when assembled

Assembles in seconds!

---

acting job and start living life for herself. But driving Mouse cross-country brings Suzanne more than just freedom. It brings her handsome young Wyoming cowboy Billy Blue. Now that she's finally on her own, is Suzanne ready for love?

#259 HARVEST THE SUN by Judith Arnold

For Abbie Jarvis, life in the big city was worth every sacrifice. But when prosecuting an emotional case leaves her needing R and R, she retreats to her small northern California hometown. In need of a friend, she walks straight into the arms of T.J. Hillyard, local hero. Like T.J., Abbie had tasted the glory she yearned for—but was it enough? Or had what she'd been looking for always been right in her own backyard?

#260 CRY FOR THE MOON by Anne Stuart

Marielle Brandt didn't have much choice after she was suddenly widowed and left alone to raise her two small children. The only legacy from her husband was Farnum's Castle, a run-down apartment house in Chicago. The building housed some eccentric inhabitants, including two psychics and a warlock— but it also was home to Simon Zebriskie, resident helper and late-night DJ. It seemed to Marielle a most unlikely place to fall in love, but how could she deny Simon's powerful sensuality?

Four believable American Romance heroines . . . four contemporary American women just like you . . . by four of your favorite American Romance authors.

Don't miss these special stories. Enjoy the fifth-anniversary celebration of Harlequin American Romance.

R5A-2

Lynda Ward's

LEAP THE MOON

... the continuing saga of *The Welles Family*

You've already met Elaine Welles, the oldest daughter of powerful tycoon Burton Welles, in Superromance #317, *Race the Sun*. You cheered her on as she threw off the shackles of her heritage and won the love of her life, Ruy de Areias.

Now it's her sister's turn. Jennie Welles is the drop-dead-gorgeous, most rebellious Welles sister, and she's determined to live life her way—and flaunt it in her father's face.

When she meets Griffin Stark, however, she learns there's more to life than glamour and independence. She learns about kindness, compassion and sharing. One nagging question remains: is she good enough for a man like Griffin? Her father certainly doesn't think so....

Leap the Moon ... a Harlequin Superromance coming to you in August. Don't miss it!

LYNDA-1B